Also by Peggy Rothschild

A DEADLY BONE TO PICK

PLAYING
DEAD

PLAYING DEAD

PEGGY ROTHSCHILD

BERKLEY PRIME CRIME

New York

BERKLEY PRIME CRIME
Published by Berkley
An imprint of Penguin Random House LLC
penguinrandomhouse.com

Copyright © 2023 by Peggy Rothschild
Penguin Random House supports copyright. Copyright fuels creativity, encourages
diverse voices, promotes free speech, and creates a vibrant culture. Thank you for buying
an authorized edition of this book and for complying with copyright laws by not
reproducing, scanning, or distributing any part of it in any form without permission.
You are supporting writers and allowing Penguin Random House to continue
to publish books for every reader.

BERKLEY and the BERKLEY & B colophon are registered trademarks and
BERKLEY PRIME CRIME is a trademark of Penguin Random House LLC.

Library of Congress Cataloging-in-Publication Data

Names: Rothschild, Peggy, author.
Title: Playing dead / Peggy Rothschild.
Description: New York: Berkley Prime Crime, [2023] | Series: A Molly
Madison mystery
Identifiers: LCCN 2022022021 (print) | LCCN 2022022022 (ebook) |
ISBN 9780593437117 (hardcover) | ISBN 9780593437124 (ebook)
Subjects: LCGFT: Detective and mystery fiction. | Novels.
Classification: LCC PS3618.O86874 P58 2023 (print) | LCC PS3618.O86874 (ebook) |
DDC 813/.6—dc23/eng/20220510
LC record available at https://lccn.loc.gov/2022022021
LC ebook record available at https://lccn.loc.gov/2022022022

Printed in the United States of America
1st Printing

Book design by George Towne

For Richard, whose unflagging love and support has been a gift

PLAYING DEAD

CHAPTER 1

Harlow hung her head out the back seat window, golden ears flapping and tongue lolling. The Saint Berdoodle nudged his way into the opening behind her. Drool broke free from the big dog's flews. Though I loved Noodle, three months living with him hadn't yet numbed me to his faucet-like slobbering. Hoping the stream of saliva hadn't hit anyone, I signaled and turned the 4Runner onto a two-lane, following the instructions provided by my GPS.

Ten minutes later, I turned onto another narrow road. A sturdy windbreak rose on my right along with a string of phone poles. To my left, avocado groves alternated with orange trees. The air smelled of eucalyptus, citrus, and hay. I noticed a flyer was stapled to each phone pole I passed. Slowing, I read the posted message: "$1,000 Reward for Information on Our Missing Golden, Freddy." Below the words, a photo of a smiling retriever along with a phone number. The flyer's edges were curled, and the picture looked sun-bleached. How long had Freddy been missing?

Or had he come home and no one bothered to pull down the fly-ers? Hoping it was answer number two, I sped up again.

Near the road's end, the GPS voice said to turn right. I bumped onto the single dirt lane. Dust swirled around us, and I tapped the brake. "Heads back inside, guys." I powered up the windows and turned on the AC. Another half mile along the driveway, Noodle began to bark.

"Can you smell the other dogs already?" This would be our first time at Playtime Academy for Dogs' training facility. Members of my Tuesday agility class swore by this place and its staff. In addition to agility, they had scent work classes, rally, and barn hunt. Only Harlow did agility, but I was eager for Noodle to take part in his first barn hunt. Everything I read assured me the rats were kept safe. An animal-loving vegan in my agility class swore the rats looked like they were having a good time. Who was I to argue with that sort of testimony?

Noodle was a gentle giant. But having adopted him from a sociopath, I often worried how he'd interact with others. I'd spent the last three months introducing him to new people, animals, and experiences. So far, the Saint Berdoodle had done great.

I guided the 4Runner around a pothole. The slope turned steep. Slowing, I continued up the winding incline through the tawny, rolling hills. Though the day was warm, friends assured me it would feel like fall soon. I missed the autumn leaves of Massachusetts, but doubted I'd miss the snow and ice when winter rolled around.

A metal sign arching over the drive—and the GPS voice—told me I'd reached my destination. I pulled into the gravel park-ing lot on the right. About a dozen vehicles were already there. I chose a spot a few feet from a large SUV with an "I Heart Boxers" bumper sticker. When I cut the engine, Harlow woofed. "That's right, girl, we're here."

I reopened the windows and climbed out. It was at least ten degrees warmer here than on the coast. I pulled off my hoodie and told the dogs to stay. A group of about twenty people were gathered near a fenced field. Beyond that sat a second grassy enclosure plus two sizable dirt arenas. Wow. The arenas even had lights for night classes. Though I'd assumed the name "barn hunt" was figurative, there was also a big red barn.

The closest grass field was set up for standard agility competition practice, the unoccupied field beyond it for jumpers. An angular woman dressed in a khaki shirtdress and running shoes stood inside the first field, her Akita already off leash. Instead of being dialed in on her person, the dog looked bored. An Akita on the course meant I'd timed my arrival well; the small dogs had already run. A cowboy-looking guy clutching a clipboard approached the woman, but they were too far away for me to overhear any pointers.

Instead of checking in, I walked to the field and leaned against the railing. I scanned my surroundings while waiting for their run to begin. The buildings looked freshly painted, and even from here, I could see that the agility equipment was rubberized. Playtime obviously ran a quality operation. Movement pulled my attention back to the ring as the woman took off.

Arriving late had its downside. Though I'd spend less time waiting, I'd missed the course walk-through. I watched the woman and her Akita carefully. Tight right after the first jump, already heading to the tunnel. Straight run to the third obstacle. A sharp left to jump number one in the reverse direction followed by a softer turn toward the next jump. Then, the elevated dog walk and a quick reverse for the second tunnel. Straight run to the tire jump. After the A-frame, the course became less complicated. The Akita narrowly cleared the long jump and trotted to the finish. She and her handler completed a flawless, if moderately paced, run. The cowboy approached and spoke with her again. He placed a hand on her shoulder before she departed the ring, head down.

An auburn-haired woman entered along with a fawn-colored boxer. I wondered if hers was the SUV with the bumper sticker. She had a brief exchange with the cowboy before beginning her run. The boxer soared through the course, looking joyful. Much faster than the previous pair and another fault-free run.

Watching was fun, but my dogs needed to stretch their legs. I spied the crating area on the far side of the parking lot and hurried back to my vehicle. Leaving the dogs in the back seat a moment longer, I loaded their supplies onto my cart and rolled everything to an empty patch. I assembled the crates and draped a tarp over each to shade them from the sun. Returning to the 4Runner, I opened the rear door. Harlow pranced with excitement while Noodle drooled onto the beach towel protecting the back seat.

I hooked on leashes and let them explore the area on the way to their crates. Once there, I pulled the water bottle from my knapsack and filled their bowls. When they'd lapped enough, we wandered to a small group of live oaks and the dogs decided which ones were worthy of their use. "All set?" They wagged their tails. "Okay then."

After urging each into their crate, I walked to the check-in table located under a blue pop-up canopy. I smiled at the stunning woman staffing the table. "Hi. Checking in."

She looked up. Her dark hair was gathered into a big puff, and the orange company polo gave her skin a warm glow. "Name?"

"Molly Madison."

She ran her finger down a printout. "You're here with a golden retriever?"

"Yep."

"You'll be up after the standard poodle."

"Thanks. I also brought along my Saint Berdoodle for the barn hunt later today. Speed isn't his strong suit, but he's got an amazing nose."

She flashed her dimples. "See, this is how people should be. Recognize their dog's strengths and lean in to them. Way too many folks can't seem to see that." Holding out her hand, she said, "Simone Beaulieu. I teach scent work."

We shook. "Nice to meet you."

"You know, barn hunt courses are designed with eighteen- or nineteen-inch tunnels. A couple of our tunnels are thirty-six by eighteen. Will your dog be able to fit?"

"Yep. He squeezes through Harlow's agility tunnel just fine."

"Perfect. If he's got a good nose, you might also want to bring him to a scent class. We have one later in the week."

"I'll think about it."

"Saint Berdoodle, you say?"

"Yep."

"Smart to get a dog like that into nose work. The combination of those breeds . . . Have you done any nose work with him?"

"Yep. Haven't been able to fool him yet."

"For classes here, we work with the usual four target odors: birch, anise, clove, and cypress."

"I've just been hiding treats."

"That's a good start. Looking forward to seeing you later at barn hunt, Molly Madison."

"Me, too." I returned to the agility ring. Another woman stood inside. Short and stocky, she wore Capri pants and a shirt that matched the black and mahogany colors of the Rottweiler by her side. She unleashed the dog and spoke to the trainer. After a moment, she gave an emphatic nod and moved into position in front of her dog. When the cowboy signaled to her, the woman started running. The Rotty took the first half of the course in stride but missed the final contact point on the A-frame. Instant five-point penalty. But the handler held it together, and the rest of the course went smoothly. Releasing her dog, the woman had another word with the trainer before exiting the ring.

Didn't any men take agility here?

An anxious-looking bottle blonde entered with a German shepherd. A brief conversation with the cowboy followed, then she got into position. It looked like she was talking to herself.

Almost as soon as she began, things went haywire. She miscued the dog on the way to the first jump. The shepherd hesitated, looking for guidance. Turning, the blonde urged him forward and he made it over. She darted toward the tunnel, and the dog plunged through like an otter in water. He soared over the next obstacle. An audible groan rippled through the crowd when she ran the dog the wrong way. Figuring it out before her shepherd back-jumped, she corrected their course. Obviously frazzled, she lost control of the dog at the following jump. She circled around to get him over it in the correct direction. After that she completely fell apart. When her dog balked at the seesaw, the woman froze and covered her face.

Yikes.

"Yeah, Ashlee's a train wreck on the course." The auburn-haired woman who had run the boxer joined me at the fence with her dog. "Don't get me wrong, Siegfried can do the work. And Ashlee's athletic and smart. But when a run is timed, she falls apart. Maybe it's a throwback to some sort of testing anxiety, but she absolutely loses it." The woman puffed out her cheeks, took a deep breath, then crouched to stroke her dog's fawn coat. "But not you. You did great. Yes, you did. You're such a good boy. Yes, you are."

Straightening, she tossed her long braid over her shoulder. The dog sat on his haunches, tail swishing an arc in the dirt, gaze on his person. "I haven't seen you here before. First time?"

"Yep. I've heard a lot of good things."

She looked back at the crating area. "The Saint Berdoodle here for barn hunt?"

"Yep. He has a great nose. I only adopted him three months ago, but he's shown real promise."

"And I'm guessing the Golden does agility?"

"You got it."

"Terrific."

Her dismayed tone surprised me.

"Sorry. I'm in a mood. Another large dog running agility won't help me advance." Grimacing, she gestured at the field. "You see my run?"

"Yep."

"Forty-five point six seconds. Royal did great. And I ran my ass off on the home stretch, but I can't seem to get under forty-five. To get to nationals, I need to get down to at least forty. Royal's good enough to win. He deserves to. I can't figure out what's holding us back."

"That why you're here today?"

"Ben's a great trainer."

"The guy in the cowboy gear?"

"That's him."

"And you want to cut five to six seconds off your time?"

She raised an eyebrow. "Why? Think it's impossible?"

"Not from what I saw."

"What? You think you can help?"

"I don't know about six seconds, but I saw how you can cut two or three."

"Three seconds?"

"Yep."

"How? Wait." She held out her hand. "I'm Felicity Gaines. And, of course, this is Royal."

"Molly Madison." We shook, then I held my hand out to her dog. The boxer sniffed and continued wagging his tail. "Don't see many boxers doing agility."

"Well, if you go to county meets, you'll see at least two of them."

"You have another dog?" I scanned the area.

"Nah. Celeste liked Royal so much, she got a boxer of her own. She's been doing agility two years less than I have and getting better times. Pisses me off."

"I'll bet." I didn't recall seeing any boxers at the local trials I'd attended. "What's Celeste's last name?"

"Simmons."

"Never met her."

"Lucky you. What makes it worse is I'm the one who suggested she try agility. I was new to the neighborhood and ran into her while walking Royal. She told me she owned a couple gyms but was looking for something to do in her spare time. If I'd only known what she was like, I never would've suggested agility. Now she's got plenty to do. Of course, she still has no friends. But that's on her."

Finished with her rant, Felicity took a deep breath. "So how can you get me three seconds?"

"Two or three. It's your hair."

"My hair?" She fingered her braid.

"Not that. The loose hairs around your face."

Felicity ran her palm from her forehead to her plait. "What about them?"

I put my left hand up to my temple, then stroked it back. "Twice during your run, you touched your hair like this. With the hand you weren't using to guide Royal. It distracted him. Just a bit, but I'd say it added up to a two- or three-second delay over the course of your run."

"No. When?"

"First time was when you were heading away from the seesaw. The dog didn't go for full speed until you brought your hand down. Lost at least a second there."

"And?"

"During the run to the final tunnel. When your back was to him—same thing. You seem to do it when you break eye contact with him."

"Crap. Why hasn't anyone told me this before?"

"You come here a lot?"

"Yeah. Why?" Her brow furrowed.

I shrugged. "They know you. They probably don't see it. Like a tic they've grown used to. It stood out to me because I've never watched you run a course before. You're doing it now."

"Sweet fancy Moses." She tucked her left hand inside her front pocket. "How do I stop if I don't know I'm doing it?"

"Maybe wear a headband? It'll feel different and hold your hair in place. Or wrap masking tape around your hand? Something like that might call enough attention to itself to keep you from unconsciously doing it."

"Worth a shot. I think I'll wear one of Royal's bandannas during my next run. I should have a few extra in the car." Her jaw dropped open and she froze. "What's she doing here?"

I followed her gaze to a petite woman sporting a white-blond bob with one side of her head shaved down to stubble. Dressed in designer jeans and a black tee bedazzled with rhinestones spelling out the letters "KIP," she looked all bone and muscle. She led a brindle boxer from the crating area. The dog probably weighed only twenty-five pounds less than she did. "Is that Celeste?"

"Yeah, and she's supposed to be in Hawaii. For two weeks. Told me she'd miss the next regional competition."

"Giving you and Royal a leg up in your category?"

"God, I'm transparent, but yes."

The blonde spied Felicity, gave a finger wave, and headed our way. When she drew near, she said, "I was hoping I'd run into you here." Her boxer lunged toward Royal. Felicity pulled her dog back. Not to be completely thwarted, the blonde's boxer lodged his nose in my crotch. The woman did nothing.

Bad manners all the way around. I nudged the dog back. "Off."

Felicity moved Royal behind her. "I thought you'd be on your way to paradise by now—or at least packing."

"I couldn't let Buster miss the upcoming meet." Celeste gave a smile that was all teeth, no heart.

"You canceled your anniversary trip?"

"No. I convinced Del that joining him at the resort a couple days late would be good for him. My husband will get time to watch all the sports he can stand, and I'll get a chance for Buster to win and earn us an invitation to the championships."

"How? The entries are closed." Felicity looked at me. "I checked for a friend."

Even though I'd just met her, I was sure Felicity was lying. If she'd checked, it wasn't for a friend.

Celeste gave a carefree flutter of her hand. "Oh, I entered over a month ago. Just in case." She bent to adjust Buster's harness, then stepped closer to Felicity. "Even Del couldn't say no when I told him how that blue ribbon was calling me. And Buster's been running like a god lately. It'd be a shame to deny him another win." She gave one more toothy smile and touched Felicity's forearm. "I'm sure the red ribbon will look good with all the others you've won." She turned and strode to the agility field.

Felicity glared after her.

"Wow. She's . . ."

"A bitch. A bitch who's only been doing agility for a year." Felicity huffed out a noisy breath. "Like everyone else, she made lots of mistakes at first. Spent maybe six months coming to meets and NQ-ing. Finally, she got frustrated and told me she was taking a month off to bond with Buster. Sounded strange to me. She and Buster should've already bonded by then. What the dog needed was more training. But when Celeste came back, she couldn't lose. It was like some sort of magical transformation. It still pisses me off."

"She looks athletic. I'm guessing she and her dog run well together."

"Sort of. She still makes a lot of errors, but the dog does the right thing anyway."

"If she's doing well, why's she so . . . snippy?"

"I think she's using agility to make up for her Olympic dreams crashing and burning."

"What do you mean?"

"She was a gymnastics champion in her teens. Blew out her knee, rehabbed, but was never as good. Several years back, she started a gymnastics program for girls—SimNastics. Huge success. She was able to open her own gym—first one, then another. Completely stopped offering her classes through other fitness centers. I'm not sure how many gyms she owns now. But however many it is, it's not enough for her. The woman still needs more victories. Don't get me wrong, I hear she's got an amazing work ethic and inspires the athletes she trains. People in the gymnastics community respect her. But the agility crowd? I don't know a single person who actually likes her."

"I can see why."

A man in a tank top, showing off bony shoulders and several tattoos, approached the ring leading a standard poodle. Apparently at least one guy trained here. But the poodle's arrival meant my turn was coming up. I excused myself and collected Harlow from the crating area. By the time we returned, the poodle was halfway through the course. He flew over the long jump and the last two hurdles. Then he balked at the panel jump. The audience groaned. Tank top man circled back to try again. Success. After a brief consultation with the cowboy, they left the ring.

When we entered, the familiar thrum of excitement ran through me. "You ready, girl?"

Harlow settled onto the ground, eyes focused on me. I unhooked her leash and tossed it aside. While we waited for the trainer's okay, I reviewed the course. Once the cowboy nodded, I took a deep breath and locked eyes with Harlow. We took off.

The Golden flew over the first jump and we raced to the tunnel. She shot inside. Then she launched and landed the next three jumps perfectly. Tight turns, good speed. Next up: the weave poles. Harlow attacked them, smiling all the way. Another tight turn for the second tunnel, then she sailed through the tire like a dart. When she hit the contact point on the A-frame, I knew we had this. My heart soared as we ran the remaining obstacles.

The trainer walked over to me as I played tug-of-war with Harlow at the finish. Her favorite reward.

"Great run. Your first time here, but not your first on a course."

"No."

"Great dog, too."

"Yep. Harlow's amazing. Aren't you, girl?" The Golden wagged her agreement.

"So what are you hoping to get out of this today?"

I let Harlow win our battle and straightened. "I wanted to see how she performs in a new place. Around new people and dogs. And pick up any pointers I can."

The cowboy nodded. "Your footwork is good. So is your anticipation and planning for the obstacles. But"—he held up his index finger—"if you arrive before we start and walk the course, I'm betting you could shave another two seconds off your time."

"Thanks." I hooked on Harlow's leash and led her from the ring.

Felicity and Royal were waiting for us. "Nice run."

"Thanks."

"We're going in for our second run in about five minutes."

"Great. Let me take care of Harlow, then I'll come back and watch."

When I returned to the railing, a deep frown marred Felicity's face. I followed her gaze. Inside the arena, Celeste and Buster were crossing the finish line. Before talking to the trainer, Celeste made a point of smiling and waving at Felicity.

Felicity peeked at the timer on her phone. "Thirty-nine seconds."

"Wow."

"Bitch loves to rub it in." She rolled her shoulders. "Not my problem, right? Karma's going to get her someday. The only thing I can control is myself. And hopefully Royal."

CHAPTER 2

During Felicity's next run, she didn't touch her hair once and shaved four seconds off her time. She left the ring with a huge grin spreading across her flushed face.

I clapped as she approached. "Well done!"

"Thanks to you."

"Huh-uh. I just pointed out the issue." I gestured toward the lime green bandanna covering her head. "You made the necessary adjustments."

"Oooh. Someone's not happy about how well Royal and I did." Felicity chuckled.

On the opposite side of the arena, Celeste glowered.

"Good."

Felicity clutched my arm. "Let me get Royal settled in his crate, then we can watch the rest together."

"Sure."

She turned away, then groaned.

"What?"

"What's Stacy doing here? With Thor?" Her hand grazed her bandanna. Snatching it back, she pointed her chin at a tall, broad-shouldered woman leading a muddy border collie to the ring.

"Why? Border collies are naturals at this."

"Thor is amazing. It's Stacy."

"She's not good with the dog?"

"Frankly, I'm amazed she even remembers to feed him. Not that anyone could blame her."

"Really. What's her story?"

Inside the ring, Stacy unhooked Thor's leash. The border collie lowered himself, a spring ready to erupt. Eager as he appeared, he held his position while the woman consulted with the trainer.

"Her daughter died a month ago. Cancer. Stacy's been a complete wreck ever since. Of course."

"That's terrible."

"Yeah. I saw her and her daughter back in June. Ramona was big into agility, and Stacy would come along to support her. Ramona hadn't been to class or competition for a while. It was a shock seeing her. The girl was pale. Gaunt. She was wearing a knit cap, sweats, and a pullover—and it was eighty degrees. I figured she'd lost her hair from chemo, but the clothes? Maybe chemo affects your circulation and makes you cold? I don't know, but it was hard to watch. There didn't seem to be any joy in it for her. She kind of did this unsteady half jog–half walk through the course. Looked like she was in pain. The dog had to keep waiting for her. That was the last time I saw her or Stacy. Then I heard Ramona passed away."

"How old was she?"

"Sixteen."

"Geez. What type of cancer?"

"Don't know. It was one of those things where everybody knew she was sick but didn't talk about it. Probably because Stacy always looked so wrecked."

"The poor woman."

"Yeah. It's weird seeing her here with Ramona's dog. And if she's planning to take over his training, why's she here so late? She'll only get one or two runs and not nearly as many pointers."

I stared into the ring, where Stacy began running the collie through the course. The dog didn't do badly—in spite of all the mis-cues—but Stacy was in tears by the end.

"Let me park Royal, then we can try to cheer her up."

When Felicity returned, she looped her arm through mine. Unused to this sort of gal-pal closeness, I tried not to tense up. Seeming not to notice my reaction, she leaned in and spoke, voice low. "This is the first time I've seen Stacy run a course. Until today, she only came as Ramona's cheering section." She led us to where the woman stood a few yards from the arena in the shade of a live oak tree.

Thor wagged his tail and looked at Stacy. When she didn't tell him to stay, he moseyed over to greet us. Gaze pointed at the dirt and shoulders slumped, Stacy looked utterly lost. I bent to pet the collie, avoiding the mud-encrusted portions. Would the woman be offended if I made a quick trip to the crating area and grabbed one of Harlow's brushes to clean up the poor guy?

"Hey," Felicity said. "How're you doing?"

Stacy shrugged.

"This is my new friend, Molly Madison. Molly, this is Stacy Marinkovic."

I extended my hand. The woman looked at it blankly. I dropped my arm to my side. "Nice to meet you."

No response.

Felicity tried again. "I was surprised to see you here."

"Because Ramona's not with me?" Stacy's voice sounded rusty, as if it didn't get much use.

"Uh . . ." Felicity reached for her hair, caught herself, and stopped. "I just . . . It's a bit of a drive coming here. You know, if you want to get deeper into agility, you can always join the club in Camarillo. They have lots of different training sessions. All levels. Plus a ton of folks you already know go there."

"Celeste mentioned this place. Said it was good."

Felicity's brow briefly furrowed. "Don't get me wrong, Playtime's terrific. But, like I said, a bit of a haul. And pricey. You can save some bucks by going to weekly club trainings."

Celeste sauntered over to our group. "Nice to see you're taking such good care of Thor." A mean smile played across her face. "Who's your groomer? I must get his number."

Stacy stared at the dog's muddy coat. Felicity surged forward. I extended my arm in front of her, blocking her progress. Celeste was a bitch, but Stacy didn't need them fighting over her dirty dog. Clearing my throat, I stepped between my red-faced friend and the serene-looking Celeste. "Wow. Your parents really screwed up with your name."

"What?" She turned, seeming to see me for the first time.

"It's Celeste, right? Means 'heavenly' and, lady, you are strictly hellish."

Her mouth dropped open.

"Great way to catch flies—since you're incapable of using honey." I touched Stacy's arm before looking at Felicity. "You two want to join me at my car? I've got chilled root beer." I was pleasantly surprised when Stacy trailed along with Thor as Felicity and I walked away from Celeste.

"You sure shut her up." Felicity squeezed my hand. "That felt good."

"I hate bullies."

After two more runs, Felicity had cut her time by another three seconds. Throughout, Stacy stood mutely by my side. If she was here trying to keep her daughter's memory alive, it didn't seem to bring her much joy. When Felicity left the ring after her final run, Celeste blocked her way, hands on hips. Neither looked like they were ready to trade blows, so I headed to the crating area to collect Harlow for our final turn. Though I missed what was said, Felicity's and Celeste's raised voices were audible as I clipped on Harlow's leash. By the time I'd returned, Celeste was stalking away and Felicity's cheeks were once again a vivid red. I intercepted her as she led Royal to the crating area. Harlow and the boxer sniffed each other and wagged their tails. Seeing they were fine, I shifted my attention to Felicity. "You okay?"

"Yeah."

"What did Celeste want?"

Felicity shook her head. "I don't want to talk about it."

"Okay. But if you change your mind . . ."

"Thanks. And thanks for your help today. I'm so glad we met."

"Me, too."

The boxer yawned. "I need to pack up Royal's equipment."

"Not staying for barn hunt?"

Celeste's sharp voice intruded. "I think poor Felicity and Royal have enough on their plate trying to master agility. Besides, barn hunt is for dogs who aren't smart or fast enough for agility."

As a former cop, I was used to having personal insults hurled at me. But implying my Noodle was stupid? Heat coursed up my face.

Felicity squeezed my forearm. "She's not worth talking to. There's nothing kind or decent inside her."

I narrowed my eyes at the blonde. Celeste's plastic smile faltered. "You're right. This woman's a waste of space." I turned back to Felicity. "Hope I see you in Camarillo."

"Count on it. Royal and I do the early class on Thursday."

"I usually go Tuesdays. It'll be fun to change things up and hang out."

When I got Harlow back to the arena, it was time for our run. As usual, the Golden soared through the course like a dream. I sometimes wondered if she'd qualify even if I wasn't in the ring with her. As soon as we'd finished, we played a brief game of tug-of-war. Cowboy Ben sauntered over. I let go and straightened.

"Good job."

"Thanks."

He pushed his cowboy hat farther back on his head. "Like I said before, your fundamentals are strong. My one thought is: Remember to keep your body low when working the contacts."

"Right. Harlow will follow my posture."

"You got it. Hope we see you again soon."

Unlike at club events, Playtime's equipment didn't need to be stowed away at the end of the day. I settled Harlow in her crate before walking Noodle to the barn. The day was turning cool as the sky darkened. Inside, bright lights pushed the shadows to the fringes of the cavernous space. Along the back wall a row of bales towered. I was momentarily concerned Noodle would be expected to climb them until I noted orange netting fencing off the area. To the right, a combination of hay bales and tarps blocked off a section of the barn. The ring sat in the center of the room with an array of bales forming pyramids, stacks, and tunnels.

Simone stood near the door greeting people. Ten dog and handler pairs entered, with me and Noodle bringing up the rear. When we were all inside, she cleared her throat. "I'm seeing a lot of familiar faces, but some new ones, too. So we'll do a brief review before we start. This course is designed to accommodate both large and small dogs, and we'll go in the order of class registration. Before running the course, we're going to give all the dogs a chance to smell the tubes—an empty one, one with a rat inside, and one with nothing but used rat bedding. Then we'll put the three tubes in among the bales, and the dogs will try to find the rat.

"Dogs all run naked—no collars, leashes, or harnesses. Once your dog begins their run, you can't touch them except to give praise and treats after the rat is found. Other than that, you can cheer, use gestures to urge them on, tell them 'in' or 'get them' or 'go'—whatever works for you and your dog.

"At this level, we only place one rat on the course and you'll be able to see where it is. This is so you'll learn how to recognize your dog's alert when they find it. Some dogs will nose the tube, others will paw it. Others will bark. Quentin, if you could bring out the tubes."

A muscle-bound man with a shaggy mop of dark hair carried a cardboard box over to the group. His complexion was the color of vanilla pudding, and acne dotted his chin and throat. "Hi. I'm your Rat Wrangler." He set the box on the ground, wiped his hands on the front of his skintight T-shirt, then lifted out a foot-long piece of perforated PVC pipe. It was about four inches in diameter and capped at both ends. "This here's an empty tube." He unscrewed one end, held it up, and turned so everyone could see it. He recapped it and set it on the ground, then hoisted a second tube. "This one here's got some rat bedding, but no rat." After opening and showing it to the group, he set it beside the empty tube. "And this is the mother lode. I'm not gonna open this one." He chuckled and placed it on the ground as well.

"Okay," Simone said. "Line up to my right, then each handler will take a turn letting their dog sniff the tubes."

With ten dogs and handlers, the process took almost twenty minutes. When Noodle's turn came, he wagged and sniffed, barking at the one with the rat and drooling on the empties.

Once each team had had a turn, Simone clapped her hands together. "Okay, everyone, now we're going to do the course." She nodded to Quentin, and he collected the tubes. "When your dog alerts, you need to yell 'Rat.' Then hand the tube to Quentin. Be sure to keep it level for the safety and comfort of the rat.

"In addition to locating the rat, your dog must go through at least one tunnel. If the dog finds the rat without going through a tunnel, you'll need to command him or her through before leaving the arena."

The first pair up was a heavyset man with an elbow brace on his right arm and a gray-muzzled German shepherd. While he removed the dog's collar, Simone held up her hand. "Can I get everyone's attention?" When we'd quieted sufficiently, she continued. "Normally in a Novice Barn Hunt Competition you'd have two minutes to find the tubes. As you can see, Quentin's placed one tube beside that stack of hay bales and another on the far side of the tunnel. The tube with the rat inside is on top of that three-bale stack. There's no time limit on this round." She nodded to the first team. "Don't start until I tell you to. The handler and dog should move into the ring at the same time, but no leading the dog. Everybody got that? Okay." She made eye contact with the man again and said, "Go when ready."

The man and his dog had obviously done this before. The shepherd gave the first empty tube a quick sniff then moved on, circling bales, retracing his steps. Simone called out, "Don't hover. But you want to stay close enough to see what the dog's doing. Not too close."

The German shepherd was methodical and thorough. He'd clambered on top of the hay bales and found the rat within ninety seconds. "Good job, Desi!" the man said. The dog scarfed up the offered treat. "Such a good boy!" He patted his dog and Simone cheered along.

Next up was a Jack Russell terrier and a twentysomething woman with a waist-long ponytail. This should be good. Terriers were natural ratters. I moved to get a clear view of the ring. To my surprise, the dog meandered about, never seeming to pick up on the idea he was there to hunt the rat. The owner urged him on until the terrier stumbled across an empty tube. When he lifted his leg to pee on it, Simone ran forward and scooped up the dog.

"The urine scent will distract the other dogs." She handed him to his sheepish-looking owner. "After he goes outside, we can try it again."

The next few dogs had greater success, though so far, the German shepherd had been fastest to find the rat. When our turn came, I removed Noodle's leash and collar, then ran my fingers through his thick coat. "You ready, big fellah?"

Noodle drooled and wagged his tail. Excitement hummed through me as I waited for Simone to speak.

"Go when ready."

"Come on, Noodle. Find the rat."

Noodle put his nose to the straw-covered floor, head swaying back and forth. Six steps forward and he raised his muzzle. Taking off at a gallop, he scaled the stacked hay bales and barked at the tube. I called out "Rat," then climbed up after him.

A muttered chorus of oohs and aahs came from behind me.

"Great job, Noodle. Good boy." I offered him a treat with one hand while passing the tube to the Rat Wrangler with the other.

Noodle gobbled the treat, then raised his head again. Leaping off the hay bale, he ran to the arena's edge and vaulted the low fence.

"Noodle! Come!"

He charged toward the tall stacks of hay along the back wall, scrambling over the orange safety fence with ease. "Come, Noodle." The dog was deaf to my commands. So much for the class being impressed by me or my dog. I ran after him and climbed the arena's fence. "Noodle. Stop!"

Finding an invisible path, the Saint Berdoodle scrambled to the top of the bales lining the wall. He nosed something out of my view, then barked.

Simone and the Rat Wrangler had joined me outside the ring. I turned to them. "Could there be a rat up there?"

Quentin shrugged. "It's possible. It is a barn, after all."

"Noodle, come!" The dog sat and barked again. "Looks like the mountain's not coming to Mohammed." Moving with care, I began scaling the bales. The stack was at least eight feet high and three bales deep. Fortunately, it felt stable. I jammed my foot between two bales and grabbed the wire circling the next bale up. How had Noodle climbed this?

Dust and bits of hay rose with each step. I fought the urge to cough. When I finally peered over the top, Noodle sat unmoving. "You okay, fellah?" I hauled myself onto the highest bale and pushed up to my knees. My stomach flipped.

Celeste Simmons lay on her back, one side of her skull caved in. Dried blood coated the shaved side of her head. Her open eyes looked lifeless, but I crawled forward and checked her pulse. "Oh no."

CHAPTER 3

I leaned my head over the edge of the hay bale. Simone's gaze was fixed on her phone while Quentin stared at me, the picture of impatience: hands on hips, lips pursed. The only thing missing was a tapping toe. Not wanting to alarm the entire class, I kept my voice low. "Celeste is dead."

"What?!" Simone's cell landed on the ground. Her head jerked up. "Celeste is up there? Dead? How?"

Definitely had her attention now. Along with that of the entire class. The group surged from the arena side of the barn toward us. "Someone bashed in her head."

Simone's jaw sagged open.

"You sure?" Quentin's eyebrows disappeared beneath his shaggy bangs. "Maybe I better come up and check."

Annoyed at having to defend myself, I said, "Don't. I'm sure. I used to be a cop. I've seen more than my fair share of dead bodies."

Quentin continued to look skeptical, but stayed where he was.

"Who would do something like that?" Simone's hand fluttered to her mouth.

"Who wouldn't?" Everyone turned to the guy with the German shepherd. He shrugged. "Come on. It's true. Celeste was a horrible person and we all know it." A few honest souls nodded in agreement. "She gave me crap about wearing an arm brace. Like tendonitis is some kind of character flaw. Said I'd never win regionals—let alone nationals—if I didn't get my arm in shape."

A full-bodied woman with a corgi in tow cleared her throat, then spoke in a tremulous voice. "She told me I needed to lose twenty pounds before I'd be fast enough to qualify. Said I should adopt out my dog to someone who had a chance of winning."

A gasp went up from the group as the woman wiped her eyes. Arm-brace man patted her shoulder, and she gave him a weepy smile. "Thanks."

Within two minutes of meeting Celeste, I'd disliked her, but this wasn't the time to say so. Simone stared, oblivious to their bad-mouthing the dead.

A pinch-faced woman holding a bichon frise said, "One time, I heard her call—"

"Someone needs to call the cops," I said. The group looked up at me, all eyes wide. Were they shocked I'd interrupted or that I'd reminded them about the dead body on top of the hay?

Quentin pulled out his phone and smirked at me. "As an ex-cop, I'd expect you to know this is county land. We're covered by the Ventura Sheriff's Department."

The Rat Wrangler was starting to piss me off. "Whatever."

I turned my attention back to the Saint Berdoodle. "Good job, Noodle." I pulled a treat from my pocket. "Come and get it." Normally a snack monster, Noodle surprised me by holding his position beside Celeste. "I know this is weird. You did good, but I need you to come." I extended my hand farther. He looked at me and drooled. Finally, he came and gobbled the treat, leaving a warm pool of slobber in my palm.

Wiping my hand against my jeans, I assessed our downward journey. The prospect of descending with Noodle appeared far more dangerous than scaling the bales had been. The dog weighed in at one hundred eighty pounds and I couldn't carry him. "Hey, Simone." She looked up at me. "I'm going to need help getting Noodle down. Give me a hand?"

That snapped her into action. Snatching her cell from the straw-covered ground, she shoved it into her pocket, then put two fingers in her mouth and whistled. "Randy! Get out here! And bring work gloves for us. We need to move some bales."

A reedy-looking teenager loped from somewhere beyond the tarp barricade and handed his boss a pair of stained leather gloves. Simone waved people back, then she and Randy shifted bales until they created a hay staircase.

When they were done, I set two treats on top of the hay. While Noodle focused on food, I slipped on his collar and leash. I gingerly led him down to ground level. "Great solution. Thank you."

"Sure." Simone gave a grim nod. "It's like what we put together for the barn hunt course. Only a lot taller."

"You probably should leave the bales there for the police."

"Right. The police." She turned and stared at Quentin. "Well?"

He tucked his cell into his back pocket. "Sheriff's Department is on its way."

Obviously, his call was long over. He'd been holding the phone to his ear until Simone and Randy finished the hard labor. Seemed his muscles came from the gym, not his job.

Unfamiliar with the department's location, I turned to Quentin. "How soon will they get here?"

He shrugged. "Depends on whether they run the sirens."

In my experience, a witness like me could be stuck on-site for a while. Miguel was supposed to drop by tonight, and I wanted to be ready to roll as soon as the officers said I could leave. To that end, I walked Noodle to the crating area and released Harlow. She jumped and licked me as I rubbed behind her ears. When she'd settled down, the three of us wandered to the small grove of live oak for another tree-marking break. Somewhere in the parking lot, a dog howled.

Back at the car, I refilled water bowls and poured some kibble. Once they'd gobbled and lapped, I urged the dogs into the back seat of my 4Runner and cracked the windows. I pulled on my hoodie and headed to the crating area. After breaking down the equipment, I lugged everything back to the car, then returned to the barn.

Class members had collected in twos and threes, while a couple students stood alone with their dogs. It looked like I was the only one who'd taken my dog to the car. I texted Miguel to say I might be home later than planned and sat on a bale of hay to wait.

At quarter to six, a Ventura Sheriff's Department SUV pulled into the gravel lot. A stocky man wearing khaki trousers and a cream-colored shirt climbed from the passenger side of the black-and-white and hitched up his duty belt. An athletic-looking woman, similarly dressed, but in long sleeves, closed the driver's side door. They moved to the front of the vehicle and seemed to study the barn. Arm-brace man's dog began to bark.

"Quiet, Desi." The German shepherd stopped barking and began to growl.

Looked like Desi didn't care for people in uniform. The dog probably terrorized their mail carrier.

Simone rushed out to meet the deputies. I edged closer to the doorway, but still couldn't hear what she was saying. The officers entered and took a few moments to survey our motley group. I scanned the faces of my fellow class members. At least half of them now looked shifty and guilt-ridden. Had one of them actually killed Celeste?

When Simone pointed at me, my heart stuttered. I took a deep breath. Of course she'd pointed me out. Next, she pointed at the stack of hay bales lining the back wall. The three of them walked to the rear of the barn, then the female deputy began climbing the hay ziggurat. When she reached the top, she disappeared for a couple minutes, before descending to join her partner.

After a brief discussion, he turned to the group and spoke in a gravelly voice. "I'm Deputy Wallace and this is Deputy Alvarez. We'll be calling in the crime scene techs. In the meantime, we need everyone—and their dogs—to move outdoors." He turned to Simone. "Is there somewhere we can speak with each person privately?"

"Yes. The office. I just need to unlock it." She spun and headed outside.

The deputy's gaze found me. "You discovered the body?"

"Yep. Well, my dog did. I went up after him and found her."

"All right. Come with me."

Deputy Alvarez stayed behind, ushering people from the barn while I trailed Wallace around the side of the building.

Simone stood beside the open door of a small freestanding structure, which looked like a converted shed. Bright light shone from within. "Let me know if you need anything else." The poor woman looked like she was going to be sick.

The office really wasn't much more than a storage room with

a metal desk crammed against one unpainted wood wall. A filing cabinet, rolls of chicken and baling wire, along with stacks of boxes, lined the remaining walls. The room smelled of kibble and spoiled apples. The deputy spun the battered chair away from the desk and sat. He nodded toward a folding chair wedged between the filing cabinet and some boxes.

Wow. Such manners. When I was in uniform, I'd never made a witness rustle up their own seat. Clamping my mouth shut to keep from saying something snide, I pulled the chair free and wrestled it open. Dust motes drifted as I sat.

He set a small notebook on his thigh. "Name?"

"Molly Madison."

"I understand you're an ex-cop? At least that's what Ms. Beaulieu said."

"I am. Worked patrol when I lived in Massachusetts. I wouldn't have mentioned it, but the Rat Wrangler—Quentin—didn't believe me when I said Celeste was dead. I figured the last thing you'd need was someone else climbing up there to see the body."

"Tell me what happened."

I recounted how Noodle went rogue after finding the rat.

"So no one gave the dog a search command before he went after the body?"

"No."

Wallace rubbed his jaw. "He just climbed up that hay staircase to the top on his own?"

"No. Simone and Randy arranged the bales so I could get Noodle down afterwards. He somehow managed to scramble up the stacks without that."

"What kind of dog are we talking about?"

"Saint Berdoodle. He's a mix of poodle and Saint Bernard. Both breeds have amazing noses."

"So, a big dog?"

"Yep. About one hundred eighty pounds."

"And he climbed up a stack of hay bales?"

"Yep."

"Damn." He shifted his weight and the chair groaned. "The dog have any experience locating dead bodies?"

"Not that I'm aware of. I only adopted him three months ago. Oh, wait! That's not true. He did find a severed hand a few days after I met him."

"A severed hand?"

"Yep. On the beach in Pier Point."

"I heard about that case. That was your dog?"

"He wasn't really my dog then—I was just training and looking after him. But he's my dog now."

"Huh. Gotta say, I'm impressed. Usually a dog gets a mess of training hours before they're able to do something like that." He turned a page in his notebook. "When you were up there, did you touch the body?"

"I checked for a pulse. Along her neck." I closed my eyes and thought back. "On her right side. Oh. And Noodle drooled on her."

The deputy grimaced. "What?"

"The dog can't help it. He's like a faucet."

"Where?"

I pictured the viscous pool. "Her left breast."

"Sheesh. I'll let the techs know. Tell me who you saw here before you found the body."

"From when until when?"

"Give me everyone since you arrived."

I bit back a sigh. I wasn't getting out of here anytime soon. After naming the various people I'd met and talked to, I described the people and dogs I'd observed, but whose names I didn't know.

We went over everything one more time before he closed his notebook and rose. "Thanks for your time."

"No problem."

When I'd reached the door, he spoke again. "If you could hang around awhile, we'd appreciate it. The detectives are on their way. They'll want to talk to you."

"You know how long that'll be? I have plans and need to get the dogs home."

"Hard to say. Shouldn't be too long."

I strode to the deserted agility ring and leaned back against the railing. One by one, my fellow barn hunt attendees entered the office, then exited and walked to their cars. Every session with the deputies—except mine—ran ten to fifteen minutes long. While I waited, I alternated between staring at the emerging stars and at the emptying parking lot. In spite of giving the dogs a snack before moving them to the car, Harlow and Noodle would be expecting dinner soon.

In the distance, a dog howled. Too high-pitched to be either of mine. A hulking black SUV remained in the lot a few yards away from mine. Did that mean Celeste was the one with the "I Heart Boxers" bumper sticker on her car, not Felicity? I crossed the driveway to the gravel lot. Yep. One of the SUV's back windows was open about five inches. The brindle boxer's muzzle stuck out through the gap. He howled again.

"Poor Buster. Hang on, boy." I stopped at my 4Runner and gave my dogs some love, then filled one of their bowls with water and another with kibble. From the next vehicle, Buster whined. "Give me a second."

I carried the water over first, reached for the back door, then froze. Celeste had obviously been murdered. Tampering with her car in any way was a bad idea. I compromised by holding the water bowl half in and half out of the window. Unfortunately, Buster managed to splash as much as he lapped. Might get me in trouble with the deputies, but I wasn't going to let the dog go thirsty. Or hungry. When he was done, I did the same with the kibble. After returning the bowls to my car and kissing my dogs on the forehead, I returned to the agility arena and leaned against the fence again.

Additional deputies arrived as did folks from the crime lab. Soon several uniforms fanned out with flashlights, searching the grounds. A powerful beam temporarily blinded me. Footsteps crunched closer.

"You work here?" a deep voice said.

"No." I raised one hand to shield my eyes. "I found the victim. Deputy Wallace said the detectives would want to interview me. I'm just waiting until they call me in."

The man pointed his light toward the office. "Wait closer to the building."

Rankled by his tone, I still managed a civil "You got it," and walked to the barn. Bright lights glowed from within as if a spaceship had landed inside. Two officers blocked the wide doorway. My nod received no response. I walked around the corner of the building and leaned against the plank wall, keeping an eye on the office.

Ninety minutes after my first interview, Wallace brought me back inside. An attractive woman perched on the end of the desk. Clad in a navy pantsuit, I pegged her as being in her mid-thirties. Her partner sat in the desk chair. His all-brown ensemble matched his mustache and beard. That, and a burly build, gave him a bearlike appearance.

The woman stood. Already tall, her braided updo added another three inches to her height. "I'm Detective DeFelice." She nodded at the seated man. "This is Detective Stern."

He pointed at the folding chair. "Have a seat."

As I got settled, Wallace entered. "Ms. Beaulieu says the list of the day's attendees is on the desk."

DeFelice turned and sorted through the scattered papers. "Got it." She perused the sheet, then handed it to her partner.

Stern whistled. "There's at least thirty-five names." He held it out to the deputy. "Go over this with her. See if there were any no-shows we can eliminate."

"Yes, sir." Wallace took the list and left.

"What's going to happen to Buster?"

Detective Stern frowned. "Who's Buster?"

"Celeste's dog."

His shoulders visibly relaxed. "Oh. We'll contact her next of kin to collect the dog."

"Her husband's in Hawaii."

Stern picked up his notepad and flipped a couple pages. "According to your interview with Deputy Wallace, you claimed to barely know the woman. How come you know where her husband is?" He leaned back and seemed to reassess me.

"One of the agility class members was surprised to see Celeste here. Said she was supposed to be on some anniversary trip. In Hawaii."

"Who was that?"

"Felicity Gaines." My cell phone chimed, indicating a text. Resisting the urge to look, I continued. "Celeste joined us and said she was going to meet her husband there in a couple days." I leaned forward. "If no one can come get the dog, what happens? To him, I mean?"

"Guess we'll have to call Animal Control."

"No! I mean, please. I can take the dog. Boxers are prone to separation anxiety. With Celeste gone, he'll need company, some-one to play with. Someone to keep him busy. If I take him, at least he'll be in a home environment—like he's used to. Whenever Celeste's husband gets back, I can bring Buster to him. The idea of him being stuffed in some cage . . ." I shook my head. "Please let me take him."

Stern rubbed his jaw again then turned to look at his partner.

"Alvarez is following up with next of kin," DeFelice said. "If no one's able to come for the dog tonight, we might let you care for him." Her gaze lasered in on me. "After all, you're an ex-cop. Means you're trustworthy, right?"

"Right. Thanks. Um . . ." I hesitated, hoping this wasn't going to wreck their assessment of my trustworthiness. "I should let you know there's some spilled water inside Celeste's car. From when I fed her dog."

Stern's face grew red. "You contaminated the victim's vehicle?"

"I fed Buster through the open window. Didn't touch any-thing, but the dog splashed some water. The poor guy was howl-ing. I had to do something."

Neither Stern nor DeFelice looked like they agreed. Stern shook his head, then took me through finding Celeste's body again before moving on to new territory. "A witness said there was an argument between the victim and Felicity Gaines. You were one of the people in the general area. What was the fight about?"

"I don't know. I heard their raised voices but was collecting my Golden from the crating area. I was too far away to tell what they actually said." I thought about Felicity's unwillingness to discuss the spat but held my tongue.

"What about the words they exchanged earlier? You were with Ms. Gaines when that happened."

"Right. Celeste said some negative stuff about Felicity and her dog. I don't remember what exactly. Just something about how she and Buster would beat Felicity and Royal at regionals."

"That's all?"

"Yep."

"Not much of a motive for murder."

I thought back to my own fury at Celeste impugning Noodle's intelligence and wondered if the detective was correct.

CHAPTER 4

Fortunately, Noodle and Harlow went into tail-wagging mode when I introduced them to the brindle boxer. Buster was a bit aggressive with his sniffing, and after a few minutes, Harlow distanced herself. "Good girl. You take care of you."

Now, how to seat them? Most agility folks ferried their dogs around inside their crates, but even with a 4Runner, I didn't have enough room. Noodle's humungo-size crate took up too much space, and I usually traveled with the dogs in the back seat, stowing their disassembled crates in the cargo area. And since Noodle loved trotting back and forth between the open windows, no way were the three of them going to comfortably share that seat. Harlow—as the best behaved of my two and the non-drooler—got to sit in front.

On the drive, Buster and Noodle shifted and shared windows without fuss. The boxer wasn't showing any signs of missing Celeste. Yet. Fingers crossed, we'd get home without him howling.

By the time we arrived, it was almost eight thirty. I led the dogs through the backyard and into the kitchen. They circled and whined as if they were starving. I opened cans of wet food, found a third bowl, and mixed in dry chow. Buster was so busy anticipating his next meal, he didn't seem to notice his new surroundings. Noodle pawed my leg. "I know, I know. Give me a minute."

I turned on the outside light and managed to set the bowls on the back deck without getting knocked over by the hungry horde. While the dogs devoured their dinner, I poured myself a glass of chilled chardonnay and stood by the open slider to watch. Buster kept his muzzle in his own bowl and didn't try to poach. Good. When they'd finished, I patted each, giving a few extra head scratches to the boxer, then brought the bowls in to rinse. I left the dogs in the yard to romp a bit before bringing them in for the night.

Taking another sip of wine, I pulled Detective DeFelice's card from my pocket. Hoping I'd never need to call her, I tucked it inside my wallet. My cell phone burred. Seeing Miguel's name on the display made me smile. "Hi. Where are you?"

"Just pulling into your driveway. I've got takeout from The Wok."

"You're my hero. Be right there." I slid the screen closed and crossed through the great room to the entryway. As soon as I opened the door, the smell of Szechuan peppers, soy sauce, and garlic hit me. My stomach growled.

Miguel's ensemble of charcoal gray suit, white shirt, and black brogues told me his day had run long, leaving him no time to change. Ignoring the signals from my stomach, I wrapped my arms around his broad back and sank into his kiss.

When we broke apart, he brushed back my hair. "Maybe we should do our macking inside instead of on the porch."

"Macking? How old are you?"

"Old enough to know how to mack properly." He pulled me in for another kiss.

He did know how to mack properly. After catching my breath, I led him inside. "My front porch isn't exactly what I'd call public. You think it's going to get back to the lieutenant that you're kissing a murder suspect?"

"Nah." He closed the front door. "I don't like that pervert across the street watching us."

"You mean J. D.?"

"Yeah. Dude's always staring out the upstairs window. Gives me the creeps."

"Well, his staring out that window helped me once."

Miguel set the to-go bag on the kitchen counter and pulled off his jacket. "Okay, I gotta give you that. But it's still weird."

"You want some wine?"

"Got any beer?" He draped his jacket over a barstool, then answered his own question by opening the refrigerator. After retrieving a bottle, he scrounged through my "miscellaneous" drawer for the opener.

I pulled out plates and silverware. "Eat at the counter or in the living room?"

"Sofa's comfier."

"Okay. Grab the food?"

"Got it."

I set out the plates on the coffee table. "Feel free to get started." I returned to the kitchen and let the dogs in through the slider. This was the boxer's first real foray inside. As I'd told Deputy Wallace, boxers were prone to separation anxiety. His howling in the lot at Playtime proved this. I needed to keep an eye on him and make sure he didn't act out and chew my belongings. I followed as he snuffled his way along the kitchen baseboard into the great room. Though he appeared house trained, I knew virtually nothing about Buster's behavior or habits.

Harlow had settled on the center cushion of the sofa, and Noodle was curled next to the coffee table. Buster continued sniffing the furniture and checked out Miguel by lodging his nose in his crotch.

"Push him back and say 'Off.'"

Miguel did as instructed and the dog resumed his tour of the room.

"Buster's apparently amazing on the agility course, but Celeste didn't teach him manners. I plan to correct that." Finally, the boxer curled on one of the sleeping pillows. Thank goodness neither of my dogs was territorial. "That went pretty well."

Miguel had opened all the cardboard cartons and was dishing up rice and kung pao chicken. He nodded at the boxer. "Why is Buster here and who's Celeste?"

"Celeste was his owner. Someone killed her today."

Miguel set down the serving spoon, brow furrowed. "How? And why'd you wind up with the dog?"

The Golden shifted her head onto Miguel's lap. It looked sweet, but I knew she was angling to catch any spilled food. I took the open cushion on the far end of the sofa by her feet. "Guess Harlow's our chaperone tonight."

"You dodging my question?"

"No. But let me eat first, then I'll tell you."

He finished dishing up food and handed me a plate. After the initial hunger pangs were quelled, I felt more civilized. But in the short time we'd known each other, Miguel was already startlingly good at reading me. Before I collected my thoughts to tell him about my day, Miguel wiped his lips and said, "So, mentioning the murder suspect thing . . . Does that mean the lawyer in Boston called?"

I shook my head and continued chewing.

He cocked his head while stroking Harlow's head. "You only bring it up when something happens with the case."

"Do I? Huh. Hadn't realized. It's probably on my mind because I found a dead body today. Or rather Noodle did."

"I take it the DB was Celeste, Buster's owner?"

"Yeah. It's been a weird, long day."

"Tell me."

I took a deep drink of wine. "This afternoon, an awful woman got her head bashed in by someone at Playtime Academy for Dogs. Noodle was getting his first try at barn hunt when he went off course and climbed a stack of hay bales. That's where he found her . . ." I checked my phone. "Wow. Over four hours ago. The place is in the unincorporated area of the county, so the Ventura Sheriff's Department responded. They did a search but, as far as I could tell, didn't find the weapon. Everyone who was in the barn hunt group was interviewed. Took a couple hours to get through us all. Then I had a long drive home."

"Any arrests? Or suspects?"

"No arrests. But I guess all of us are suspects."

"Which is why the Boston case is on your mind."

"Yep." Seven months earlier I'd been hired to find out if a man's wife was cheating on him. The case had blown up my life when he killed her and my husband—the man she was cheating with—leaving me widowed and high on the Kingston Police Department's suspect list. Didn't seem to matter that the shooter was locked up awaiting trial. As much as I dreaded having to go back and testify, it would be a relief to be done with the case and the suspicions that had followed me across the country from Massachusetts.

"So you knew the victim?"

"Just met her today."

"Then how come you called her awful?"

"I saw her in action. She was awful and didn't hide it. She may even have been proud of it."

We talked through the rest of dinner. Miguel's questions were focused, never leading, and he gave me plenty of time to answer. When the food was gone and I felt talked out, I shifted Harlow's legs off my lap and stood.

"How about we go up to the deck to enjoy another round of drinks without canine supervision?"

A smile replaced Miguel's serious expression. "Sounds good to me."

I went to the kitchen, refilled my glass, and opened another beer while Miguel cleared plates and tossed out to-go containers. On the rooftop deck, the murmur of waves greeted us along with the briny night air. I leaned against the cool metal of the railing and stared out at the Pacific. A fog-free night, the full moon's reflection rippled on the dark water. A siren howled in the distance. I held my breath. When the dogs didn't react, I relaxed again.

Miguel's bottle clinked against the concrete deck, then his hand journeyed up my spine. I nestled against his solid chest as his lips worked their way along the side of my neck. My knees turned to jelly and I spun, my mouth seeking his.

When we broke apart, I gazed up at him, breathing hard. "How about I settle the dogs downstairs and we head to bed?"

"You read my mind."

I slept all the way until 8:00 a.m. before the dogs woke me by charging the door and whining. Since I didn't have a crate for Buster, I'd left them all loose for the night. It was amazing they hadn't woken me sooner. I reached my hand across the cotton sheets. Miguel's side of the bed was already cold. He must've gone home to change before reporting in. Sighing, I stared at his rumpled pillow.

After a quick shower, I dressed in jeans and a T-shirt, then opened the bedroom door. All three dogs tumbled inside, tails wagging. "Anyone hungry?" Noodle pawed my leg and drooled. "Okay. Breakfast it is."

I was setting their bowls on the back deck when my cell rang. Once the dogs were eating, I checked the screen: "Unknown Caller." "Hello?"

"Hey, Molly. You coming to agility class tomorrow?"

I stared at my cell's readout. Still said "Unknown Caller." "Uh, who is this?"

"Oh. Sorry. It's Felicity Gaines. We met at Playtime yesterday."

"Hi. I didn't recognize your voice." Felicity sure sounded chipper. Did that mean the deputies hadn't contacted her yet with the news about Celeste? Or maybe they had and that was the source of her happiness? Time to find out. "I'm not sure about tomorrow. I've got Buster and don't know when I'll need to take him back."

"Buster? As in Celeste's dog?"

"Yep." I waited, curious to hear her reaction.

"Why do you have Buster?"

So she didn't know. Or was a terrific actress. "The detectives haven't contacted you?"

"What detectives? And why would they contact me?"

"Celeste was killed yesterday. At Playtime."

"What?"

The horror in her voice sounded genuine. Feeling bad about dumping the news rather than breaking it gently, I went over the events of yesterday evening. After finishing the dregs of my coffee, I added, "The detectives asked me to tell them everyone I saw there. From the moment I arrived."

"Oh."

"And during my second interview, I heard Simone gave them a list of all the registered students who were at Playtime, so I imagine someone will be calling you soon."

"I can't believe it. Well, that's not true. Not really. Celeste was a horrible person. Tough and a hard worker, but still horrible. Dear God, do they think someone who goes to Playtime did it?"

"It's possible. That is where she was found."

"Yeah, but she was terrible to everyone. Not just the agility crowd. I mean, one time I had to meet her at her gymnastics studio. I was dropping something off for the boxers' club we both belong to. Belonged to, I mean." She took a sharp inhale before continuing. "I've gotta say, the way she talked to those kids was awful."

"Talked? Not yelled?"

"No. She was subtler with her cruelty. She'd smile as she said something completely demoralizing to one of the girls. It was clear her students didn't know how to fight back."

"I imagine the deputies will need to talk to them, too."

"And what about her husband?"

"Isn't he in Hawaii?"

"That's what Celeste said. But maybe he hasn't left yet. Or maybe he paid someone to get rid of her for him."

Felicity was right; the spouse was always a potential suspect—
as I knew far too well. "I thought they were celebrating some big
anniversary."

"Five years. Which—with the way she treated him—was a
miracle."

"Wait. How do you know how things were with her and her
husband? It's not like you two were confidants."

"We used to be neighbors. That's how we met."

"Right. You mentioned that yesterday."

"Thank goodness they moved to Pier Point a few months later.
But before then . . . Let's just say, those two didn't close the windows when they fought. Or made up. And Celeste never kept her
volume down with him. In either situation."

CHAPTER 5

Harlow and Buster were playing tug-of-war on the grass in the backyard while Noodle chewed and drooled on a tennis ball. I couldn't believe how well the boxer was adjusting to this drastic change in his life. Granted, having Harlow to play with probably helped distract him, but still . . . Did Buster's seeming indifference to Celeste's absence say something about how she treated him?

Shaking off that thought, I checked the time: five minutes until I was due at Ava Greenwood's. Over the past few months, the girl had done a great job with her Basset-Retriever, Butterscotch. Nevertheless, we continued our training sessions—as much for me as her. Most people were surprised by my friendship with the eight-year-old prodigy, but we enjoyed each other's company.

I crossed the lawn, petted and kissed the dogs. Just one day of telling Buster "off" and "down" had worked wonders with his behavior. I gave him an extra kiss. "Okay, be good. I'll be back soon." Leaving through the gate, I headed down the alley. As always, I stopped when I reached what local papers called "Slaughterhouse Five." "Slaughterhouse" for the dismembered woman and "five" because the address was 555. The press would eventually cease their stories and the ugly reference would be forgotten—but not by me. Empty now, I'd heard the home would be sold to help pay for legal fees. But who'd want to move into a murder house? I imagined whoever did would get a great break on the price.

Deep breath in. I turned my attention to the opposite side of the narrow lane and the Italianate two-story with all the wrought iron. Ava and Butterscotch were already waiting for me on the front porch.

She grinned and waved. "Hi, Molly."

"Hey, smart stuff." In spite of the dog's short legs and low body, Butterscotch jumped high enough to lick my face as I bent to greet her. I stroked her long silky ears before straightening.

"*Buenas dias,*" Ava said.

"Excuse me?"

"That means 'Good day' in Spanish."

"I know what it means, but why are you wishing me a good day in Spanish?"

"I'm studying with an online tutor. I'd been learning on my own but was worried I might get the pronunciations wrong."

"Ah. And the tutor's helping?"

"*Sí.*" She turned and waved me toward the side gate. "*Venga conmigo.*"

"What?"

"It means 'Follow me.'" She looked down at the dog. "*Venga conmigo,* Butterscotch."

"No 'please' in there—for me or the dog?"

Ava paused and cocked her head. Off-the-charts smart, the

girl spent most of her time studying or playing chess. Her social skills needed work. She licked her bottom lip. "*Venga conmigo, por favor.*"

"Better." Not that I was a paragon of civility or gracious behavior—probably why we got along. I took a step forward. "Glad to hear Spanish is going well. What else are you doing?"

She opened the side gate and led the way, tossing words over her shoulder. "I'm writing an essay on the effects of climate change on the fishing industry and working on quadratic equations and nonlinear systems of equations. Jemma thinks I should be able to move up a grade next month."

"Wow. Is the pace all right for you? Not too hectic?"

"I like it." She grinned, exposing a gap where her right canine tooth had been.

Stopping, I pointed. "What happened there?"

"Lost an incisor. Made ten dollars."

"The tooth fairy's more generous than when I was a kid."

Ava settled her free hand on her hip. "We've talked about this. I know the tooth fairy is Jemma."

"True. But there's no harm in adding a little whimsy to every-day life."

Her forehead wrinkled at this foreign concept, then she shrugged and continued to the backyard.

When we'd reached the small grassy area, her mom opened the slider and waved. A breeze fluttered her dark hair. "Hi, Molly. Got a minute?"

"Sure." I turned to Ava. "Since you and Butterscotch have the basics nailed, how about reviewing the 'drop it' command?"

"Okay." Ava hurled the tennis ball across the yard and But-terscotch ran after it on stubby legs.

I joined Jemma on the deck. "What's up? Everything all right?"

Jemma smoothed her locks. "Yes, I just wanted to thank you."

"For what?"

"The last few months have been tough. Especially since . . ." She lowered her voice. "Rick left. Having this new challenge of training the dog—and having a friend—has been a game changer for Ava."

"You don't need to thank me. I get as much from hanging out with her as she does from being with me."

"Regardless, you're the one who showed me Butterscotch could live inside with us and not destroy everything. That's made a huge difference for Ava. She laughs more, worries less, and sleeps through the night."

"Probably tired out from running around with the dog."

"I'm sure that's part of it. But I know you have a lot to do with her being happier."

Not sure what to say, I shrugged. "She's a great kid."

"You and I know that. But it hasn't always been obvious to others. Especially the neighborhood children. Ava tended to be rude when they didn't understand what she was saying. That's changed. Training Butterscotch has been good for her. And, added bonus: The neighborhood kids adore that dog. Which means Ava now has something to talk about with them. They love her dog stories. I mean, how many children get excited hearing about Magnus Carlsen's shift from an attack style of chess in his early years to a more mature and measured approach?"

I snort-laughed. "Not a whole lot of adults are excited by that, either." Ava wasn't the only one who had changed; Jemma was no longer the spaced-out, disengaged mom I'd met the first time I came home with her daughter.

"Having the dog and the training . . . it's extra-important right now."

The jingle of Butterscotch's tags pulled my attention to the yard.

"Drop it," Ava commanded. The dog complied.

I turned back to Jemma. "Because?"

Jemma sighed. "It's official. Rick and I are getting divorced." She crossed her arms over her chest. "I always knew reconciliation was a long shot. I mean, it's not like it was the first time he cheated. But it was definitely the last." Her gaze landed on Ava.

"Good for you. How's she taking the news?"

"Better than I expected. Rick feels so guilty, he's making an extra effort to spend time with her. He's even paying attention to the dog. That's a major improvement."

We chatted another minute before I rejoined Ava on the grass. Butterscotch raced back again with the tennis ball and dropped it when told to. "Good job, you two. Now, let's try working on a long stay."

When it was nearing time for Ava to resume her studies, I grabbed the tennis ball and tossed it to the dog. "You going to that chess competition next week?"

"Uh-huh. I've been watching YouTubes about Bologan and Michael Adams, and reading up on the Karpov-Kamsky match."

"Feeling confident?"

She shrugged. "This will be my first time playing against adults. I can't say I'm confident, but I'm looking forward to it." When Butterscotch returned and Ava picked up the ball again, she looked at me. "Is everything okay?"

"Huh?"

"You seem distracted."

Knowing it was inappropriate to talk about Celeste's murder with an eight-year-old—no matter how smart she was—I weighed my answer. "I went to Playtime Academy for Dogs with Harlow and Noodle yesterday."

"Did they like it?"

"Harlow had fun and did great. So did Noodle." Technically, finding a dead body hidden on top of a haystack could be called "great" in the nose work department. "And we met some new people. One of them—a really nice woman—got into a yelling match with another less-nice woman. But she won't tell me why. I can't stop wondering about that."

Ava tossed the ball. After Butterscotch trotted back with it, she said, "Drop it." Ava threw it again. "Why do you care?"

Normally I wouldn't. Damn, the kid was smart. "The reason's not important."

She tossed the ball again, then turned to face me, hands on her narrow hips. "The reason is always important."

I bit back a sigh. "Right. Guess I just don't want to get into it."

"Kind of like your friend."

I couldn't help but smile. "Got me." Butterscotch returned with the ball, and I took a turn tossing it across the yard. "I think there're a few reasons she might not answer my questions. Like, she's stonewalling because the reason for the fight is embarrassing."

"And makes her look bad?"

"Maybe. Or maybe it's because she has the same breed of dog as the other woman and keeps losing to her at competitions. And the less-nice woman hasn't been doing agility as long."

"That'd make me mad. Maybe the less-nice woman cheated?"

"Interesting. Not sure how she could've swung that, but worth considering. Also, they used to be neighbors so it might have nothing to do with their dogs."

"Maybe she cheated the other way."

I raised my eyebrows.

"With the other woman's husband."

Yikes. Her own father's straying was understandably on Ava's mind. I cursed myself for inadvertently sending her thoughts in that direction.

"Come on. Enough of this. Let's run around the yard with Butterscotch for the last couple minutes." The simplest answer might well be the correct one: Felicity killed Celeste.

The next day I headed to the club-sponsored agility class in Camarillo, hoping to meet up with Felicity. When I reached the large park, I drove past the dusty BMX raceway and the concrete roller hockey rink before finding parking near the open grassy area. Harlow bounded from the car, tail swooshing like an enthusiastic plume. The smell of airplane fuel and eucalyptus hung in the air. I loaded the cart with our equipment and headed across the blacktop. The class area was marked off by a low fence. About fifteen people were setting out crates, chairs, and shade cover beyond the boundary.

I rolled our supplies across the sidewalk and onto the grass. I'd set up the crate and was clipping a shade cloth to the top to shield Harlow from the sun when Felicity and Royal joined us.

"You made it."

"Yep." I opened the door to the crate and the Golden burst out. Her tail continued wagging as she and Royal sniffed one another.

"You're going to be glad you came today. This instructor's amazing." Felicity glanced around us. "You didn't bring Buster?"

"Didn't want to confuse him by adding a new handler to the mix. Besides, this way Noodle's not home alone. He hates that." I debated broaching the topic foremost on my mind. Knowing it was probably a mistake, I said, "You willing to tell me now what you and Celeste fought about?"

She waved away my question. "It was no big deal."

No big deal? Celeste was dead. "Have the detectives been in touch with you yet?"

"Some guy named Stern left a message."

"When?"

"After you and I talked yesterday."

"And?"

"And what?"

"You didn't return his call?"

"I've been busy." She took a step back, resting one hand on her hip.

Defensive much? "Felicity, don't mess with the Sheriff's Department. Call Stern and get it over with. They're investigating a murder. You don't want to look like you're not taking it seriously."

Her mouth dropped open. "I'm not . . . That's not what . . ." She shook her head, then took a deep breath. "I wasn't even there when it happened."

"You may not want to hear this, but we don't know when it happened. And you were there that day. Everybody heard you and Celeste argue. The detectives already asked me what you fought about."

Her face paled. "What'd you say?"

"The truth: I was too far away to hear what either of you said. But they're going to ask you. There's no way around it."

"It's none of their business."

"That's not going to cut it. They're going to want to know what you said."

"It's got nothing to do with what happened to Celeste."

"How can you be so sure?"

"I just am."

I stared at her. Not a ringing endorsement for Felicity's innocence. The instructor's raised voice broke the tense silence.

"Thank you for asking me to lead today's class." Standing in the center of the fenced area, a striking blonde in her forties pulled off her sunglasses. "I'm Dixie Walcott and we'll be covering advanced agility techniques. Crate your dogs and come help set up the equipment for today. Let's go, people."

In spite of Felicity's obvious irritation at my nosiness, we worked together carrying the club's teeter-totter from the trailer. With the help of a bronzed twentysomething man named Joel, we got it set up. I scanned the area. Arm and knee braces abounded among the club members. I raised my eyebrows at the other two. "Ready for another load?"

Joel grinned. "You bet."

The three of us retrieved the A-frame—the largest of the obstacles—and put it where Dixie pointed. Once all the equipment was situated, the instructor walked the course, directing minor adjustments to the placement of each obstacle, then called us to order again.

"Those who have large dogs can walk the course now."

I went through a few times: the first to learn the order of the obstacles, the second to determine which side of Harlow to take on our approach, and the third to figure whether I'd run in front or behind her as we raced to each. Returning to my camp chair, I watched the few folks still doing their final passes.

When everyone had filed out, Dixie held up her hand. "Okay, we're starting with the twenty-inch jumpers and will work our way down. Line up with your dogs over to the right."

Felicity coaxed Royal from his crate and I did the same with

Harlow. The first dog and handler pair were a thin anxious-looking man with an equally nervous-looking greyhound. The man alternated between pulling on his right earlobe and rubbing his bald scalp as he and Dixie spoke in advance of his run. She pointed and he moved to the start and called his dog.

Between the second and third obstacles, he misjudged a front cross, causing the dog to slow. He sped up and the greyhound nearly back-jumped the next obstacle. The handler froze, then re-directed the dog. After that, he never got the dog back up to speed though the rest of the course went more smoothly. When they'd finished, the man stood red-faced as Dixie spoke quietly to him for at least two minutes. Next she beckoned Felicity into the ring.

After talking to Dixie, Felicity told Royal to stay and walked a few feet out. At her command, Royal took off like a dart. They raced through the course, making smooth transitions and modulating speed at the contacts. Felicity didn't touch her hair once. When done, she met with the instructor then trotted Royal back to his crate, a huge smile on her face.

"Great job. You two looked totally in sync."

She huffed out a breath and sat. "I can't believe I actually got a compliment from the great Dixie Walcott. Those are rarer than diamonds in a dung heap."

A woman with a Weimaraner ran next. By the second obstacle, it was clear they had no business attending an advanced class. At the end, Dixie spent five minutes talking to the woman and walking her through the course.

When my turn came, I led Harlow inside and took a deep breath to still the butterflies.

Dixie waited until we were toe-to-toe before speaking. "How are you guys going to do this?"

"I'll start with Harlow on my left. We'll use a rear cross between obstacles two and three and I'll do a one-eighty between numbers three and four. I think a front cross will work best before the second tunnel and a blind on the way to number eight."

"Plan of attack for the teeter?"

"On that and the A-frame, I want to stay in front of her so she doesn't jump the gun and skip the contacts."

"Good. Go when you're ready."

The butterflies had flown. I unclipped Harlow's leash and tossed it to the side. "Okay, girl. Let's go!" We ran toward the first jump. Harlow landed a little rough, then angled with me to the tunnel. It was one of those runs where almost everything went perfectly. Harlow was focused, her speed just right. When she raced across the teeter, I yelled, "Bang it." The plank thudded down, then she bounded toward the next jump.

As Harlow cleared the panel at the end, Dixie called out, "Beautiful!"

Warmth spread through my chest. I played tug-of-war with Harlow before clipping on her leash and walking over to the instructor.

"Good blinds and rears. A little rocky on that first hurdle. What do you think went wrong there?"

"I didn't get my feet pointed to the right soon enough. Think that messed her up."

"Good. You got it."

I dragged my chair next to Felicity's to watch the few remaining large dogs who'd yet to run. Joel was the last in our size category. Turned out he had an Australian shepherd who handled the course like a dream. Bright and completely tuned in to his handler. When they'd finished, Felicity and I went onto the course to reset the jump heights for the medium-size dogs while Dixie gave Joel his review.

As we headed to our chairs, Felicity called Joel over. He and his dog loped across the grass. I suspected she'd beckoned him to keep me from asking about her fight with Celeste as much as to rehash how class had gone.

"You're so strong on the blinds," she told him.

Joel crouched and stroked his Aussie's merle coat. "From an early age, Philly picked up what to cue in on. He's such a smart boy, aren't you? Aren't you?" The dog's tongue lolled as Joel scratched behind his ears. Straightening, he thrust his chin toward Royal. "You guys really tightened up your times. What's your secret?"

Felicity pointed at me. "This lady. She made me see a behavior I'd been doing that confused Royal. Now that I'm aware of it, I'm hoping we can shorten our time even further as I feel more in control. And Dixie gave me some good tips for handling the blinds."

"Good for you." He held out his hand to me. "We moved equipment together, but I never properly introduced myself. Joel DeCarolis."

"Molly Madison. You from Philadelphia?"

He looked blank for a moment, then chuckled. "No, the breeder where I got Philly said this guy was shaped like a Philly Cheesesteak when he was a puppy. The official name on his papers is Rising Blue Tide, but he answers to Philly."

I studied the dog's long slender snout and low sloping neckline. "Gotta say, it's hard to picture him looking like a cheesesteak now."

"Right?"

Tail wagging, Harlow moved forward to sniff the new dog.

"Philly's great with other dogs. Gets a little nervous around new people."

"Got it." I stayed where I was and didn't try to pet Philly. After my Golden and the Aussie circled and sniffed, Harlow returned to my side. A brief hesitation, then Philly followed. He snuffled along my tennis shoes and up the leg of my jeans. I let my hand dangle at my side and soon felt a wet nose on my skin. "Think it's okay if I pet him now?"

"You're good to go."

Crouching, I met his glacier blue gaze and held out my hand. He sniffed then licked, and I stroked his coat. "You're smart and handsome, aren't you?" Philly wagged his tail.

While I'd been paying attention to Joel and his dog, Felicity had packed her equipment onto her cart. She gripped Royal's leash. "We've got to go. Good to see you, Joel, and glad you could try the class, Molly."

"Thanks for the recommendation."

"You new to the area?" Joel said. "I mean, you're obviously not new to agility."

"Newish. Moved to Pier Point three months ago."

While we chatted, Felicity practically jogged to her SUV, escaping before I could talk to her about Celeste again. Nothing guilty looking about that, right?

CHAPTER 6

The next morning, the female deputy I'd met at Playtime called to inform me that Celeste's husband was home from Hawaii. "His name's Del Kaminsky," Alvarez said. "He told me I could give you his address and phone number."

"Thanks." I wrote down the information. "I'll get the dog to him ASAP."

The first call I placed to Del went to voice mail. I left a message. Around noon, I tried again. Voice mail. I left another message. At four o'clock I called the number once more. When his voice mail kicked in, I hung up. Leaving another message seemed pointless. Either he hadn't heard the others or was too busy to respond.

Good thing I'd promised to get Buster back home "as soon as possible" rather than "immediately." I supposed Celeste's husband was dealing with the Sheriff's Department or her funeral arrangements. I looked at the boxer. "I bet he needs your love more than ever. Let's take a chance and drop by."

When I picked up Buster's leash, all three dogs began to caper. "Okay. Road trip it is." I piled him and Noodle into the 4Runner's back seat, and Harlow, once again, rode shotgun.

The Kaminsky-Simmons house was only six blocks away—on the opposite side of Pier Point's small restaurant row. I parked and checked the address. The house was a white two-story cube with black trim and a galvanized steel roof. Leaving the windows cracked with the Saint Berdoodle and the Golden inside, I walked Buster up the slate path.

I pushed the bell and startled when a fanfare played. Buster howled. "Don't like that bell, huh? Can't say I blame you."

While we waited, I patted the boxer's flank. I was considering pressing the bell again when the door swung open. A man with a sunburned nose, close-trimmed hair on a square head, and scraggly scruff on an equally square jaw towered over me. His smile turned to a scowl. Reflexively, I took a step back. Buster gave a low growl. I bent to soothe him. "It's okay, boy."

"What's he doing here?"

Not the reaction I'd expected. Straightening, I studied Celeste's husband. His gray T-shirt had a brown splotch running across his stomach and he wore red plaid Bermuda shorts and no shoes. His eyes were bloodshot. From crying? Scotch fumes assaulted me. Okay, maybe not due to grief. "Del Kaminsky?"

The big man's frown deepened. He pointed at Buster. "I said, why's that mutt here?"

"Um, I figured you'd want your dog."

"What the hell am I supposed to do with that thing?"

That thing? The dog's growl grew throatier. Heat rushed up my face. I took a deep breath and told myself to stay courteous. After all, the man had just lost his wife. "I take it Celeste was the one who looked after Buster."

Del lifted a rocks glass filled with amber liquid. After drain-
ing the contents, he slurred, "It was her damn dog, not mine."

Apparently, Deputy Alvarez had asked Celeste's husband if it
was okay to give me his number, but not whether he wanted
Buster. "Uh, look, I know you've had a terrible loss. And I don't
want to add to your stress." And Buster obviously disliked the
man. "How about I take care of him? For now. If you feel differently about wanting him back in the next couple weeks, let me
know." I offered Del one of my business cards.

He took it reluctantly. "What the hell's a dog wrangler?"

"Just another name for dog trainer." I studied the man. How
drunk was he? Clumsy drunk or loose lips drunk? Suspecting the
latter, I said, "But I used to be a cop. Back in Massachusetts. I'm
the one who found Celeste."

"Bully for you."

Wow. Maybe not grief-stricken at all. Time to try a new approach. "I couldn't help wondering if your wife had any enemies?"

"You mean other than that snake pit she called an agility
club?"

Snake pit? Feeling like we were speaking different languages,
I retreated another step. "I've gone to a couple events and the
people seem pretty nice."

"Yeah?" His hairy nostrils flared. "Wait until you win a few
meets. I guarantee things will turn nasty then."

Buster gave another growl, this time baring his teeth. I short-
ened the leash. "Are you saying people made negative remarks to
Celeste? Stuff like accusing her of cheating? Or did someone
from the club threaten her?"

He stepped forward, his bulk filling the doorway. "That's none
of your business." He jabbed a thick index finger near my face.
"Any problems Celeste and I had were between her and me. I

don't need some sad sack ex-cop trying to give their life meaning by poking around my wife's murder." He stepped back and slammed the door.

I looked down at Buster. "Sad sack?"

The boxer wagged his tail.

"Well, at least someone's happy to have my company." I bent to stroke the poor dog's coat. "And I'm happy to have yours, too." He licked my hand and I blinked back tears. "You're such a good boy. How could that man not want you?" I straightened and ran my sleeve across my face as we headed to the street.

Why did Del bring up "problems"—plural—between him and Celeste? Guilty conscience, maybe? Or too drunk to understand my question had nothing to do with the state of his marriage?

When I opened the car door, Noodle and Harlow greeted me as if I'd been gone for days, not minutes. After loving them up, I loaded Buster into the back seat. I started the engine and gave Del's house a final glance. "Well, whatever he meant, he doesn't look much like a man in mourning." I turned to Harlow. "We need to dig deeper, right?"

The Golden woofed.

It wasn't until after we'd finished our evening walk and the dogs had gobbled their dinners that I had a chance to log on to my Trackers account. Keeping my membership active—even though I wasn't licensed as a private investigator in California—had proved helpful more than once since the move. I typed in Del's name and address.

Turned out he owned a sportswear business. From the corporate report, it looked like they made a cheaper version of the clothing lines that had made Under Armour a household name.

Additional digging indicated a similar level of achievement had eluded him so far. The previous year's annual report showed the business had turned a profit—but just barely. Had Celeste been more successful than her husband?

I did a quick search on her business, SimNastics. Wow. Celeste didn't just run a couple gyms. She owned two locally and had franchised a string of gyms up and down the California coast. After checking the company's corporate records, I gulped. Who knew there was so much money in teaching girls to fly through the air like gravity didn't matter?

California is a community property state, and it appeared Celeste had no business partners or children. Unless I'd missed something, old Del stood to inherit a healthy chunk of change. That, and his mention of "problems" between him and Celeste, added up to a possible motive for murder.

My cell rang. A photo of Ava's Basset-Retriever appeared on the screen. "Hey, Ava. What's up?"

"I'm worried about J. D."

"What happened?"

"I was walking Butterscotch this morning when J. D. stepped onto his front porch. I waved at him. He smiled and took another step. Then his face got all sweaty and he ran inside. I think he's getting worse."

When my neighbor J. D. returned to Pier Point after spending a year in Costa Rica surfing and working at a turtle conservation program, he'd been overwhelmed by the number of people everywhere. What started as panic attacks when too many people were around quickly spiraled into agoraphobia. Recently, though, I'd had some success prying him out of his house to do what he loved best: surfing. "He did okay going to the beach with me on Thursday. Surfed for almost an hour."

"Maybe he needs a handler."

"Huh?"

"Like I'm Butterscotch's handler. I keep her from getting too scared by new things. Maybe we could get J. D. a handler who could take him to do things he loves and help keep him from getting overwhelmed."

"That's an idea. I wonder if he'd be open to it."

"We should ask."

Out of the mouths of babes.

Miguel texted as Ava and I wrapped things up: I've got pizza. Can come by and share.

I sent back a thumbs-up and happy face emojis, then took the dogs into the backyard. Pizza and pups were rarely a good combination. Even when the dogs were well behaved and didn't actively beg, they'd give me the big eyes and I always wound up sharing more than I should.

Minutes later, Miguel knocked. I opened the door and he entered, holding the pizza box aloft. The smell of melting cheese and pepperoni trailed after him. He wrapped his free arm around me and I sank into his kiss. "Wow." I gazed into his tawny eyes. "Maybe we can put the pizza in the oven to keep warm."

His hand traveled down to my hip. "You read my mind."

Later, when we were sprawled amid the sheets, he traced the line of my clavicle. "We kind of skipped the small talk. How was your day?"

"Ah. Time to act like civilized folks?"

"Not completely." Miguel leaned in and kissed me.

When I'd caught my breath again, I finally answered his question. "I tried to return Buster to Celeste's husband."

His eyebrows rose. "Tried?"

"Yep. The guy didn't want him."

"So you've got three dogs now?"

I waggled my hand. "Time will tell. I told him he had a couple weeks to change his mind."

"Do you want another dog?"

"I . . . You know me, I love them all. But I only adopted Noodle three months ago. Even though he's done a great job adjusting, it's a little soon for me to permanently take in another." I rolled onto my side. "You want a dog?"

"Whoa." He held up his hands before reaching out to stroke my cheek. "Don't try to drag me into your dog-mania."

"Oh, come on. You love the dogs. And Buster's already trained."

"Yeah, but with my hours, I don't think I'd be around enough to make a good home for him."

"Point taken." I checked the time. "Speaking of which . . . There are three dogs in the backyard I should bring in."

Miguel sighed as I climbed from bed and strode into the bathroom. After a quick shower, I emerged dressed in sweatpants and a T-shirt.

"See, that's another thing I like about you."

"What?"

"You never dress to impress me. You're always you."

My cheeks grew warm and I shrugged. I was still getting my bearings in Pier Point and knew getting involved with Miguel this fast was probably a mistake. So far, we'd managed to avoid talking about our feelings. I changed the subject. "Are you familiar with Celeste's gyms?"

"No." Miguel sat up and leaned his back against the headboard. "Why?"

"I did a little digging. The woman owned a number of gyms—not just the two local ones. She and Del didn't have any kids. I imagine her husband stands to inherit her entire estate."

He frowned. "Ah, Molly. Don't go there."

"Where?"

"I get it. You've got a cop's nose for crime. But leave the woman's death to the Sheriff's Department. This is their investigation."

Irritation flashed through me. It wasn't like I'd been trying to snoop. Except that's exactly what I'd done on the Trackers website. "I left a clean towel on the rack. I'll let the dogs in and warm up the pizza."

"But we're not sharing it with them this time."

"We'll see."

He gave a rueful grin. "A losing battle, I know."

As I headed down the stairs, I realized Miguel was right: Celeste's death was none of my business. I'd barely known the woman and didn't much like her. It was time to butt out.

CHAPTER 7

While Miguel and I ate, the dogs stared at us, alert and hopeful. I was the first to cave, tearing small sections from my slice and offering a tidbit to each. Tails wagged as the dogs gobbled. Following my lead, Miguel tore a strip off his piece and divided it into three sections. Licking and more wagging ensued.

"Okay. That's all." I wiped my hands on a napkin. "Everybody lie down." Harlow circled then settled on one of the dog pillows. Seeing an opening on the sofa, Noodle hopped up on Miguel's right. The big dog needed more space and Miguel scooted closer to me. "Way to go, Noodle." I grinned.

"Believe me, I'm not complaining." His stiff posture was at odds with his warm tone.

The boxer remained seated near the sofa, eyes focused on me. "I'm guessing Celeste used to give Buster a lot of table scraps." I stood. "Lie down."

He cocked his head, then snuffled to the other dog pillow.

After circling and giving it a thorough inspection, Buster stretched across it and sighed.

I sat and took another slice. Normally conversation flowed easily between Miguel and me. But tonight, he was uncharacteristically silent. "How're things at work?"

"Got an interesting case. High-end car thefts. We suspect a ring of pros is shipping them out of the country."

"You getting anywhere with it?"

He waggled his hand. "Not a lot to go on. But it's high priority because . . ."

"Because what?"

He picked up a paper napkin and wiped his mouth. "Probably shouldn't say."

I leaned back. "Are you kidding me? Those words are like . . . pizza to a dog. I want more."

"Okay. But you didn't hear this from me. The mayor's on our ass about the thefts because the cars of a couple top donors were taken."

"Ouch." Maybe that was why Miguel seemed wound so tight. "When cases get political . . ." I shook my head.

"Tell me about it." He grabbed another slice from the box. Strings of melted cheese stretched from the adjacent piece. Breaking the connection with his free hand, he dropped the slice onto his plate. "I talked to Lupe earlier today. Said she was looking forward to seeing you tomorrow." His voice sounded strained.

I turned to face him.

He kept his gaze on the pizza and took a bite. After swallowing, he added, "How often do you two get together? Is it just to train Ulysses?"

"We train, then hang out. It's only once a week now. I think Lupe likes having a set day because it guarantees she gets some social time, and since we call it a training session, it gives her an excuse to leave work on time. You know how she usually stays late—except on cooking class days. And now dog-training days."

His brow furrowed.

"Don't worry—I'm not charging her."

"Oh. No, I didn't think . . ." He cleared his throat. "I still can't believe she and Andy didn't know their dog was deaf until you told them."

Surprised he was bringing up old news, I shrugged, then rose and took my empty plate to the kitchen.

Miguel's phone burred. He checked the screen. "Sorry. Gotta take this." He cleared his throat. "Vasquez here. Uh-huh. Uh-huh." After a long pause, he spoke again. "Okay. Be right there." He tucked his phone inside his pocket and grabbed his jacket. "Gotta go. Got a lead on a stolen Maserati."

The tension in his jaw was gone—as were the furrows crossing his forehead. Maybe pressure from the mayor was why Miguel seemed on edge. I set the plate in the sink and rounded the counter. "At least we did the uncivilized thing early."

He bent down and gave me a quick kiss. "It's no 'We'll always have Paris,' but I can live with that."

I snort-laughed and walked him to the door. The three dogs roused themselves to follow. "You be careful."

"Always."

After he'd left, the house felt empty—in spite of the dogs. I rinsed our plates and tucked them into the dishwasher. Drying my hands, I grabbed my laptop and sat cross-legged on the sofa. Harlow hopped up, followed by Noodle. Buster settled nearby on the floor. Surrounded as I was by canine goodwill, I still missed Miguel. Even if he'd been acting squirrelly tonight.

Three episodes of Bosch later—each accompanied by a glass

of wine—I stood and stared at the room. Right. I didn't have a crate for Buster. I plodded up the stairs to bed, dogs at my heels. I patted the comforter. "Dog free-for-all!"

Noodle jumped up and commandeered Miguel's pillow. Harlow took over the foot of the bed. Buster cocked his head as if trying to figure things out. I rubbed his head and flank. "It's okay, boy, you can hop up if you want."

I got ready for bed, then fit myself into the narrow space on the mattress left by the three dogs. When sleep didn't come immediately, I turned onto my back and stared at the dark ceiling. Maybe I was making a mistake avoiding "The Talk" with Miguel. Was it his case—or my lack of candor—that had caused his seeming eagerness to head back to work? I liked the guy. Maybe more than liked. Was that so awful to admit?

Noodle rolled against me and began to snore, his warmth and size reassuring. Dogs were ever loyal. Unlike my dead husband. The man cheated on me after I miscarried. Talk about a crap move. Maybe being cautious sharing my feelings wasn't such a bad idea. No need to make myself more vulnerable than I already was.

Closing my eyes again, I hoped the chardonnay gods would smile upon me and let me sleep.

I awoke at dawn with something dripping onto my cheek. All three dogs hovered, but only Noodle drooled. "Okay. Okay. I'm on it. Give me a minute." Wiping my face, I climbed from bed and made a quick detour to the bathroom before trailing the dogs downstairs. I let them outside to do their business and opened cans of dog food. After mixing in kibble, I took the bowls onto the back deck. The three inhaled their breakfasts.

Once the coffee maker was going, I returned upstairs to strip the drool-splattered bedding. I carried it downstairs and loaded the washer. As it churned, I poured myself a cup of coffee and joined the dogs outside.

I pulled out my phone. Nothing from Miguel. He usually texted from work. Hopefully the lack of a message meant he was tracking a solid lead. Harlow scavenged a forgotten tennis ball from alongside the fence and brought it onto the deck. "Always ready to play, aren't you? Drop it."

The Golden complied and I tossed the ball. She and Buster flew after it. Noodle found a sunny patch of grass, where he sprawled and drooled. As much as I loved Harlow, was it wrong for me to wonder if Noodle might be smarter?

Harlow and Buster raced back together. This time the boxer had the ball. "Drop it."

Buster let go and wagged his arc of a tail. I'd barely known Celeste, but she seemed more the sort to crop a boxer's tail and ears. Maybe she adopted him at an older age? Whatever the reason, I was glad she'd left Buster's ears and tail intact. They gave him a ton of personality. I tossed the soggy ball again. How often had Celeste worked with him? I'd done nothing since bringing him home two days ago. The boxer was an up-and-coming agility star. I should run him through some fundamentals to keep him sharp. My hangover whispered training could wait.

After eating a bowl of oatmeal, I tossed the ball some more, then called Buster and told him to sit. Not wanting him to lose his rear cross skills, but not feeling like running myself, I had him follow me with his eyes. "Stay. Watch me." First, I walked to his right, then to his left. When he held his position, I circled him clockwise. He only turned his head. I circled in the opposite direction. The dog was a rock. An alert, engaged rock, holding position, gaze on me, never moving his feet.

"Wow. That was easy. You make me look good at this." I leaned down and stroked his soft ears. We went through the exercise a few more times before I called the other two dogs. "Okay, guys. Who wants to take a walk?"

Harlow pranced and Noodle drooled. Buster remained seated but thumped his tail. I grabbed leashes and hooked them on. We left through the gate. I urged the dogs across the street to J. D.'s, hoping to kill two birds with one well-aimed stone.

The door opened before I knocked. "Wow. You expecting someone?"

"Nah." He shook his shaggy blond head. "I was looking out the window and saw you heading this way." He crouched and petted Harlow and Noodle, then extended his hand to the boxer. "Who's this beautiful fellow?"

"This is Buster."

Buster leaned into J. D. as he rubbed his coat. "Come on in." He led the way through the austere high-ceilinged house to the backyard. "I can't believe you got another dog." He dug in the toy box he'd assembled for my dogs and tossed a tennis ball. Once again Harlow and Buster chased after it while Noodle spectated.

"He's not exactly mine. His owner died and her husband says he doesn't want him. I'm giving him a couple weeks to reconsider."

The dogs ran back to J. D. He took the ball and petted Buster again. "How could someone not want you?"

"Exactly."

The next trip back with the ball, the boxer rose up on his hind legs and pawed J. D.'s chest. "He really likes you. He hasn't done that with me."

"Yeah?" J. D. threw the ball and the dogs ran it down again.

"Would you like to take them for a walk with me?"

He rubbed the back of his neck. "Uh . . ."

"I'll take Harlow and Noodle, and you can take Buster." I decided to play dirty. "I know it's a challenge for you, but you'd be doing me a big favor. Three big dogs are a lot to handle. We can walk on the beach. Shouldn't be crowded right now. And we can turn back anytime you need."

"Okay." He wiped his palms along the sides of his jeans.

Sweat beaded his forehead even before he stepped out the front door, and I was aware of J. D. doing his deep-breathing exercise as we walked the short distance down the alley to the cul-de-sac. As always, the crashing ocean seemed to calm him. "You doing okay?"

"Yeah." He gave me a tight smile, then looked at the boxer prancing along. "Let's keep going."

"All right." We crossed to the hard-packed sand by the water. A half-dozen surfers were past the break, waiting for the next decent wave. "I can come back with you after Ava's lesson if you want to surf today."

"You shouldn't have to babysit me so I can have some fun."

"I'm not. You're my friend and I want you to get better."

"Better, right." His tone sounded bitter.

I looked around. The sun hadn't yet burned off the cloud cover and we had the beach to ourselves. "How about we let them off their leashes?"

When J. D. unhooked Buster, the dog seemed baffled by the action. Harlow bounded into the water, scattering shorebirds along the way, and Noodle went snuffling along the dune grass. The boxer remained by J. D.'s side.

"Should I tell him to run?"

"No. If he'd rather stay close to you, let him. He's been through some big changes. But back to what we were talking about—"

"You mean my inability to function in the real world?"

"Don't be that way. You're a great guy who has a problem which I think can be managed."

"Oh, I'm doing great 'managing' things." A pair of seagulls flapped down a few yards ahead of us, squabbling over the remains of a muffin.

"You know, Ava had a suggestion that might help."

"What?"

"She thought you could use a handler. To help keep you calm in stressful situations."

"This is bad. An eight-year-old thinks I need a caretaker?"

I took his free hand. "Not just any eight-year-old. An eight-year-old genius. And she suggested a handler, not a caretaker."

"Yeah, right. Big difference."

"There is. I was thinking about how I went with you to the beach last week. You were able to surf because you knew I'd swoop in if anything went wrong."

"That's kind of your default setting."

I chuckled. "True. I'm a swooper. But it's not like I actually did anything. It was someone being there who had your back. That's what let you be out in the world. I was your safety net."

"Maybe."

"Maybe nothing. You were able to do something you love—in the middle of a group—because you knew someone was watching who'd stand up for you. Like you once did for me."

"Are you applying for the job as my handler?"

"Nope. I've got someone even better. Loyal. Smart. Fast. Someone who I can see is already smitten with you."

J. D. stopped and rubbed the nape of his neck. "Since I never go out, I'm at a loss as to who this devotee might be."

I pointed my chin at Buster, the dog looking up at J. D. with total adoration. "He'd be a terrific defender." Not exactly what Ava had in mind, but J. D. was already well on his way to earning Buster's love and trust.

"Huh. Thought you said you gave his new owner a couple weeks to change his mind."

"That's what I told him. But unless Buster suddenly starts pooping gold nuggets, that man isn't going to want him."

"Let me think about it." He bent down and patted the dog, then began to jog. "Come on, Buster, let's go."

The two ran along the water's edge, the boxer occasionally jumping with joy. Harlow started to head toward the pair and I called her and Noodle back to me. I bent down to pet them. "We're gonna let those two get to know each other a little better, okay?"

CHAPTER 8

As we neared the end of our walk, I turned to J. D. "You want to keep Buster with you today?"

"Really?" He grinned, then reached down to pat the boxer's flank.

"Yep. He's good company. And you already have a box full of dog toys. Along with water bowls for these guys. Are your parents here or at their place in Pebble Beach?"

"Neither. They're in the Hamptons. Wanted a little fall color. They won't be in Pier Point again until December. They never miss the holiday boat parade."

I spread my arms wide. "In that case, Buster won't bother them."

"You are a master manipulator."

"That's me. A manipulative swooper. Look, Buster's even better behaved than my dogs. Except for nosing crotches. But he's already improved a ton. Just tell him 'off' or 'down' and he'll stop. He sleeps well. Eats well. If things go smoothly, I can bring by a dog bed and food and, if you want, he can spend the night. Your call. But I don't have a crate for him."

He crouched and rubbed Buster's ears. The dog leaned into J. D.'s hands, rolled his eyes back, and sighed. "Sounds good to me. We'll see how it goes and I'll text you later."

"Great."

After saying our goodbyes, I took Harlow and Noodle into the backyard. After drying off the Golden, I refilled their water bowls, then headed to Ava's for her lesson. Like with Lupe, there really wasn't much more I could do to help Ava train her dog. She wasn't interested in agility or other competitive dog sports; she just needed her Basset-Retriever to behave well enough to be allowed inside—and she'd already mastered those basic skills. Still we continued to meet twice a week, more as an excuse to spend time together than anything else.

If my friend Murph in Massachusetts could see me now— voluntarily socializing with a variety of people—her eyes would bug out like in a cartoon. Knowing Murph, she might discount it because they were mostly dog people, but it was still a big change from the old me.

Ava and Butterscotch weren't waiting out in front of the two-story home. That usually meant she was engrossed in an online class. I knocked and waited. Jemma opened the door. "Hi, Molly. Come on in. Ava's almost done with Earth Science."

"No problem." Not so long ago, Jemma would've had no idea what her daughter was studying. Nails scrambled against tile and Butterscotch scurried around the corner to greet me. "Hi, girl." I bent down and rubbed her curly coat. "Sorry, no treats until the lesson."

"Want an iced tea?"

"No, I'm good." Butterscotch and I went out on the deck to wait for Ava. A few minutes later she joined us, her hair in its usual tidy braids, wearing blue jeans and a pullover. "Hey, smart stuff. Don't think I've ever seen you in a pair of dungarees before."

She wrinkled her nose. "Dungarees?"

"It's an old-timey word for jeans."

Her face cleared. "Oh. I have a play date with one of my on-line chess friends. Jemma's taking me to his house later, and we're going to build a paper airplane launcher. We were going to make a catapult, but his mom thought that sounded too dangerous."

"Sounds like you'll have fun. Is he another smarty pants like you?"

"Yep."

"What's his name?"

"Lincoln."

It looked like I wasn't the only one who was blossoming so-cially. "We better get started. I don't want to make you late. What do you want to work on today with Butterscotch?"

Ava looked over her shoulder at the open slider and lowered her voice. "Butterscotch chewed up one of Jemma's sneakers. I hid it so she doesn't know yet. Maybe we can work on that?"

"Come on. You know that's not something we can practice. Preventing Butterscotch from chewing is more about keeping those kinds of things out of reach, making sure she gets plenty of exercise and engagement, and interrupting the behavior when it happens. Were you able to catch her in the act?"

Ava's gaze seemed glued to her shoes. "No."

"You found the evidence later?"

"Uh-huh."

"Do you know when it happened?"

"Yeah. When I skipped her afternoon walk to play chess on-line with Lincoln."

"Okay. And what do you do if you can't make time to play with Butterscotch?"

"I should put her in the crate, then take her outside to play fetch as soon as I'm able."

"So that's what you'll do next time, okay? Now, stop looking guilty and let's give Butterscotch some extra fetch time today."

When I returned home, I went out back to groom the dogs, then brought them inside and checked my phone. Still nothing from Miguel, but I'd missed a text. Someone wanted to talk to me about training their dog. She noted that Lupe had referred her. I called the woman back.

"Izzy Harmon," a brusque voice answered.

"Hi, this is Molly Madison. You texted about your dog, Sky."

"Right. Look, I'm late for a meeting. Can you come by tomorrow at noon to meet her? At my house. We can go over what I'm looking for then."

"Sure. You live in Pier Point?"

"Yes." She gave me the address and I wrote it down. "I'll see you tomorrow. Twelve o'clock sharp." She hung up without saying goodbye.

Hopefully the woman's lack of social graces was due to being rushed and not because she was obnoxious.

The dogs and I took another walk during midafternoon, this time at Hillside Park. I herded them up an unpopulated trail. Halfway to the crest, I paused to check our surroundings. Still seeing no other hikers, I let them off leash. Harlow went in search of small critters to bark at while Noodle meandered by my side, occasionally lifting his head to woof at circling hawks. After Noodle let loose with a barrage of barks when a raptor dove into the nearby scrub, I crouched and grabbed his collar. Once the bird had flown off with his trophy, I released Noodle. "Don't worry, big guy. You'll get him next time."

Aware of my upcoming appointment at Lupe's, I led the dogs back down the trail to my 4Runner at quarter past five. Tuckered out, they snoozed through the short drive home, then flopped down in the living room for part two of a well-deserved nap.

Before heading to Lupe's, I texted J. D.: **Things going good with Buster?** He texted back a thumbs-up.

Molly: Want me to bring a dog bed and food?

J.D.: Yes

I gathered the supplies. Neither Harlow nor Noodle lifted their head as I left the house. This time J. D. wasn't waiting by the door. I knocked. When he opened it, Buster at his side, J. D. looked relaxed and happy for a change. So did Buster. I realized the boxer may've been a little cowed while at my house. Getting thrown into the mix with two big dogs would've been a huge change for him.

J. D. took the offered items. "Thanks. Did you see the sign?"

"What sign?"

He pointed at the tan Mediterranean two-story home next door. A wooden post with a "For Sale" sign hanging from it was planted in the center of the small yard.

"I guess probate finally closed." I hadn't known Seville well, but she'd been the first one to welcome me when I moved to the neighborhood.

"Yeah." J. D. shook his head. "I knew it was coming, but it was still a shock when I saw the agent hammering in the post."

Sadness over our neighbor's death seemed to steal both our voices.

"Well, I've got to go to Lupe's now. I should be back in about an hour. If you think Buster could use another walk, let me know and we can go together."

"Appreciate the offer, but we played fetch and tug-of-war for a couple hours today. I think we're both ready to take it easy."

"All right. Let me know if you need any other supplies."

I made it to Lupe's at six o'clock as scheduled and rang the bell.

A few moments later, she greeted me with a smile. "Come on in." Her thick hair was up in a loose bun and she wore jeans, a baggy sweater, and no shoes.

Some time ago, Lupe told me she only knew Seville well enough to wave and say "Hi" to. I chose not to mention the "For Sale" sign in front of Seville's now-empty home. "You look ready to relax. Tough day?"

"You said it." Ulysses bounded over to sniff and lick my hands. Lupe signaled for him to follow her. "Maybe we should take care of this guy and chat after."

"Sure."

Lupe slipped on a pair of red-checked Vans and turned on the outdoor lights. We went into the backyard and ran Ulysses through the basic commands to keep them fresh. Lupe had mastered all the hand signs and was communicating beautifully with the deaf dog. After we'd finished the training session, Ulysses and I followed Lupe into the kitchen, where she filled the Dalmatian's bowl and poured two glasses of wine. Ulysses gobbled his meal, then flopped onto his bed while she and I headed back out to the deck.

I took a seat, then a sip. Tart with a hint of pear. "Yum. Andy buys the best wine."

"Right? One of the perks of being married to a wine snob."

"And of having a friend whose husband is a wine snob." I saluted her with my glass before taking another sip. "Your friend Izzy called me today."

"Who?"

"Izzy Harmon. She said you told her about my work with you and Ulysses. Said she wanted me to meet her dog, Sky, and see if I could help."

"Oh, right. She's in my cooking class."

Lupe and her husband regularly attended cooking classes covering an ever-changing range of menu items. "What're you learning to make now?"

"We decided it was time to try French cuisine. Next week we'll be tackling canapés. And if this past Wednesday's class on soufflés is any sort of predictor for what's coming, 'tackling' is the operative word."

A bat swooped overhead, an inky silhouette against the darkening sky. "What happened at your last class?"

"Andy and I dropped our soufflé. Somehow our potholders got wet. We're lucky we didn't get steam burns. But the dish crashed to the floor and cracked. Our soufflé deflated faster than a stuck balloon."

"Yikes."

"Izzy was nice enough to share hers. And we got to talking about our dogs. She can be a bit . . . high-handed, though." Lupe poured herself more wine and cleared her throat. "So how're things going with Miguel?"

Something struck me as off in Lupe's tone. I eyed her then said, "Fine. But he had to bug out early last night. Got called back in to work."

"You saw him last night?"

The angry edge to her voice surprised me. Was I walking into some sort of sibling conflict? "Yep. Why?"

Lupe stood and paced the wood deck. "I can't believe him." She spun and faced me. "I had it out with Miguel yesterday morning. Said if he didn't tell you, I would."

My gut tightened. "Tell me what?"

She strode to the side table, picked up her wineglass, and drained it. A loud exhale, then her shoulders slumped. "He's married."

"What?" I understood the words, but they made no sense. "Your brother's married?"

"Yes." She thudded her glass onto the table. "He promised he'd tell you."

My stomach bunched like a fist. "Why would you let me get involved with him? You could've mentioned it before things got . . ."

"When? You guys went from adversaries—with me trying to convince you Miguel was a good guy—to whatever your relationship is now, in, like, a nanosecond. When was I supposed to warn you?"

I rubbed my face. This wasn't happening. I was the "other woman"? "Tell me they're at least separated."

"You could say that." Lupe collapsed into her chair. "I can't believe he didn't tell you."

"He did get called away suddenly." If he'd promised Lupe to tell me the truth, his eagerness to leave last night now made sense.

"Yeah? How long was he at your place before that happened?"

"About an hour-and-a-half."

Lupe rolled her eyes. "Plenty of time."

I downed half of my glass and waited for the alcohol buzz to ease the growing ache inside. "What did you mean by 'you could say that' they're separated?"

She puffed out her cheeks, then let out another long breath. "I shouldn't be the one telling you this. Miguel should."

"Well, he didn't. And you can't stop now."

"Right. Sloan's in prison."

"What? Your brother's married to an inmate?"

Lupe shrugged. "She wasn't one when they met. They'd been married maybe eight years when she got hooked on Oxycontin. Miguel claims he didn't realize she had a problem until she started running through their money. She swore she'd stop, but she just got better at hiding what she was doing. Took out a bunch of credit cards in both their names. Started kiting checks. Miguel complained about the situation to his partner. Wright's the one who arrested her. Miguel and he fought about it. But the guy did the right thing. Otherwise Miguel would've been ruined financially." Lupe massaged the bridge of her nose. "She got ten years with the possibility of parole in seven."

"I thought check fraud was a misdemeanor."

"Yeah, but at the time, she was a pharma rep and had been ripping off her company and clients. Miguel had no idea that was going on, either. At least that's what he says. Once she was in custody, Sloan told the cops everything. The resulting theft charges added a lot more years to her sentence. Plus, she got a hard-case judge who thought the wife of a detective should comport herself at a higher standard than the average person. He threw the book at her."

My eyes stung. I blinked several times. I would not cry here. "When did this happen?"

Lupe refilled her wineglass. "The arrest was almost five years ago and the trial maybe six months later."

"So she could get out soon."

"I guess. Maybe." She took a drink, then offered the bottle to me.

"No, thanks." I set down my glass and stood. "I need to go."

"No." Lupe jumped to her feet and grabbed my hand. "Stay. We can talk. I'm furious with Miguel and will happily curse his name."

"Thanks, but I need to be alone. To think."

I barely noticed the dark alley as I jogged home. Tears made me miss the keyhole on my first try, but I got inside before the dam burst. Stumbling to the sofa, I curled up sobbing. Noodle and Harlow took turns pressing their damp noses against my face.

Over the next few hours, I polished off the remains of the chilled chardonnay in my fridge and opened a fresh bottle. Every time my cell burred, I lunged for it. Each time it was J. D. sending a photo of Buster looking adorable.

Miguel didn't call, didn't text. Finally, before pouring myself into bed, I texted him: You're married?

I turned off my phone and tossed it onto the bathroom counter.

CHAPTER 9

I crawled from bed, cursing my decision to numb myself with wine and—even worse—for trusting Miguel. The dogs sensed my mood but couldn't contain their joy and excitement over the prospect of breakfast. Swallowing three aspirin, I ignored the drool-spattered sheets and trudged down the stairs after them. While the dogs went about their business in the yard, I filled their bowls with a mix of wet and dry food. Once they'd eaten and I'd had the chance to down a cup of coffee, I turned on my phone. Still no message from Miguel. "Coward."

Wanting to check on J. D. and Buster, I texted: How's it going?

Within seconds he replied: Great. Wanna take dogs for walk?

At least J. D. and Buster were doing well. I answered: Be there in 5

Walking the dogs would be the perfect distraction from the hamster wheel of recrimination running inside my brain: Why hadn't I known? I should've seen it. Spotted some sign. How could

Miguel do this? Why hadn't Lupe told me sooner? Did everyone in town know?

Enough.

After leashing the dogs, I guided them through the front door. Even the brilliant blue sky failed to improve my spirits. Harlow barked at a seagull standing in the middle of the alley, Cheeto in its beak. Noodle joined in, his deep woof the bass to her alto. The large bird flapped away with its prize.

I knocked and J. D. opened the door, Buster already leashed. "Wow. Someone's raring to go."

"We've been up since six. Someone"—J. D. pointed at the boxer—"is an early riser. I may want to get him a crate after all."

We made it to the cul-de-sac without J. D. noticeably sweating or struggling to breathe. The sunny September morning had lured a fair number of people to the beach to walk and jog. Too many for J. D. to handle? "You good to walk the dogs here today?"

"I'm willing to try." He bent down and patted Buster.

"All right then."

J. D. took several deep breaths as we stepped onto the sand. Nerves taut, I did my best to appear unconcerned. Relief washed through me when he smiled at the boxer capering alongside him. This might just work.

Tail swinging, Harlow eyed a Frisbee sailing back and forth between two kids. "Heel, girl. That's not your toy."

A strong breeze came off the water, carrying the scent of brine. A wave crashed high on the beach. J. D. and I exchanged a look, then urged the dogs toward dry sand. Buster clamped his leash between his jaws and J. D. chuckled. "Think you're ready to walk yourself, bud? Maybe when things are less crowded."

I stared at the choppy water, the sun spilling golden coins

onto its surface. Seagulls screeched above. Twenty feet out, a lone surfer caught a wave. Mesmerized, I watched her ride it in. I turned to J. D. to comment on her form. The look of longing on his face stopped me. I wished I could drive away his demons. "Know her?"

"Nah. Gorgeous ride, though."

In spite of the wild brew of emotions churning within me, walking with J. D. and the dogs did improve my mood. It was good to focus on something besides myself. We were halfway to the playground marking the beach's end when Noodle wrenched against his leash, nearly ripping it from my hand. It took all my strength to rein in his 180 pounds. "Noodle, heel."

Once I had the big dog under control, I scanned the beach for what had caught his attention. A small orange cat peeked at us through the dune grass. "That's not good. Who'd leave a cat outside here?"

"Let's hope it's only a clueless person visiting for the week and that the cat wasn't dumped."

"Noodle." I pulled the Saint Berdoodle back again. "Sit. Stay." I turned to J. D. "Can you handle all three of them for a minute?"

"Sure."

I handed him the leashes, then walked slowly to the dune. The small face disappeared, then the striped cat bounded over a tuft of grass. Not a cat. A kitten. Such a young cat probably didn't have the skills or coordination to catch and kill a shorebird, but why take that risk? Plus, a kitten could easily become prey out here. Crouching, I offered my hand. "Hey, kitty." The little tiger walked closer and rubbed against my fingers. No visible collar. "You're fearless, aren't you?"

I scooped her up and scratched under her chin. Her purr

roared like a tiny motor revving. "You understand I can't leave you here, right?"

Continuing to cosset the kitten, I scouted the nearby beachfront homes, but saw no open windows or doors, or anyone frantically searching for a lost pet. I knocked on the doors of the three closest but got no answer. Most likely summer places.

J. D. agreed we should abort the walk and managed the three dogs while I carried the purring cat. Fortunately, only Noodle seemed interested in the little fuzz ball. When we reached my front door, I pulled one hand free and unlocked it. The kitten began to wriggle. I hustled inside and J. D. followed with the dogs. After considering my options, I took her into the half bath off the great room. "You think she'll eat dog food?"

J. D. shook his head and began removing Noodle and Harlow's leashes. "Got any tuna?"

"Maybe." The kitten mewed piteously as I shut her inside the room and went to the kitchen. I filled a bowl with water, then rummaged through the cupboards. I found a pop-top can at the back of the pantry and put a small portion on a plate. When I returned to the bathroom, the Saint Berdoodle was tracking a white paw as it appeared and disappeared beneath the door. "Noodle, sit. I know you don't get it, but you're, like, a bajillion times bigger than the cat. You need to treat her gently."

Grabbing the big dog's collar, J. D. said, "Got him."

I opened the door and the kitten bolted out.

J. D. chuckled. "That went well."

Putting down the water and tuna inside the bathroom, I hoped the smell would lure the kitten back. "I guess I should buy some kitty litter and make a bunch of 'Found' signs."

"Let me check our garage. We used to bring our Maine coon,

Trixie, with us each summer. There may still be a box and some sand."

"Thanks. Sorry about the walk."

"No worries." He handed off Noodle to me.

Seeing no sign of the cat nearby, I released the Saint Ber-doodle. He raced into the bathroom and hoovered up the tuna. "Guess I didn't really think that through."

J. D. laughed again. It was good to see him happy. "Back in a few."

While he and Buster were across the alley, I searched for the small cat. I was standing on the step ladder, checking the top of the refrigerator, when the front door opened.

"We're back."

"I'm in the kitchen." I climbed down and moved the ladder to check an upper cupboard that was ajar.

"At least Harlow and Noodle were in plain sight when the cat ran off, so you know they didn't eat him."

I snorted. "I think she ran so fast, Harlow didn't even see her."

"Her?"

I shrugged. "She's so pretty, she must be a girl."

"Says the dog expert. Want me to put the litter and cat box in the bathroom?"

"That'd be great. Hopefully I'll find the owner right away, but it'll be good to make the cat feel at home. Now all I have to do is locate the damn thing so I can take a picture for the flyer."

"How about we put the dogs in the backyard. But carefully, so the cat doesn't slip out. Then we can do a room-by-room search."

I climbed down again. "Sounds like you've done this before."

"When we brought Trixie home as a kitten, she managed to climb up the backside of a desk drawer and fell asleep inside on a stack of files. We frantically searched for hours before finding her."

"Hopefully we'll succeed more quickly than that." I walked to the kitchen slider. "Harlow, Noodle, come." I urged the dogs through the opening, then J. D. guided Buster outside. I closed the screen behind them.

He clapped his hands together. "All right. Start upstairs or down?"

"I've done a pretty thorough search of the kitchen. There's not much to check in the great room—just under the sofa—so let's do that, then head upstairs."

Thirty minutes later, I found the kitten snug inside an open shoebox in the bedroom closet—halfway inside one of my sneakers. I shook my head. "She's here." When J. D. joined me, I continued. "I swear the door was only open two inches, but she managed to worm her way inside." I picked up the box containing the dozy kitten. As I carried her downstairs, she stretched and yawned. Since the dogs were still outside, I didn't lock her in the bathroom when I put more tuna on the plate. The little cat nibbled, a much daintier eater than my dogs. When done, she climbed back into the box. Pulling out my cell, I snapped several photos.

"You should post a notice on the neighborhood website."

"Right. And I'll print a few up and hang them near where we found her."

"Safe to bring Buster through?"

I stepped out of the bathroom and softly closed the door. "Sure. Heading home?"

"Need to spend some time tossing him the ball."

I went to the kitchen and opened the screen door. All three dogs trotted inside. I petted Harlow and Noodle while J. D. hooked on the boxer's leash. "Thanks for your help."

"No problem."

Noodle raced to the bathroom door and began snuffling along the gap at the bottom. After Harlow had received her share of love, she sauntered to her pillow and sprawled across it.

A few minutes after J. D. and Buster had left, it hit me: I hadn't told him about Miguel being married—nor thought about it since spotting the cat. Keeping busy might just get me through this day.

I posted the kitten's picture on the online neighborhood site with a "Found" header, along with a description and my phone number, then printed two dozen flyers. Walking back to the stretch of beach where Noodle had first spotted the cat, I took the access path between two mammoth homes to the street behind them. I stapled flyers to six of the wooden phone poles located along the sidewalk and taped another eight to concrete light stanchions. When done, I hurried home to change clothes for my meeting with Izzy and Sky at noon.

Izzy Harmon's home was a sleek three-story glass and concrete structure located on the water. Though my house was only six down from the beach, that difference probably equaled a cool two or three million in price. The nine-foot-tall front door made me feel teeny. Was this how the kitten Noodle had found viewed the world? If so, she didn't act like it made her feel small in spirit. Food for thought. I rang the bell and waited.

Izzy opened the door and frowned. About five foot two, not counting the four-inch heels, she had short red hair and wore a tailored peach suit with matching shoes. What did this woman do that she was decked out in business attire on a Saturday?

"Come on in." A stocky French bulldog trotted over to greet me. "This is Sky. She has a chewing problem. Ruined a pair of my Christian Louboutins last week."

Sky was gray with a white chest and a wiggly butt and was downright adorable. "How old is she?"

"I think the breeder said she was one."

"So she's no longer teething?"

"No idea."

"Okay. Is this a new behavior?"

"You think I've been letting her regularly gnaw on my eight-hundred-dollar shoes?"

Touchy. "No, my point is, if this is a new behavior, we might be able to pin down the cause. Has something in Sky's environment or schedule changed?"

"If I wanted a pet psychiatrist, I would've hired one. I want you to teach her not to chew. Period."

Was the woman acting rude in an attempt to hide the fact she knew nothing about dogs? Positive she wasn't going to like what I had to say, I nonetheless soldiered on. "Chewing's not something you can exactly teach a dog not to do. It's not like teaching her to sit or stay. First thing, you need to keep your closets closed and all clothes and shoes out of her reach."

"I suppose I could do that." Izzy crossed her arms and led us through a state-of-the-art kitchen into a huge sitting room. Floor-to-ceiling windows gave a 180-degree white water view.

"This is amazing."

"Thanks." She leaned against the back of one of the two sofas, seemingly uninterested in the view.

"How often do you walk her?"

"We walk on Sunday mornings. That's the only time I have to spare."

Then why had she gotten a dog? "I know that Frenchies can be stubborn and hard to train, but the bigger issue is they don't do well when left alone for extended periods."

"Well, I can't do anything about that. I'm out of here by seven-thirty six days a week and usually back again around twelve hours later."

Poor Sky. No wonder she was chewing. "Is there any way you could make time to walk her before or after work?"

"Not a chance. I work out every morning and bring files home to review at night."

"Well, you could crate her during the day to keep her from chewing. But if you do, I'd recommend coming home at lunch to let her out so she can run around the yard a bit before she has to go back inside."

"That won't work. Making time to meet you today has already thrown my entire day out of whack. Is six hundred a week good?"

"For what?"

"Your pay."

Not needing the money, I rarely charged anyone, and when I did, I topped out at ten dollars an hour. "What exactly do you want me to do?"

"Whatever it takes. Walk the dog. Play with the dog. Keep her busy so she doesn't chew the place up." She headed back into the kitchen, dug through a drawer, and pulled out a key. "You can come by anytime after I leave for work. Just be gone before I get home. I need my alone time then."

The woman was gone for almost half of each day. "How much time do you want me to be with Sky?" Hearing her name, the Frenchie nosed my calf. I bent down to stroke her coat.

"As long as it takes to keep her happy."

"I have my own dogs to take care of. To walk, play with. I can't spend my days at your house."

For a petite woman, she seemed to grow in stature as her frown deepened.

Izzy seemed like she'd be difficult to work with, but as much as I wanted to turn down the job, Sky desperately needed someone to play with during the day. "What I can do—if you'd like—is come by on weekdays, pick up Sky and bring her to my place. She'll get at least two walks a day—either on the beach or around the neighborhood or at Hillside Park. When we're home, she can play with my dogs. And I can work on her training. That should keep her occupied."

"Make it seven days a week and I'll pay you eight hundred."

I glanced down at Sky's eager face. "Okay."

"Good." She glanced at her cell phone. "Take her with you today. I need to get back to work."

"Sure." I accepted the offered key.

Izzy walked me to the entryway and retrieved a hot pink leash from the coat closet.

As I attached it to Sky's rhinestone collar, the Frenchie looked up at me, butt wiggling. How she remained happy in this ice palace was a mystery. "I'll have her back by seven."

Izzy nodded and shut the door behind me.

I slowed my normal pace to accommodate the Frenchie's short legs. Walking her with Harlow and Noodle might prove a challenge. Maybe she and I should take solo walks? When I got home, I paused in the entryway and shook my head. Three months ago, it had just been Harlow and me. Now I also had Noodle, and maybe Buster—depending on how things went with J. D.—plus I was providing daycare for Sky and was temporarily (I hoped) responsible for a kitten.

Maybe I shouldn't be surprised. When had my life ever gone as planned?

CHAPTER 10

By 3:00 p.m., Miguel still hadn't called or texted, and the kitten was crying to be set free from the bathroom. Though the dogs were snoozing, I hooked on their leashes—just in case they freaked at the sight of the little cat. Unfortunately, that made them think we were going for a walk. The three sat up, tails wagging. I gave a firm "stay" command and hoped for the best.

When I opened the bathroom door, the kitten gamboled out, all big eyes and paws. Whoa. Really big paws. She had at least six toes on each front foot. Didn't seem to slow her down as she made a beeline for the living room. I hurried alongside, ready to snatch her up or grab a leash if any of the dogs acted threatening. Harlow stared at the kitten, unimpressed. She gave a deep sigh and lay back down on her pillow. Looking worried, the Frenchie scuttled under the coffee table.

Noodle shook himself, then snuffled across the room to inspect the fuzzy interloper. When his nose brushed her ear, she whapped him with her front paw. The big dog retreated a few paces, looking at the kitten with a mix of curiosity and respect.

"Okay, pups. Let's go for a walk." Leaving the kitten in charge of the house, I loaded Harlow and Noodle into the 4Runner's back seat and put Sky up front. I hesitated before starting the engine. Would the cat be okay on her own? How much trouble could the tiny tiger get into over the course of a couple hours? I never left out sharp objects or things the dogs shouldn't eat. The cat should be fine. I reversed out of the garage.

Ten minutes later, I pulled into the lot at Hillside Park. Noodle and Harlow nosed the air, recognizing our destination, while Sky wiggled her butt and barked.

My phone rang. I checked the screen: Felicity, not Miguel. I cut the engine and answered. "Hi."

"Where are you?"

Odd question. "I'm at the park. About to take the dogs for a walk."

"Can you come to my house? Right now?"

The urgency in her voice sent my pulse racing. "What's wrong?"

"According to my lawyer, I'm about to be arrested. I need you to take Royal."

"Arrested?"

"For Celeste's murder. My lawyer's on his way. He got a heads-up from the Sheriff's Department. They claim they've got enough evidence. Blake—my lawyer—says it's all circumstantial." A soft sob followed. "They're going to charge me with second-degree murder."

"Oh no."

"Since it's Saturday, he says I'll probably be held until Monday."

"Are you okay?"

"No. Can you take care of Royal?"

"Of course. Give me your address."

By the time I'd reached Felicity's home in Camarillo, several black-and-whites lined the street. Two officers stood blocking the driveway to the ranch-style home. Both wore the county uniform of khaki pants and cream-colored shirts. Dark glasses and peaked caps shielded their clean-shaven faces. Leaving the windows cracked, I crossed to their side of the street.

Deputy 1 held up his hand. "You're gonna have to stop there."

"I'm a friend of Felicity Gaines. She asked me to get her dog."

The deputy remained impassive.

"Someone's going to need to feed and care for him while she's in custody."

He turned to Deputy 2. "I'll keep her here. You check out her story."

Story?

Deputy 2 nodded, then strode to the porch and disappeared inside. Four frustrating minutes passed as Deputy 1 ignored my questions about what was going on with Felicity.

Finally, the other deputy emerged. "The lawyer says someone named Molly Madison is allowed to take the dog."

"That's me."

Deputy 1 held out his hand. "I.D.?"

Seriously? Did he think I was some gawker who'd stopped by on the off chance of stealing a dog? "I left my purse in the car." When his expression didn't change, I sighed and crossed back to my 4Runner. Sky jumped into the driver's seat and tried to lick my face. "Down." She either didn't know that command or was a master at playing dumb. I gently pushed her back. "We'll work on that later."

Once I'd retrieved my wallet and produced the requisite I.D.,

Deputy 2 escorted me down the driveway and I tried, unsuccessfully, to get a glimpse of Felicity through the windows. The deputy unlatched the tall wooden gate to the backyard. It swung open with a creak. Patchy grass covered most of the area, a half-full kiddie pool sitting near a large elevated pet bed. Royal dropped the rawhide bone he'd been chewing, then bared his teeth. The boxer gave a throaty growl.

Was he freaked by the uniformed stranger? Hoping that was the case, I moved away from the deputy. "Hey, Royal." I held out my hand. "It's me. Remember?"

The dog took two tentative steps forward then froze and cocked his head. I waited. Three more steps, then he sniffed my fingers. His tail began to wag. "Good, Royal." I stroked his coat as I turned to the deputy. "I'm going to need his leash."

"Oh." He looked at the back door, then at me, undecided.

"Considering the circumstances and Royal's jumpiness, taking him from the yard without a leash is a bad idea."

Finally, the deputy nodded and climbed the back steps.

I continued petting the boxer, trying to soothe him. It was one thing for Felicity to cart him hither and yon for competitions and classes, but another thing entirely for a semi-stranger to remove him from his home.

Deputy 2 returned, holding a no-pull harness and leash.

"Perfect. I'll need his crate, too."

"What?"

"Felicity probably has one in her car and one in the house. Either will do."

A deep frown and a strong huff of breath. "Anything else?"

"Not unless he needs special food."

"It's a damn dog, not a sick kid." He stalked back into the house.

I slipped the harness around the boxer's back and chest and continued petting him until the deputy returned, lugging a disassembled crate. "Thank you."

He acknowledged my words with a curt nod. "Let's go." He led the way through the gate, slamming it after us.

I asked the deputy to put Royal's crate on top of the two folded crates in the 4Runner's cargo area, then walked the boxer along the sidewalk to the back door. Noodle stuck his nose out of the window and Royal stood on his hind legs to sniff him. Harlow shoved her muzzle through the gap, too. Royal's tail began to wag. Next, I let him meet Sky. The Frenchie wiggled her butt, unafraid and oblivious to their size difference. I scooped her up, opened the back door, and directed Harlow into the front, then nudged Noodle to the other side of the car. "Stay."

Royal sniffed the air and kept wagging. "Ready to climb in? Go on. In."

The boxer scrambled up. Sky began to squirm and I tightened my grip as I watched the bigger dogs get reacquainted. Once everyone seemed happy, I closed the door and turned to the deputy. "Thanks again."

He nodded and crossed the street to Felicity's driveway.

I climbed behind the wheel with the Frenchie in my lap. "This is like a clown car for dogs." I looked down at Sky. "Can you manage to sit still while I'm driving?" Her tongue lolled and she wiggled her butt again. "I'll take that as a yes. I'm thinking we'll scrub the walk and head home. Okay, guys?" No one complained as I pulled away from the curb.

Back at the house, I unloaded the dogs in the driveway and led them through the gate to the backyard. Royal and Sky sniffed their way around the fence line and adjacent plants, peeing several times. Then Royal found the abandoned tennis ball and grabbed it. Harlow ran across the grass and tried to take it away. The two play-fought over it while Sky scampered around them, snorting. Noodle sprawled in a patch of sunshine and drooled. Leaving the sliding door open, but the screen shut, I went inside to check on the cat.

The kitten had curled on Noodle's pillow, a tiny orange-and-white circle on the fuzzy gray expanse. I picked her up. "Hello, sleepyhead." I kissed her forehead. "Your fur's so soft." Cuddling the little fuzz ball, I checked my phone. No responses yet to my "Found Cat" notice. I carried her to the kitchen and stared out the screen at all the dogs. "How did this happen?"

The kitten pawed my face in answer.

"Right. Because I'm a sucker where animals are concerned." I kissed her again. "Back in a sec." After setting her on the floor, I slipped out through the screen door and returned to the 4Runner. There, I unloaded Royal's crate and hauled it inside. As I set it up in the great room, alongside Harlow and Noodle's home crates, the kitten provided assistance by climbing the metal framework like a monkey. When the crate was assembled, I tested the door and latch. I didn't know whether I should crate the dogs tonight. What would be best for Royal in a new place? Almost as important, what would be best for my furniture?

My thoughts turned to Felicity. For the first time the weirdness of her call hit. We'd just met. Hung out twice. And she trusted me with her dog? Did she have no one else who could help her? Or were none of her family or friends dog people? If it was the former, once Royal settled into the routine here, I needed to see if there was anything else I could do to help her. No matter what Miguel said.

Miguel. Damn. It didn't matter what he said or thought. Not anymore.

An odd thump came from the front porch. Like something had been thrown against the door. Weird. I didn't get any newspapers delivered to my home. Careful not to let the kitten escape, I cracked the door and peered out. A burgundy Tahoe blocked the driveway. Del Kaminsky headed toward it. A manila envelope lay on the mat at my feet. Slipping outside, I picked it up and yelled, "Hey!"

Del stopped and turned.

I hoisted the envelope and stepped off the porch. "What's this?"

"Open it and find out."

Jerk. "Fine. Better question: Why are you leaving whatever this is on my porch?"

He jammed his huge hands inside the pockets of his baggy shorts. "Those are Buster's papers. Figured you'd want them. Celeste thought that stuff was important. It's got his breeding or some such nonsense. I don't know how many times I told her it's a dog, not a rare piece of art." He resumed his march to the Tahoe.

At a loss for how to respond, I shook my head. "Okay. Guess this means you haven't changed your mind about taking in Buster."

He swung around, face turning red as he reversed course.

I didn't like the look in his eyes as he strode up the walkway. My cop training kicked in. I opened the front door a couple inches, tossed the envelope inside, and snapped it shut. Shifting my feet to shoulder width, I dropped into a universal fighting stance.

"I told you, I don't want the damn dog." His chest rose and fell with alarming rapidity. "I never wanted him. I told Celeste that but she got him anyway. She always did whatever she—" He froze, then took a step back, seeming to realize he was yelling at the wrong person. "My life's none of your business."

I shrugged. "Never said it was. I'm just making sure you don't want the dog."

Movement across the alley caught my eye. J. D. stepped from his house with Buster. "Everything all right over there?" At the sight of Del, Buster began to growl. J. D. grabbed the boxer's collar.

The pair's presence seemed to make Del shrink. "We're fine. Just dropping something off for the lady."

The lady. I snorted.

Del glared at me, then stalked back to his Tahoe and climbed inside.

J. D. crossed the asphalt, tightening his grip on Buster as they neared. The boxer's gaze followed Del as the dog continued to growl.

When they reached my side, I bent to pet him. "You don't like that man much, do you?" I straightened. "Thank you both for the assist."

"What's his deal?"

"He's the fool who didn't want to keep Buster."

"I knew there was a reason I didn't trust him."

I jerked my thumb toward my closed front door. "He brought by Buster's papers." The stealthy way he tried to dump them without talking to me spiked my curiosity. "Mind if I take a look before handing them over?"

"So"—a grin played across J. D.'s face—"we're abandoning all pretense that Buster's not my dog?"

"Yep."

He chuckled. "Great. And of course you can look over the papers. Call if you need us. Come on, boy."

As he headed back across the street, I stared after him. Buster was already doing wonders. J. D. had crossed the alley without hesitation—something I hadn't seen him do in weeks.

Feeling guilty for doing nothing with Sky all day, I dropped the manila envelope on the coffee table and joined the dogs in the backyard. I tried to get Royal to play with the others, but he lay down on the grass instead. For the next hour, the rest of us played fetch and tug-of-war, then wrapped up with some basic training. The familiar commands caught Royal's attention and he came over to join in.

Sky understood sit and stay but didn't always comply. I was unsure if she knew heel, down, or drop it, or was simply ignoring me. For the next fifteen minutes, I focused on those commands with all four dogs. After that, I took them for a walk on the beach, two leashes in each hand, fully expecting I'd need to carry Sky part of the way.

Royal perked up when we approached the water's edge, running into the foam and biting the waves. When we got far enough down the beach, I let the dogs off leash and he joined Harlow chasing shorebirds. I had to admit, the Frenchie was a trouper, never flagging, in spite of her short legs. Since hers wasn't a swimming breed, I snatched her up when she followed Harlow and Royal into the foam on our return trip. "Time to leash you guys again anyway. Harlow, Noodle, come. Royal, come." After hooking on their leashes, we continued toward home.

We were almost to the side gate when my cell rang. Unknown caller. Wondering if it might be Felicity calling from jail to check on Royal, I shifted the leashes to one hand and answered. "Yes?"

"Hi. Are you the person who put up the 'found cat' flyers in Pier Point?"

"Yes. Is she yours?"

"I hope so. I didn't see the flyer—a friend did and sent me a photo. It's a bit fuzzy. My cat's an orange tabby with white paws."

"How many toes?"

"Seven on her front right paw, six on her front left. Normal in back."

"Can you hang on a sec?"

"Sure."

I undid the gate's latch, then nudged it open with my shoulder before herding the dogs into the yard. Once I'd unhooked their leashes, I slipped into the house. The cat was once again snoozing on Noodle's pillow. I gently lifted her front paws one at a time. She stretched, then licked my hand with a raspy tongue. I held the cell to my mouth again. "You're right. I thought they both had six."

"Oh my God. Thank you. This is such a relief. I've been worried sick ever since I came home last night and realized my ex-boyfriend took her."

"That's terrible."

"And the police were no help at all. They treated it like a joke. Riffing about catnappers and catnapping. I'm so glad she's safe. Unfortunately, I can't come pick her up right away. I've got a long shift and won't be off until eight p.m."

"I'm happy to keep her tonight if you can't get her until tomorrow."

"Thanks, but I want Cinnamon back as soon as possible."

"Cute name. If you want to swing by after your shift ends, that's fine. I'll be here."

"Great. What's your address?"

After giving it to her, it finally occurred to me to ask: "What's your name?"

"Shondra Davis."

"I'm Molly Madison. Look forward to meeting you."

As I hung up, the kitten bolted from the pillow and tried to jump onto the sofa. Failing, she raced into the kitchen. Seeming to sense her, Noodle rose from his patch of grass, shook himself, and trotted to the screen door. His gaze followed Cinnamon as she explored. Noticing the big dog, she sauntered to the screen. He pressed his nose against it and she rubbed her shoulder against him. "Talk about an odd couple."

I went outside and toweled off Royal, Harlow, and Sky. The Frenchie wriggled to be free of my ministrations, eager to join her pals playing. Happy to see Royal and Harlow playing together in the yard, I left the dogs outside, scooped up the kitten, and carried her and the manila envelope to the sofa.

CHAPTER 11

I emptied the envelope and Cinnamon immediately pounced. While she savaged the hollowed-out paper carcass, I pawed through the innards. After reading the first page, I looked at the cat. "Why did Celeste buy Buster from a British breeder? It's not like we don't have boxers here." Cinnamon's only answer was to bite the envelope again.

Risking life and limb—or at least a finger—I scratched beneath her chin as I flipped pages. Oh. The breeder was located in the United States. It was Buster's first owner—the guy Celeste bought him from—who lived in England. Odd he'd choose to import a dog. Maybe he preferred the look of the U.S. boxer over the U.K. breed? The U.K. boxer had a larger head and body while the U.S. dogs had a tight, shiny coat. Maybe those differences drew him to buy his boxer from a U.S. breeder. And then what? After going through all the cost and paperwork, he changed his mind? Unlikely.

Maybe Buster had originally been bought to show rather than

for dog sports? If his conformation didn't match the breed's ideal, that would sadly explain his first owner selling him. Having never explored this area of canine competition, I had no idea whether Buster met the standard criteria. But if someone was vying for a win at Westminster, it wouldn't matter how smart and loyal a fellow Buster was if he didn't have the right look.

Finding the seller's name, I carried the kitten, along with the envelope and its contents, to the kitchen. I pulled out a barstool and turned on my laptop. Cinnamon hopped onto the counter and explored, first sniffing the toaster, then pawing the can opener.

"Oops. That's sharp, sweetie." I airlifted her back to my lap and clicked on my Trackers account. Within minutes I had the seller's contact information. A half hour later, I had a whole lot more.

David Smythe lived in Hertfordshire, England, in the town of Ware. A former Olympic gymnast, he'd suffered a career-ending back injury. After recuperating, he returned to school and became a veterinarian. He now treated large animals. Different career choice, but a similar history to Celeste's. Maybe they'd met at an international gymnastics event. That could explain why she bought Buster from him rather than a local breeder. I wrote down Smythe's number. Might be worthwhile to find out why he sold Buster. If there was some sort of undisclosed medical problem with the dog, J. D. deserved to know. I checked the time. It was the middle of the night in England.

Exhausted by the epic battle of kitten versus envelope, Cinnamon yawned and curled up in my lap. I stroked her soft coat. She began to purr.

I studied the last sheet in the pile. "What the . . ." Celeste bought Buster only eight months ago? "I could've sworn Felicity said she'd competed against the pair for over a year." The dozy kitten had nothing to add.

The discrepancy nagged at me during the day, distracting me as I fed the kitten more tuna and freshened the dogs' water bowls. I finally let it go when it was time to return Sky to Izzy's. I put the kitten back inside the downstairs bath, then headed out with the Frenchie. When I approached the front door, instead of following me, Sky pulled toward the street. "What's up, girl?" A tall man with dark hair loitered on the opposite sidewalk. When I nodded at him, he hurried away. "That was weird. Right, Sky?"

Upon my return home, I fed the dogs, then tried to interest Royal in a game of fetch. The Golden raced after the ball, but the boxer lay down on the deck, head on his paws. Poor fellow. He missed Felicity and his home.

Five more tosses and I brought the dogs inside. After freeing the kitten from the bathroom, I shadowed her for twenty minutes while she explored. She was way too fast for any of the dogs to catch, but the myriad ways she might get hurt were unnerving. When nothing went awry, I began to relax. Picking up the contents of the manila envelope, I carried them and the cat to the sofa. She curled into a tight fuzzy ball on my thighs. I hoped she'd nap again as I reread Buster's history and lineage. A few pages in was a four-generation pedigree for the boxer along with paperwork showing the date and types of vaccinations he'd received. The papers listed his formal name as Kodiak Sun. Not unusual for a pedigreed dog to have two names: a registered name and one for day-to-day use. But there was a handwritten note from Smythe I'd missed during my first reading that listed the dog's common name as Dervish.

Something was off. I raised my head. Oh no. Cinnamon

wasn't in my lap. I scanned the room, spotted her, and sighed. The goofy little orange-and-white cat was curled on top of Noodle. Both were snoozing. Go figure.

Once I felt I'd gleaned all I could from Buster's paperwork, I opened my laptop and started an episode of *Bosch*. Harlow jumped onto the sofa to join me. At 8:30 p.m. the doorbell rang. To my surprise, none of the dogs barked or roused themselves. I paused the show, extricated my legs from beneath the Golden's head, and stood. Checking to make sure the cat was still sleeping on top of the Saint Berdoodle and nowhere near the door, I opened it three inches. A trim woman, locs pulled into a ponytail at the base of her neck and dressed in blue hospital scrubs, stood on the porch. "Shondra? Come in. But quickly. That little cat of yours moves like lightning."

"I appreciate you being so careful about that. She's supposed to be indoor only. Or was until Leonid took her." After I closed the door, she held out her hand. We shook. "Where is she?"

I led the way to the great room and pointed to Noodle sprawled on his pillow with Cinnamon curled on top of his back.

"Oh, I have to get a picture of this." Shondra pulled her cell from her bag and snapped several shots.

I chuckled. "She hasn't even been here twelve hours and is already at the top of the pack. I know you've had a long day—and we've just met—but would you like a glass of wine? I've got some chilling in the fridge."

"That sounds great. Thanks." She set a pink cat carrier on the floor. "I'd love to hold Cinnamon. Will the dog mind?"

"Noodle's a gentle giant. He won't bite, but he may drool on you." I walked to the Saint Berdoodle and crouched. "Noodle, meet Shondra." I looked up at her. "Just hold out your hand so he can sniff it." She did. "There. Now you're pals."

She ran her fingers through his thick coat, then picked up the kitten. Cinnamon squirmed then put a paw on Shondra's cheek. "Oh good. I was worried she'd forget me. She's so young."

Harlow hopped from the sofa and sniffed Shondra's shoes. "Sit." The Golden sat and looked up at me. "Good girl."

I went to the kitchen and poured two glasses of chardonnay and brought them back to the coffee table. "Sorry. The sofa's a bit furry."

"Don't worry about it."

I set a glass in front of Shondra on the coffee table. "A friend loaned me a litter box, but I didn't have any cat food. She ate a little tuna. Hope that's okay."

"Perfect. Thank you for taking such good care of her." Shondra smiled as Cinnamon sprawled on her lap. "I missed this."

I settled on the opposite end of the sofa. "Your ex just took her?"

She took a sip of wine. "He kept calling, saying I had some of his T-shirts. I told him I didn't. He took all his clothes when he left. Apparently, he didn't believe me."

"And when he didn't find the shirts . . ."

She picked up the kitten and nuzzled her. "I was frantic. A window in the kitchen was open, the screen unlatched. I didn't remember unlocking either one, but was beating myself up, thinking I'd somehow let Cinnamon get out. Then I found Leonid's ball cap on the kitchen table. He returned his key when he moved out, so he must've jimmied the window to get in."

"Wow. And left incriminating evidence behind."

"Not the brightest mind. Though he could be sweet."

"And he dumped Cinnamon at the beach?"

"I'm guessing it was an accident. Leonid and a group of friends are taking advantage of the off-season rates and renting a place near the water. I'm betting he didn't tell the others he had the cat and that they needed to keep the doors and windows shut."

"I'm glad Noodle spotted her."

"The big dog? He's the one who found her?"

"Yep. Saw her peeking through the dune grass."

"No wonder Cinnamon feels safe with him."

"I've never had a cat—though growing up, my best friend did. It was fun being around her. The place was a bit of a menagerie today. Fortunately, she doesn't seem any worse for wear." I pointed at the boxer sitting at the kitchen slider staring out at the yard. "I took in Royal this afternoon." I told her about dog-sitting the Frenchie and my brief stewardship of Buster. "It's been a busy couple days."

"And the other boxer's owner died?"

"Right."

"How sad." She turned to look at Royal. "What about this guy?"

I hesitated. Celeste's murder had already hit the news. Felicity's arrest soon would, too. I wasn't breaking any confidences. "His person's been accused of killing the other dog's owner."

"Wait." Her hazel eyes widened. "Are you talking about the Celeste Simmons murder?"

"Do you know her? Sorry, I mean, did you?"

"Unfortunately. Don't get me wrong, I was sorry to hear the woman was killed, but not surprised."

"Why?"

"You ever meet her?"

"Yep. Not the most pleasant sort."

She lifted her glass and sipped. "She was one of the worst people I've ever known."

I'd witnessed the woman's rudeness, but this sounded like something more. "I don't mean to pry, but what'd she do to you?"

"When I was younger, I made the mistake of training with her. She ruined my gymnastics career."

"How?"

"Pushed me too hard. For athletes, there's always a fine line. You want to be the best, and when an expert believes you can do more, you push. And push." She drank again. "The problems come along when a coach cares more about the win than the athlete."

"What happened?"

"When I was sixteen, our team was preparing for a meet. I'd strained my rotator cuff earlier, but Celeste told me to get off my ass and onto the uneven parallels. She'd always say: 'Winners work through the pain, losers' tears run down the drain.'

"As soon as I grabbed the low bar, I knew it was a mistake, but she kept yelling, 'Kip, kip, kip.' So I did. I swore everyone in the gym heard my rotator cuff tear."

"That's terrible."

"Not 'kill her' terrible, but I loved the sport. Even though I got the surgery, did the rehab, the damage was so bad . . ." She shrugged. "I never competed again."

"I'm sorry that happened to you." I remembered Celeste's bedazzled tee. "'KIP.' That's what it said on her shirt. The day I met Celeste. The day she died."

Seeming to force herself back into the moment, Shondra said, "What?"

"Her shirt. It said 'KIP.'"

She rolled her eyes. "I hated those 'message' shirts. Celeste had a whole bunch of them. KIP. STICK IT. TUCK. FLICK-FLACK. SALTO. She had them specially made somewhere."

"What does 'kip' even mean?"

"You kip on the uneven parallel bars. It's when you move from below the bar to a position above it." She lifted her glass again and swirled the wine, staring as if mesmerized. "You know, it wasn't just that Celeste pushed some of us too hard; she could also be cruel."

"How so?"

"I was lucky. My metabolism burns through food. But some of the other girls she trained . . ."

"What?"

"She'd pinch the meat at their waists, hips, thighs. Tell them they were too 'thick' to fly. More than one of them developed an eating disorder during the years I trained with her."

"Why would they stay?"

"Because she turned her girls into winners."

The next morning, J. D. and I were walking the five dogs on the beach when my cell rang. Another unknown number. I handed off Noodle's leash to J. D. and answered. "Hi."

"Molly Madison?" a husky voice said.

"Yep."

"I'm Blake Namaguchi, Felicity Gaines's lawyer. She wants an update on her dog."

"Is she with you? Can I talk to her?"

"No. But I promised I'd check in with you before I see her today."

"Oh." I shook off the wave of disappointment. "I'm walking Royal right now. He seemed a bit depressed last night but is in better spirits today. He ate a good dinner and breakfast, and we'll spend some time playing in the yard later."

"I can't believe I'm taking notes about a dog's mood and activities. Anything else?"

"She'll be out Monday, right?"

"That's the plan."

"Let her know I'll do my best to keep Royal happy and ask her to call as soon as she's out. I can bring the dog to her or she can pick him up if she prefers."

"Got it. Hopefully she'll be satisfied with the information. If she does have more questions, is this a good number to reach you in the evenings, too?"

"Yep." Once the lawyer had disconnected, I relayed the information to J. D.

When we turned back at the children's play area, he said, "Between you and me, you think your friend did it?"

"I . . . I have to say I never seriously considered it."

"Why not? Obviously, I haven't met her, but how well do you know her?"

"Not very. But she loves her dog."

"A huge point in her favor." J. D. grinned.

I had to stop myself from staring. Once again, J. D. looked genuinely at peace. Giving him the dog was working better than I'd dared hope. "I've only met Felicity twice. We hit it off immediately, but I was kind of shocked when she asked me to take care of Royal. I don't know her well, but I like her. Could she have done it?" I shrugged. "As a cop, I saw a lot of mild-mannered people turn violent when pushed too far. So who knows? What I do know is she and the victim argued about something earlier that day, but neither of them had to be restrained or appeared close to throwing a punch. Or slapping the other. My gut says Felicity didn't do it."

"Your gut is good enough for me."

We stopped in front of J. D.'s house. He handed over Noodle's and Sky's leashes, then brushed back his hair. "I'm thinking about taking a trip with Buster."

Whoa. J. D. rarely left his house, let alone went out of town. "Really?"

"Nice attempt at sounding blasé about it."

"I try."

"There's a dog beach in Santa Barbara. I know we're always breaking the rules here and letting these guys off leash when no one's around, but this beach is dog friendly. I figure I can take my board and Buster can wait on the sand for me while I catch a few waves."

"Not to be a wet blanket, but would you want to do a trial run first? I could sit with Buster on the beach here and see how it goes."

"I appreciate the offer. Lemme think about it."

"Okay." Hoping I hadn't squashed J. D.'s desire to stretch his boundaries, I took the dogs through the house to the backyard. I didn't want him to overreach, have a panic attack, and retreat into his house again. But maybe I should've kept my mouth shut.

After grooming the dogs, I refilled their water bowls. The four dogs seemed content and I went inside, but left the slider open. I found David Smythe's number and tapped it into my cell. It was 10:00 a.m. here, which meant it should be 6:00 p.m. in England.

Voice mail. Rats. I left a message, explaining I had a couple questions about Kodiak Sun and asked him to call me back when he had a moment.

CHAPTER 12

Monday arrived and still no word from Miguel. Though I told myself not to obsess, I continued checking my phone throughout the afternoon and evening. No calls, no texts. Even if Miguel had been working nonstop since he left my house Thursday night, Lupe would've found a way to contact him. He had to know she'd told me his secret.

And this was how he responded?

The anger simmering inside me threatened to erupt.

I took several deep breaths. Miguel would get in touch when it suited him. And I needed to be ready. His rumbling promises and puppy dog eyes weren't going to suck me in again. Feeling calmer, I quietly opened the slider and sat on one of the deck chairs. I loved the dogs, but needed to deal with these feelings without their wonderful distractions.

As much as I hated to admit it, Lupe was right. She didn't deserve my fury. There had never been a good time for her to warn me about her brother. He and I had spent most of the ten weeks since we'd met building a friendship. After my cheating husband, Stefan, was murdered, I'd grown cautious. Because of my "once burned, twice shy" state of mind, we'd only crossed the "just friends" line three weeks ago. Now I felt foolish. I wished I'd waited a little longer.

A chill was creeping into the air. I returned inside and grabbed my hoodie, then stared at my phone. I'd been in the wrong with Lupe. No reason not to admit it. I found her number in my contacts and hit the call button.

Two rings, then a gruff voice said, "Lupe's phone."

"Andy?"

"Oh, hi, Molly. Lupe's outside with Ulysses. Gimme a sec."

I heard him calling Lupe's name.

Then, "Molly? I'm so glad you called. I was feeling terrible about how we left things. I should've—"

"No. You did everything fine. There are no more 'should'ves' for you. The person I'm pissed with is your brother, who—and this stuns me to say—still hasn't called me back since I left a message letting him know I learned he's married. But it's not your fault. It's not your job to police your brother. Or supervise my relationships. I was just . . . thrown. I thought Miguel was a stand-up guy."

"So did I."

"But you and me—we're good?"

"As far as I'm concerned," Lupe said.

"Me, too."

"I'm glad you called."

"So should I come by for our usual training day?"

"Of course."

"Great. See you then." I disconnected, then rested my hands on the cool granite counter, grateful Lupe and I weren't going to torch our friendship over her brother. I took a deep breath in, straightened, and woke the dogs. "Let's go. It's training time again." Harlow, Royal, and Sky raced outside while the Saint Berdoodle made a more leisurely exit. We went through the basics for the second time today, reviewing sit, stay, heel, down, and drop it. Sky soaked up each new command, seeming happy to learn. Had Izzy never trained her?

Each time I distributed treats, the dogs' joy warmed me. These amazing critters knew how to appreciate every moment. Doing my best to follow their example, I shoved away my angry thoughts about Miguel.

The sun had been down awhile before I realized I needed to take Sky home. I gave everyone dinner, then put on the Frenchie's leash. The other dogs began to prance. "Sorry, no walk for you guys right now." Faster than the stubby-legged dog probably would've liked, we trotted to Izzy's. When we reached the house, Sky pulled toward the road. I turned. Once again, the dark-haired man stood on the opposite sidewalk. "Hi."

He turned away and jogged out of sight around the corner. "Have you got a secret admirer, Sky?"

The Frenchie panted and wiggled her butt.

I unlocked the door and stuck my head into the gap. Silence. "Lucky break for us," I said to Sky as I unhooked her leash. "Izzy isn't home yet." As I leaned down to kiss the Frenchie, the clack of heels on the marble floor approached. I straightened.

Izzy strode from the kitchen, frowning. "You're late."

"Right." The woman shifted her glare from me to the dog, making no move to welcome Sky. Not exactly the behavior of someone eagerly awaiting her dog's return. Was her anger just about me not sticking to her schedule? "Sorry about that. Lost track of time."

"Don't do it again." Izzy crossed her arms over her chest, frown deepening. Sky scampered toward her. When she drew close, the woman aimed a kick at the dog, but stopped before connecting. Sky whimpered and retreated.

Fury boiled up inside me. "What the hell was that?"

"What?" Izzy's frown deepened. "I didn't touch the dog."

"You threatened to kick her."

"Nonsense. I didn't touch her. And don't try changing the subject. You're late and I need you to leave. I work hard and need my downtime."

I crouched and called Sky to me. The Frenchie gave Izzy a wide berth but trotted to my side. I kissed her forehead then provided her with a full body rub. I shot Izzy hard eyes as I stood. "She understands stay, sit, heel, come. There's no reason to threaten her."

"How I choose to handle my dog is none of your business."

I bit back my angry retort. Sky needed me. Getting fired wasn't going to help the dog. Giving the Frenchie one more reassuring pat, I left.

Rage fueled my walk home. Once I was inside, I spent the following half hour pacing and fuming. At first the dogs trotted alongside. But soon they grew bored and found cushy spots to nap. Finally, hunger beat out anger and I went to the kitchen and nuked a burrito. After eating over the sink, I watched another episode of *Bosch* on my laptop, Harlow sprawled beside me on the couch. When ten o'clock rolled around, I realized I hadn't absorbed more than twenty percent of the show. What was I going to do about Izzy? If she didn't want to listen to me, how could I teach her about interacting positively with her dog?

I closed my computer with a sigh, then took the dogs outside for one last pee. When we returned to the great room, I got each of them settled in their crate. Royal seemed happier than he had on the previous night. Harlow pawed my leg and I bent down to stroke her head, then did the same with Noodle. "Sleep well, you guys."

Feeling melancholy, I headed upstairs to bed.

Hours later, I jerked awake. Miguel's imagined touch lingered on my skin. I scrubbed my hand across my face and rolled onto my side. Balanced on sleep's knife edge, I jerked awake again. I checked the time. Five a.m. The idea of more Miguel dreams turned my stomach. Switching on the bedside lamp, I picked up the latest Margaret Mizushima mystery, flipped to my bookmark, and resumed reading.

At 7:00 a.m., the squawk of the alarm clock startled me awake. The book was open beside me on my pillow. I untangled myself from the covers and made the bed. After washing my face, I pulled on jeans and a long-sleeve tee, then trotted downstairs to release the dogs and take them outside. While the three determined the best spots to do their business, I got the coffee maker going, dished up a mix of wet and dry food, and carried the bowls out to the deck. Dew coated the grass and furniture. A gray day to match my mood.

By the time I'd downed a hot mug of coffee and brought in the empty dog bowls to wash, it was time to collect Sky. Leaving Harlow and Royal to play in the backyard while Noodle looked on, I walked the short distance to Izzy's. Prior to entering, I scanned the street. The dark-haired man was nowhere in sight. Maybe it had nothing to do with Izzy or Sky and the guy stopped here at night to sneak a cigarette before heading home.

Izzy's house didn't grow any less imposing with each visit—or any less sterile. The Frenchie's nails clicked on the marble floor as she dashed to greet me. She slid to a stop then began jumping and snorting. I crouched to pet her. "Yes, I'm happy to see you, too." How could Izzy not be nuts about this dog? Straightening, I found Sky's leash and hooked it to her rhinestone collar. "Come on, girl. Let's go."

After locking up, I set a leisurely pace for home, Sky investigated dozens of interesting smells along the way. The entrance to the alley proved especially fascinating to her, and I waited until she'd sniffed her fill. We entered the yard through the side gate. Noodle, Harlow, and Royal raced to greet us, giddy to see their new friend again. Once they'd calmed down, I clapped my hands. "Okay, everyone. Training time."

We ran through a few basic commands. Sky continued to improve. The treats were as big an encouragement for her as they were for Noodle, but I suspected seeing the other dogs following my orders also influenced her. We had a good fifteen-minute session, then I held up a tennis ball. Sky, Royal, and Harlow jumped and barked. I tossed the ball and the three raced after it. Noodle wandered onto the deck and sprawled on the doormat. "Don't feel like lying in the wet grass, huh?" He looked up at me and drooled. "Smart boy."

While the other dogs played, I deployed my pooper scooper. By the time the lawn was clean, it was closing in on 9:00 a.m. J. D. hadn't texted me yet about walking our dogs. Weird. My nerves sparked. I pulled out my cell to make sure I hadn't missed a message. "Settle down. He's fine."

At the sound of my voice, the dogs stopped and looked at me. Feeling bad, I found another tennis ball and tossed it to them. The scramble for control of the magical orb resumed.

Okay, J. D. hadn't texted. Big deal. The guy could've slept late. The tightness in my gut argued against this sunny conjecture.

Caving to my unease, I texted him. Ten minutes passed with no response. Hoping I was overreacting, I leashed the dogs and walked all four to the beach.

Our late start meant many of the dog lovers had already come and gone. I nodded at a guy with the two Weimaraners. He waved and called out, "Got your hands full today."

"Yep." In spite of the smile I flashed, my uneasiness about J. D. grew. Before taking in Buster, my neighbor rarely ventured outside of his house. Had adding the dog to his life—along with walks outdoors—been too much too soon?

A few surfers were still out. At least a dozen people walked and jogged along the hard-packed sand by the water. With two leashes in each hand, I doubted I'd be able to keep the dogs out of everyone's way. I urged them away from the crashing surf. Ever obedient, Harlow complied, but shot longing glances at the waves and shorebirds. "Sorry, girl. Maybe tomorrow."

The dry sand made for tougher going. With Sky's stubby legs, I'd need to keep the walk short. When my hands began to ache from gripping all the leashes, I turned the dogs back. Though Sky was panting when we reached the cul-de-sac, she looked happy.

My cell rang. I shifted the leashes to my left hand and pulled out my phone. J. D.'s name brightened the screen. With a sigh of relief, I hit "Accept." "What's up?"

"I need your help." He sounded like he was struggling for air.

Alarm wildfired through my chest. "We're almost to the alley. I'll be there in a sec."

"I'm not home."

My heart began to hammer. "Where are you?"

"Hendry's Beach. In Santa Barbara." Raspy breaths filled the line. "I was feeling good. I thought . . ."

"Where are you, exactly? On the beach? Nearby?"

"I'm sorry, I—"

"J. D., you don't have to explain. Tell me where you are."

"My car. In the parking lot."

"Okay." I turned into the alley and started jogging. Rats. Too fast for Sky. I scooped her up and continued. Dammit. I couldn't get the cell close to my mouth. Hoping I didn't sound like I was shouting, I said, "Focus on your breathing. Is Buster with you?"

"Yes," he gasped.

"Good." Reaching my house, I set down Sky, opened the side gate, and unleashed the dogs. "That's perfect." I took a deep breath, then tried for a normal volume as I continued. "Now close your eyes and pet him. Feel his coat beneath your hand. Keep doing it." Slipping inside the kitchen, I found my purse and car key. "You still there?"

"Yeah."

Cutting through the backyard to the garage, I climbed into the 4Runner. "My cell's on speaker and I'm not hanging up." I started the engine. "Talk if you want or just breathe. I'm listening. I'll be there as soon as possible."

Fortunately, the lights timed my way and I was on the freeway in three minutes. Driving like the posted speed limit of sixty-five miles per hour was merely a suggestion, I wove around slower drivers, trying to keep the needle below eighty-five. The last thing I needed was to make J. D. wait because the highway patrol had pulled me over. Within fifteen minutes I was passing the greenhouses marking the south edge of Carpinteria. At this rate, I'd get to Santa Barbara in less than thirty minutes. Good thing it wasn't yet noon and traffic was relatively light. I wiped my sweaty right palm against my jeans, then did the same with my left. When I neared Summerland, I spoke again. "You still with me?"

"Yeah." J. D.'s voice sounded weak.

"I'm about ten minutes away. How's Buster doing?"

Voice stronger, he said, "He's a champ."

"Hang in there." When I reached Las Positas Road, I pulled off the 101. Bowing to the laws of physics, I slowed for the round-about. I took the first exit, Cliff Drive, and a few minutes later was pulling into the narrow palm-tree-lined lot for Hendry's.

"I'm here," I called out. Finding a space halfway down the aisle from J. D.'s Toyota Land Cruiser, I screeched to a stop. "I'm on my way." I jumped out of the car and ran.

When I reached his vehicle, the back seat was down. J. D. was curled up in the cargo area, arms around Buster. His keys sat on the front passenger seat. The door was unlocked. I decided against opening the back—fearing it might make him feel too exposed. I climbed onto the front seat and kneeled facing him. Reaching between the seats, I touched his wet suit–encased shoulder. "I'm here."

He nodded, keeping his eyes closed.

"How's your breathing?"

"Better."

"Where's your surfboard?"

"On the beach."

"You okay if I leave you here for a moment to get it?"

He shook his head. "No. It's . . . on the far side . . . of the creek. It'll take too long."

"Okay. Let's get you home."

"Gimme a minute. Then I'll get in your car."

"Stay where you are. I'll get a ride back and pick up my car later."

"Sounds good."

Unfamiliar with J. D.'s vehicle, I set a more sedate pace for the return trip. I kept up a stream of chatter, hoping to distract him from the symptoms of his panic attack. Ten minutes from Pier Point my cell rang. My first instinct was to let it go to voice mail, then I saw the number. Not one I knew, but it still struck a familiar chord. "Hello?"

"Hi. I'm out."

"Felicity?"

"Yeah. I just got the bail taken care of and I'm heading to your place. I need to see Royal. I'm hoping he'll help me feel normal again."

"Um." I glanced at J. D. huddled in the back. "I'm not home right now. I should be there soon. If you get to my place before me, all the dogs are in the backyard. Let yourself in through the side gate. The house is locked, so you'll have to wait for me to get his crate and leash."

"Okay. Thank you so much for looking after him. See you soon."

I disconnected and eyed the rearview. Buster lifted his head and met my gaze before resettling against J. D.

When I pulled into our alley, the tightness in my chest eased. I backed into J. D.'s driveway and cut the engine. "I'm going to walk to the rear and open the hatch. You ready?"

"Yeah."

Sunlight streamed into the cargo area. Sweat covered J. D.'s face. He kept his eyes clamped shut. "Buster, come." The boxer hopped out. I touched J. D.'s ankle. "You're next." He opened his eyes. His pupils were dilated, his breathing ragged. "We're home. Take my hand and we'll get you inside."

He pushed himself up and staggered from the car. Buster leaned against his leg as I guided J. D. into the house. Side by side we tottered down the hall to the family room. Once he was settled on the sofa, Buster hopped up beside him. I brought him a blanket, pillow, and glass of water. I checked that Buster had water, too, then squeezed J. D.'s clammy hand. "I'm so sorry, but I have to run. I'll check in on you later, okay?"

"Okay." His eyes appeared unfocused.

"Hey." I put one hand on either side of his face. "Look at me." When he did, I continued. "If you need anything or just want someone to be here with you, call me. Promise?"

"I will."

"All right." Feeling guilty for leaving, I hurried across the alley to my gate. When I opened it, I smiled—in spite of all my worry. Felicity held a tennis ball aloft and ran around the yard's perimeter, Royal, Harlow, and Noodle at her heels, Sky trailing along after. If the woman grinned any more broadly, I swore part of her face might break off.

I closed the gate and stood silently, not wanting to interrupt the magical moment.

Felicity spied me and dropped the ball. Royal and Harlow dove for it, while Sky snorted and jumped. Noodle panted and drooled.

Spell broken, I hurried to her. We hugged. Though we'd only known each other a short time, it felt right. "How're you holding up?"

"I'm just glad to be out." She took a step back, her hand wandering up to smooth her hair.

"Royal missed you."

"I missed him, too. I don't think I could survive being locked up again." She watched the boxer cavorting with Harlow and Sky. Chewing her lip, she turned to face me. "Can you help me?"

"With what?"

"You used to be a cop and a P.I., right?"

"Yep."

"I hate to ask, but I don't think the Sheriff's Department is looking at anyone but me for Celeste's killing. I was hoping you could poke around."

Was there more to her arrest than I realized? "Why'd they focus on you?"

She massaged her temples. "The argument I had with Celeste at Playtime. That public fight and my apparently 'well-known jealousy' about her wins have convinced the sheriff I hit her in a fit of rage or something. I wish I could press rewind and erase that whole day."

"Are you ready to tell me what the fight was about?"

She balled her fists, knuckles whitening. "No."

"You want me to look for other possible suspects, but won't trust me with this?"

"I can't. It's not about trust. It's just . . . It's too awful to talk about. But it has nothing to do with her death. I swear." Harlow ran back with the ball and dropped it at her feet. Felicity wiped her eyes and tossed it across the yard again.

I debated whether to push harder. She seemed so fragile. Saving the topic for another day, I said, "Have they found the weapon?"

"She was hit."

"She was hit with an object, not someone's fists."

"Oh. I didn't know." Felicity pulled her gaze from the dogs and frowned. "The cops have to tell my lawyer if they find the weapon, right?"

"They're supposed to."

"Good. I wish I hadn't gone straight home after agility class. Then someone besides Royal could've seen me to support my alibi."

"And they're not about to take his word."

"I wish." The boxer ran back with the ball. "Drop it." Felicity picked it up and hurled it across the yard.

"I take it you didn't talk to any of your neighbors that afternoon or evening?"

"Nope. We just went inside and flaked. Can you dig around? There have to be dozens of people who hated Celeste enough to kill her. I can pay you for your time."

"Not necessary. I want to know what happened, too. But can you do me a favor first?"

She tossed the ball again, forehead furrowed. "What do you need?"

"A ride to pick up my car. It's at the beach in Santa Barbara."

The tension left her face. "You got it."

Felicity didn't want to be separated from Royal, so we loaded his crate into the back of her Jeep Wrangler. He jumped right in. As she drove, I told her about J. D.'s agoraphobia and his recent progress.

"He's taking care of Celeste's boxer?"

"They're taking care of each other."

"And today was, like, a setback?"

"A big one. But it may be hard to convince him that's all it was." We lapsed into silence.

When we entered Santa Barbara, Felicity cleared her throat. "So this friend of yours, he's probably not going to do agility with Buster?"

"Maybe someday he'll want to run him through a few jumps in my yard or the weave poles. But I don't see him competing in public. Which means you don't have to worry about Buster beating Royal."

"I am so transparent." She signaled for the exit at Las Positas. "That said, I'm glad you found him a good home."

"Speaking of which, Celeste's husband brought me Buster's

papers. When I went through them, they got me wondering . . . How long ago did Celeste start doing agility with Buster?"

"Thirteen months."

"That's precise."

Felicity took the first exit from the roundabout. "I remember because Royal and I had just double-Q'd at the regional meet in June. We were both hyper afterwards and walking off some energy when Celeste said hello. She said something nice about Royal and I got to talking about agility. I'd only moved into the neighborhood the week before and hadn't had a chance to meet anyone. Celeste admired Royal and I told her about the competition. She said it sounded like fun. Said she was looking for something to do with her spare time. It took her a few weeks to find a dog. One who was old enough to begin training for agility."

"Huh. She left his puppy training to others?"

"I don't think she had the patience for it. She wanted to dive right into competing. And that early training can be such an important part of bonding." Felicity wrinkled her nose. "With Celeste, the more I learned, the less I liked her. I was glad when she and Del moved to Pier Point."

"Weird."

"Why? She wasn't exactly likable."

"No, I mean the time line is off. Did she work with another dog before Buster?"

"No. Got him right off the bat. Wanted a boxer like Royal." Felicity pulled into the parking lot at Hendry's Beach. "Why all the questions?"

"Because, according to the papers from Buster's previous owner, Felicity bought him eight months ago."

"That's impossible."

"Maybe it's a typo."

"I guess."

"I left a message for the seller. I'll ask him about it when he calls back." I climbed out. "Thanks for the ride."

"Sure. Thank you for looking after Royal."

"No problem."

"And you'll look into Celeste's murder?"

"Count on it." I waved as Felicity and Buster drove away. Before getting into the 4Runner, I struck out toward the water. A fair number of people were walking along the shoreline. Turning away, I headed up the beach to Arroyo Creek and the dog-friendly beach.

When I'd reached my destination, I stared out at the water, hands on hips. Not that I was any expert, but the waves seemed crowded for a Monday. I scanned the beach and shallows for an abandoned board but saw nothing. I continued up the sand. When I'd watched J. D. surf in Pier Point last Thursday, he'd taken a teal-and-tan board. I saw nothing that matched, but he had three others, so who knew which board he'd brought today?

Abandoning my search, I walked back to the parking lot.

CHAPTER 13

When I returned to Pier Point for the second time, I did a quick check on the dogs before hurrying to J. D.'s. Buster nosed through the door when J. D. answered. Though looking wan and shaky, he'd managed to change out of his wet suit into jeans and a Sweet Johnny T-shirt.

"Hey." Waving me in, he trudged through the entryway, past the living room, kitchen, and dining room to the den, where he flopped onto the leather couch. The boxer wedged himself between the coffee table and J. D.'s bare feet. He rubbed the dog's head, then looked up at me. "Thanks for coming to my rescue."

"No problem. What happened?"

He raised his eyebrows.

"I know you had a panic attack." I plunked myself onto the armchair. "What I meant is: Were you already in the water? Or had you just gotten to the beach? Or . . . ?"

Leaning forward, J. D. picked up an open bottle of beer from the table.

Seemed a little early to me, but I kept my mouth shut. He'd had a rough morning.

"I was on my board. I'd got Buster set up on the beach and paddled out. I felt good. Excited, even." He tilted his head back to drink, Adam's apple bobbing. After clunking the empty down, he wiped his mouth with the back of his hand. "I got past the breakers and it hit like a brick. How huge the ocean was. I looked back at the shore. Buster was this distant speck. My heart started racing, my mouth went dry. The fastest way in would've been to catch a wave, but my legs were shaking too hard for me to stand. I paddled back like a total loser and hauled my board out. But my breathing was bad and my legs too weak to hold me. I had to crawl to Buster's side." He looked near tears.

"You didn't have your phone?"

"Left it in the car."

Having just made the trek from the dog-friendly beach to the parking lot, I knew it was a four- or five-minute walk. But in the midst of a panic attack, a five-minute walk might as well be fifty miles. "How did you make it all the way to the parking lot?"

"With Buster's help. My knees kept giving out every few yards. He'd huddle next to me until I could move again. A nice older couple spotted me kneeling with my arms around him at the edge of the lot and helped me to my Land Cruiser. They wanted to call 9-1-1, but I told them I had someone who'd come get me."

Swallowing the lump in my throat, I rose from the chair and went to sit beside him. "I'm so sorry. It must've been awful for you."

"Who am I kidding?" He scrubbed his face with both hands. "I'm never gonna be normal again."

"I don't know about normal. I mean, who's ever really normal? The thing is, I'm sure you'll improve. You just overreached today."

"No. There's something wrong with me." He curled forward to

rub Buster's ears. "I've been thinking about this since you left earlier. You need to take this guy back. It's not fair to him. He needs someone who can go outside and play with him."

"What?" I had a brief flare of the panic J. D. lived with every day.

"I can't take him for walks, run on the beach. I'm no good for him."

"Look at me. Now." My voice came out like a drill sergeant's.

He lifted his face, red-rimmed eyes finally meeting mine again.

"You're my friend. Maybe the best friend I have here in Pier Point. But you're starting to piss me off."

His already pale face blanched while his mouth dropped open.

I pointed at Buster. "That dog loves you. He's already lost one person and I'm not taking him away from you. You had a setback. A big one. But it's temporary. And until you feel up to walking him yourself, I'll walk him twice a day. And I'll keep doing it until you can do it yourself. I don't care if it takes a week or ten years. You got it?"

He straightened. "Got it."

"All right." I stood. "I'll come by about five o'clock today to pick him up."

"Okay."

Relieved J. D. had heard me—even if he didn't believe this was only temporary—I stepped outside and took a deep breath. J. D. and Buster needed each other. I hoped he realized it.

Feeling wound up from our conversation, I went straight to the backyard and romped with the dogs. After we'd all blown off some steam, we did another fifteen-minute training session. Each time, Sky grew more responsive. When done, we went inside and everyone—including me—took a much-needed nap.

At five o'clock, I collected Buster from a chagrined-looking J. D. "I'll have him back in an hour."

"Thank you."

"You'd do the same for me."

He nodded.

The next morning, after collecting Buster and Sky and taking the four dogs for a walk, I returned the boxer to J. D. Heartened by the color in his face, I took a chance and said, "Feeling better?"

"Yeah. Getting steadier." He ruffled his already messy hair. "Thanks for talking some sense into me yesterday."

Not sure which bit of sense he was referring to, I cocked my head and waited.

Crouching, he gave the boxer a hug. Buster bobbed and licked his face. J. D. laughed. "I don't know what I'd do without this guy."

"Or what he'd do without you. It's a two-way street, bud."

He stood. "You're right. Again." Buster shook himself, tags jingling.

"I'm heading out to Playtime Academy in a little while. I won't be right across the street, but it'll only take thirty to forty minutes to get back. Call if you need me. Okay?"

"Okay."

After refreshing the water bowls in the backyard, I brushed the three dogs then went inside to grab my keys and wallet. I left Noodle snoozing on the deck while Harlow and Sky played tug-of-war with the knotted rope. The Frenchie really had no idea how small she was compared to her new dog pals.

Not sure what I hoped to find at the training facility, I climbed into the 4Runner. Traffic consisted mostly of tractor trailers loaded with produce and the journey went more slowly than I'd anticipated. Since the dogs weren't with me, I kept the windows closed, enjoying the AC as I trundled down the two-lane road. I wondered if I should've brought Harlow along for cover. Probably not. I wasn't signed up for a class so that ruse would quickly fall apart. This was one of those times when honesty was the best policy.

Once again, the series of "missing dog" flyers posted along the road saddened me. I hoped he'd found his way home and someone had merely neglected to remove the notices. When I reached the narrow driveway, I slowed and bumped my way up the incline to the parking lot.

Though only Tuesday, the lot was half full. I found a spot and climbed out. At least twenty dogs and handlers stood inside the far dirt arena with Cowboy Ben facing them. I continued to the office, pausing when I spied a now-familiar flyer tacked to the side of the building: another notice about Freddy the missing golden retriever. The print and photo were less sun-faded than the ones lining the road.

The office door was open so I poked my head inside. Simone Beaulieu sat at the desk, engrossed in paperwork. I knocked on the door frame. She gasped and jerked her head.

"Sorry. Didn't mean to startle you."

She swiveled her chair to face me. "Oh. Hi." She gave a strained-looking smile. "I know you. You came with the Saint Berdoodle who . . . um . . ." Her eyes widened. "Right. Found Celeste. Sorry, I've forgotten your name."

"Molly Madison."

A small crease appeared between her eyebrows. "I don't remember seeing you on today's class list."

"I'm not. I just came by . . ." No reason not to say it; I'd already decided to try honesty. "Felicity Gaines was arrested for Celeste's murder."

"No. I—" She shook her head. "I can't believe that."

"She's out now and asked me to look into what happened."

"Oh. So she didn't do it. Good." This time her smile looked genuine. "She's just too nice, you know?"

Realizing how what I'd said could be misconstrued, I started over. "I meant she's out on bail. The charges still stand."

"Oh."

"I admit, I don't know Felicity well, but I do know she's not stupid. It makes no sense for her to have a public argument with Celeste then kill her. I get why the cops suspect her, but I think they're wrong."

Simone tugged at a curl. "And you came by just to tell me this?"

"No. I wanted to get your okay to walk around. See if anything here speaks to me."

"Why would I do that?"

"Oh, right." I silently chided myself for not being on my game. "I used to be a cop. And I was a private investigator after that. Felicity hoped that, with my experience, walking around the place might trigger some ideas."

Simone chewed her lip and continued pulling on her curl. "The area on top of the hay bales is still taped off, so you can't go up there. But if you want to look around the barn and walk the premises, it's all right by me. The sooner this gets settled, the better it is for us."

I glanced out the office door. "Doesn't seem to have hurt business. Pretty busy for a weekday."

"Those guys?" She frowned. "They're all newbies. We've lost

a few regulars over this. And we'd already lost several because of . . ." Simone snapped her mouth shut.

"What?"

She shook her head, curls softly swaying. "Sorry. That's Playtime's business. Suffice it to say, we don't need another problem."

Another? Had Celeste stumbled across this other problem? Hoping to draw Simone out, I continued. "Of course. Still, that's a good-size class."

"Most of them don't even know how to make their dogs sit. They're strictly here to gawk. Though Ben's hopeful he can convert some of them to agility." She turned back to her desk. The conversation was over.

"Well, thanks for letting me look around." As I exited, the missing dog's picture caught my eye and I reversed course. "Sorry to disturb you again, but I couldn't help noticing the flyer. And all the flyers along the road. Has the dog turned up?"

"No." She turned back, eyes damp.

"Oh dear. Is he yours?"

"No. Freddy belongs to Playtime's owner. He lives on an adjacent piece of land."

"I take it he brings the dog here to visit?"

"Sometimes. He's got a big spread, so Mr. Hopkins lets Freddy run loose during the day and early evening. The dog would stop in for a treat almost every day." She huffed out a breath. "But he didn't return one night."

The faded quality of the flyers added to my worry about the dog. "How long ago was this?"

"It's been three weeks now. I remember because I was closing up the place after an evening agility class when Mr. Hopkins came storming in to see if Freddy was here."

In an area that was home to bobcats, coyotes, and mountain

lions, three weeks was way too long. "Sorry to hear that. I'll get out of your hair now."

I began my site tour by walking along the barbed wire fence marking the property's perimeter, looking for any possible object which could've been used to bludgeon Celeste. While a fence post could've done the job, all the ones I saw were still in place and secured by wire. Where did they keep the old rotted posts?

The fence line circled back toward the class area. I skirted the two dirt arenas and the agility fields and headed for the barn. Stepping inside, I waited for my eyes to adjust to the dim interior. Checking along the wall, I found the panel and flipped the light switch. A brief hum, then the bright overheads popped on. In the center of the huge space, the setup for barn hunt was unchanged. I walked to the rear of the building and tilted my head back to stare at the bale stack where Noodle found Celeste. A portion of the orange net fencing off the bales had been torn away. Had it been that way when I'd scrambled to the top a week ago? I couldn't remember. Like Simone had said, yellow crime scene tape cordoned off the hay bale ziggurat.

I stepped back and tried to picture the killer luring Celeste to the top of the stack, then hitting her. Nope. No way would Celeste climb up there dressed like she was in designer jeans and one of her special bedazzled shirts. Besides, there was far too little blood on the straw where I found her. Far more likely someone killed her, then hauled her to the top. That spoke to physical strength, as did the blow that ended her life.

Turning, I walked around outside the barn hunt arena, scanning for likely weapons. When I'd reached the tarped-off area on the right side of the barn, I flipped the plastic sheeting up. Light filtered in from the main part of the barn. Spying a hook jutting out from the wood lintel above, I looped one of the grommets edging the tarp over it. Here, too, hay bales lined the walls. A rustling sound came from inside. I froze, then spotted the stack of cages along the rear. At least twenty rats stared at me. I walked to the closest and stuck a finger near the bars. A large black-and-white rat scuttled over and sniffed. "Don't worry. I'll only be here a few minutes."

I scanned the cramped space. Lots of tools. Stirrup hoes, spades, shovels, and bow rakes. Plus a crate full of what looked like sections of metal pipe. Each piece was about ten inches long and four in diameter. I crouched to get a closer look. Yep, if swung with enough force against someone's skull, these could prove lethal.

"What're you doing?"

I jumped and turned.

Quentin the Rat Wrangler smirked at me. "Did I scare you?"

"Startled. Not scared." I pointed at the pipe sections. "What're those for?"

"Why should I tell you?" He ran a large hand through his shaggy mop of hair.

"A woman was killed here." Times like this—and sneering guys like him—made me miss having a badge. "Simone gave me the okay to look around. And ask questions." Okay, the second part was a lie, but Quentin rubbed my nerves raw. "What're they for?"

He frowned and crossed his arms, looking like a muscle-bound toddler. "We used them for barn hunt before switching over to PVC." Picking up a metal section, he swung it like a miniature bat. It made a whistling noise as it cut through the air.

"What's that sound?"

"Had to drill air holes in them to keep the rats alive. Much easier doing that with the PVC."

"If you don't use them now, why are they here?"

"You never know when you might have an emergency and need some extra pipe."

"Pipe that has holes in it?"

He found his smirk again.

I didn't know if it was my dislike of Quentin or his behavior that sparked suspicion. "Mind if I look through them?"

"Why?"

"Just checking something. Like I said, I got Simone's okay to look around."

"That may be, but this is my area. I'm the Rat Wrangler and I don't want you messing with my stuff. Or upsetting the rats." His glare raised the fine hair on my forearms.

"Okay." Keeping my eyes on him, I sidled past, then backed out of the tarped-off area. The tension in my jaw eased when I reached the portion of the barn visible through the open front doors. After taking a couple steadying breaths, I continued my tour, peeking behind and between the bales. I didn't expect to find an actual weapon but thought it possible I'd spy a potential hiding place. The killer could've stashed the weapon then removed it as soon as the coast was clear.

Nothing besides Quentin's rat pipes jumped out as a convenient and effective weapon. Too bad I didn't get the chance to examine them in good light. I might need to return when Quentin wasn't around.

I wrapped up my tour of the barn. Cowboy Ben had moved the class from the dirt arena to the first agility field. I walked to the railing to watch. As I leaned against the cool metal, I examined the rail. A section of railing would've made an effective, if cumbersome, weapon. I saw no loose, rusted sections. Playtime kept their grounds and facilities in good shape. Could any of the agility equipment have been used as a weapon? The weave poles were designed so they wouldn't injure a dog if they ran into one rather than between them. Far too pliable to do the kind of damage inflicted on Celeste. I studied the elevated dog walk. From here, all parts looked securely attached. The components of the teeter and A-frame were too large and awkward to use as weapons. Unless the weapon was short and easily hidden, it made more sense for it to come from the barn.

I turned my attention to the class. Cowboy Ben had divided the group into two sections and was teaching one group basic skills such as come, stay, and sit, while the other group walked the course. Most of the students appeared to be having fun—as did their dogs. One face looked familiar, but I couldn't place her until I spied the border collie at her side. Thor. That meant she was the woman who had lost her daughter to cancer. Stacy something. It looked like she planned to go on working with her dead daughter's dog. Maybe it helped her feel connected to what she'd lost; I wasn't sure I'd have the strength to do that.

I crossed to the second agility field and examined the various jumps inside. Again I found nothing that seemed a convenient, viable weapon. Returning to the barn, I scouted behind it and the office. I still didn't know what Playtime did with rusty or failing bits of equipment, but they didn't appear to dump them anywhere outside. Feeling I'd done all I could for today, I returned to the parking lot. When I'd reached my car, I stopped and stared at the training facility. The fact that Celeste was attacked here made her killing seem a crime of opportunity. And the way she was killed made it look like a crime of passion. Whoever hit her must have hated her. And from what I'd heard, there were a lot of people who felt that way. I just needed to figure out who struck that fatal blow.

CHAPTER 14

I took the dogs to the beach for their last walk of the day. The wind had picked up. As each wave crested, salty spray gusted. Only a handful of people were out enjoying the crisp evening. When we approached the dunes, Noodle lunged forward, leash straining my arm muscles. "Heel." My voice came out sharper than I'd intended. In spite of that fact, the Saint Berdoodle continued charging forward. Both his and Sky's leads slipped from my hand.

Oh no. What had he found now? "Noodle, Sky, heel!"

The Frenchie froze and I collected her leash. The big dog didn't stop until he'd reached the top of the dune.

The other three dogs and I caught up to him. I grabbed his leash. "What is it, big guy?" I looked down at the other side of the small dune. "Oh." Some beachgoer had left behind a half-eaten sandwich. "No." I reversed course.

As we crossed the sand, Noodle kept looking at me like I'd deprived him of the world's greatest treat. At the end of our walk,

I deposited Noodle and Harlow inside the house before ringing the bell at J. D.'s. He came to the door, beer bottle in hand. Setting his drink on the tile floor, he crouched and hugged Buster. "You have fun, fellah?" The boxer answered by licking his face.

"He chased three seagulls."

"Three? Good job, Buster." J. D. rubbed the dog's back, then grabbed his beer and straightened. He met my gaze and gave a half smile. "Thanks."

"No problem. Need anything? Food?" I nodded toward his beer. "Drink?"

"Nah, I'm all set."

His mood seemed improved from when I'd picked up the boxer. Was it a real shift for the better or the beer talking? Hoping for the former, I walked Sky to Izzy's, keeping an eye out for the dark-haired man. While he didn't seem interested in me, it didn't pay to be careless. Tonight, no one loitered on the opposite side of the street.

I stepped inside the house and sucked in a breath. It felt like a meat locker. Izzy must be rolling in money to leave the AC cranked to high when no one was home. "Okay, Sky. I've got to go. Sit."

The Frenchie complied and I unhooked her leash. She was a sweet dog. I needed to find out more about how Izzy treated her when no one was around. Not that the threat I'd seen wasn't bad. Izzy's attitude could be fixed—if the woman was willing. But if she was actually hurting the dog, that was another story. Soon, the Frenchie would lose her sweet temperament. Become hand shy. Foot shy. Scared of her own shadow.

Since Izzy had a top-notch security system—I'd already noted a camera in the foyer and one in the kitchen—I wouldn't be able to hide a camera of my own or get the chance to access her video feed without her seeing me.

I wiped my eyes, then patted the Frenchie again. "You have a good night. I'll be back tomorrow."

The night was shifting from indigo to slate. With the days growing shorter, I had maybe three more weeks until I needed to bring the other dogs along as escorts when I walked Sky home. But for now—as much as I loved them all—it was nice to have moments like this to myself and get some time to think.

My standing Friday evening appointment with Lupe and her Dalmatian was still three days away. Even though I checked with her yesterday to make sure she wanted to have a session this week, I was tempted to cancel. It wasn't like Ulysses needed the training anymore. And though I'd already told her she wasn't to blame for Miguel's behavior, I didn't feel like talking about it. With her or anyone else. Not even Miguel. Not after he'd lied his way into my bed. Knowing Lupe's need to thoroughly analyze things, she'd want to examine the situation from every possible angle. Listening to my better nature, I elected to wait another day before deciding whether to cancel.

My cell rang. I pulled it out and checked the screen. Speak of the devil.

Stomach tightening, I declined Miguel's call and pocketed the phone. A couple minutes later, it burred inside my pocket. I waited until I got home before looking at the screen again. Stopping under the porch light, I opened his text: Need to talk

Anger surged through me. My fingers flew across the keys before my inner censor stopped me from answering.

Piss off. Your 'need to talk' is way too late.

I stormed inside. As if they'd read my text and knew I needed support, Harlow and Noodle rushed me, tails wagging. Dropping to my knees, I hugged and kissed them. "Thank you. I'm so lucky to have you two."

Since the night had turned chilly, I fed the dogs inside the kitchen. While they gobbled, I poured myself a glass of wine. After rinsing their bowls, I pulled on a sweatshirt, grabbed my phone, and carried my glass to the rooftop deck. I sat in one of the two director's chairs and breathed in the smell of salt and seaweed before scrolling through my messages. While ignoring Miguel, I'd inadvertently missed a text from my mom.

You're all grown and live far away, but I want your approval. Things are getting serious with Bruno. Call me.

Who the hell was Bruno?

Widowed at twenty-five—with a six-year-old daughter to raise—my mom had proved she could handle anything. All cops' wives were tough, but Mom was like a diamond drill bit, cutting through whatever got in her way. Through the years, she'd had many suitors, but never took any of them seriously. She'd say to me, "I already have two jobs. The most important one—the job I love best—is taking care of you. The second is making enough money to keep a roof over our heads and food in our bellies. I don't need some guy who just wants a free cook, housekeeper, and convenient sex." The first time she said this, I'd cringed at her uttering the word "sex." But over the years, I got used to it. It was her mantra.

I checked the time. Too late to call back now. I took another sip of wine, accepting the fact I wouldn't learn more about Bruno until tomorrow.

Wednesday morning came way too early. My phone had buzzed repeatedly during the night—both before and after I'd tumbled into bed. Texts from Miguel interrupted my sleep until I convinced myself it was unlikely J. D. would have a panic attack inside his own home, turned off my cell, and stuffed it inside the nightstand drawer.

After dressing in jeans and a long-sleeve knit top, I retrieved my phone. No messages from J. D. Thank goodness. I hurried downstairs and released the dogs from their crates. While they did their business, I filled food bowls and carried them to the deck. As I watched the dogs eat, it hit me: Bruno was Mr. Calabrese, the owner of The Most Delicious Deli. We'd met him when we moved to Brockton after Dad's death. Back then, Mom swore Calabrese sold the best capicola and porchetta in town. I remembered her telling me a few weeks before my move west that Mr. Calabrese's wife had passed away. And now he and Mom were an item?

I finally counted the number of texts that had come from Miguel during the night. Twelve. Curiosity warred with anger over their possible contents. Anger won. I shoved the phone into my pocket and leashed Harlow and Noodle. After picking up Buster from a sleepy-looking J. D., I walked the dogs to Izzy's. Tying the three to the post of her mailbox, I told them to sit. I waited a beat to make sure they obeyed, then went inside to retrieve Sky. The Frenchie greeted me with butt wiggles, snorts, and kisses. "I missed you, too, girl."

Leash on, I took her out front to join her friends. After a joyous reunion, we cut between Izzy's house and a neighbor's, heading toward the crashing surf. The misty marine layer still huddled along the coast, turning the surfers into wraiths on the water. In spite of Harlow's hopeful gaze, I decided against letting the dogs run loose. Even on a cold day like this, at least three of them would want to charge into the surf and come home drenched. Harlow and Buster made the best of it and woofed at shorebirds while Sky panted and snorted. Always one to follow his own drumbeat, Noodle kept his nose to the sand, following various scent threads. As usual, we turned back at the children's play area.

Midway down the beach, a sixty-something man launched a kite. The wind caught it and the blue bat shape rose and cut across the sky. I paused to watch the arial acrobatics until Harlow sighed. "Okay, girl. We're heading home now."

I gave the kite master a wide berth, then cut across the sand to the cul-de-sac. Buster began to pull against his lead. "Eager to see your boy, huh?"

When we'd reached J. D.'s porch, I told the dogs to sit, then knocked. J. D. opened the door, still looking sleepy-eyed. Crouching, he petted the dog. "You have fun, fellah?" Buster licked J. D.'s face. "I missed you, too."

"No going in the water today, but he still had a good time."

"Thanks for taking him."

"No problem."

By the time I'd led the dogs into the backyard, they were ready for a drink and a nap. Once they'd all drunk their fill, I brushed each and left them resting on the grass. I went inside and busied myself vacuuming and sweeping, then took a quick shower. Seeing the time, I hurried downstairs to kiss and pet the dogs before hustling along the alley to Ava's. She and Butterscotch were waiting for me on the front porch. "Hey there."

Both jumped to their feet. Instead of one of her usual dresses, Ava once again wore jeans. "*Hola.*"

"*Hola* to you, too. How'd your project with Lincoln go?"

The girl beamed as she led the way through the house. "Great. The paper airplane launcher worked perfectly. Our longest flight was eight feet. We need to modify our plane design to reduce drag if we want to get anywhere close to the world record."

"Which is?"

"Two hundred twenty-six feet, ten inches."

"Are you kidding me?"

"No."

She and Lincoln obviously had a whole different way of looking at paper airplanes than I had as a kid. "Wow."

"It was only our first time trying. And we decided that, rather than focusing on the wing design, we'd try making a Ping-Pong ball launcher."

"How far did the Ping-Pong balls fly?"

Ava gave a weak smile. "The ball went over the fence on our first try. We didn't have any other Ping-Pong balls for tests."

"The neighbor wouldn't give it back?"

"She wasn't home. According to Lincoln, the woman's not very friendly. So no more test flights. But we used the rest of our time to figure out what we'd do next."

"And what's that?"

"We're both going to research thrust and drag and paper airplane design. But before we do any more test flights, we're going to build a dumbwaiter for his tree house. Then we can use his tree house as our workroom. Everything's all planned out. We're going to build a plywood box and install an eyebolt and pulley system that we'll attach to a large branch. We discussed building an I-beam joist but that would take too long. We want to get it done in an afternoon."

"You're going back to Lincoln's today?"

"Uh-huh."

"This Lincoln sounds all right to me."

"He is."

We turned to training. As usual, we began with the basics. Ava had Butterscotch sit, stay, and come, then we reviewed heel, down, and wait. "Any more chewing incidents?"

"No. I just can't let new enthusiasms blind me to my responsibilities."

Her answer brought me up short. "Responsibilities" sounded like her father, but "new enthusiasms" had Jemma written all over it. "I think I get what you're saying: Our dogs count on us to take care of them."

She nodded.

"I know you're the only one taking care of Butterscotch. Is it too much for you?"

Ava's eyes widened. "No. She's my best friend. Like you. And Lincoln. It's just that . . ." She gulped. "When I met Lincoln at my online chess group, we had so much in common. But in a different way than I do with Butterscotch." Ava watched the dog chewing on a treat. "Does that mean I'm not good for her?"

"Oh, sweetie. No. Look at her. Butterscotch is happy, loved, well fed, and exercised. You're doing a great job. The thing is, your world is bigger than her. But that's a two-way street."

Ava's brow crinkled again. "What?"

"Her world is vast and you can't explore it all with her. Yes, you're her caregiver and best friend, but her nose takes her on journeys you can't even imagine. That doesn't make her disloyal, does it?"

"No."

"And your time exploring worlds that she's not a part of, those don't make you disloyal, either."

Ava's brow cleared. "I get it."

"Of course you do."

To wrap up, we worked on the "watch me" command, then played fetch with the Basset-Retriever. While I was in Ava's yard, my cell signaled the arrival of new text messages four separate times. I ignored them, knowing J. D. would call if he had a problem. On the walk home, I checked the screen. All were from Miguel.

The dogs still seemed logy when I returned. Perfect time to call my mom.

The phone rang three times before going to her voice mail. "Hi, Mom. It's me. What's going on? You been dating Mr. Calabrese? I mean, good for you, but call me back. I want details. But not too many."

Way to blow the landing. Shaking my head, I grabbed my laptop and sat on the sofa. I opened my browser and checked the schedule for Playtime's barn hunt. During the fall, classes met Tuesday, Thursday, and Saturday. Did that mean Quentin wouldn't be there guarding his lair today? One way to find out. I tapped the office number into my cell.

An efficient voice answered. "Playtime Academy for Dogs."

"Hi. Is Quentin there?"

"Who is this?"

"Molly Madison."

"Oh, hi. Simone here. Sorry if I sounded abrupt. We've been getting a lot of weird calls since Celeste's death."

"Weird how?"

"Like, messages with people yelling 'You love dogs more than people.' We got a few claiming we're protecting her killer. It's nuts."

"Sorry to hear that. Have you told the Sheriff's Department?"

"You think I should?"

"I do. It's probably not related to the crime, but you never know."

"I'll think about it. To your question, Quentin's not in today."

"No problem. I was planning to come by again this morning for another look around."

"Why?" Her voice sounded like this was the last thing she wanted to hear.

Hoping I hadn't already strained Simone's patience past its breaking point, I said, "To make sure I didn't miss anything. It's always best to look more than once."

After a weighty silence, she said, "I get that. Come on by. Just don't bother any of the students."

"Sure thing. Thanks. I should be there in thirty to forty minutes."

I debated whether to let J. D. know I'd be away from the house but decided against it. No reason to make him feel like I didn't think he could take care of himself. On the way to my 4Runner, I topped off water bowls and petted the dozy dogs.

Traffic was light all the way to Playtime. I found myself slowing at the sight of the "missing" flyers for Freddy the golden retriever. Sadness tugged at my heart. "Poor dog."

At the top of the driveway, I noted the parking lot was once again half-full. More lookie-loos? Or were students showing their loyalty to the place? I parked and stared at the agility fields. A slender woman was running her Australian shepherd through the course while Cowboy Ben supervised. The rest of the class spread out along the rail, watching. I hurried to the barn.

For the first time, I wondered what the building had originally been used for. In addition to the off-center main door—large enough for a tractor—there was a smaller door near the right front corner. It had the pitched roof of a traditional barn, but neither stalls nor hayloft. With the scattering of old walnut trees on the property, I wondered if it had once been used as a curing shed.

Before entering, I took a few minutes to circle the barn. Nothing had changed since yesterday's visit. Rounding to the front again, I scanned the grounds for Quentin. Not seeing the muscle-bound man, I stepped inside. This time, I welcomed the darkness. Standing still, I waited for my eyes to adjust. The quiet reassured me I was alone. Instead of flipping on the overhead lights, I pulled out the compact, but high-powered, flashlight I'd stashed in my pocket.

The straw-covered floor muffled my steps. I stopped at the tarp separating the Rat Wrangler's area from the rest of the barn and watched the front door. When no one entered after me, I slipped behind the plastic sheet. Breathing softly, I clicked on my flashlight and ran the beam across the cramped space. Dozens of tiny eyes stared back at me. I gasped and stumbled backward but managed to stay upright.

The caged rats. Of course. I shifted the beam to the floor and continued searching for the crate. The tubes were still there. My shoulders relaxed a notch. I hadn't wanted to acknowledge my fear that Quentin might've removed them. I crouched beside the crate. No blood was visible on the exposed portions of pipe.

Tucking the light under my arm, I pulled a pair of latex gloves from my pocket. My phone burred. Cursing myself for failing to silence it, I quickly turned off the sound, noting another text from Miguel. Careful not to smudge any prints—or wipe away other potential evidence—I lifted one of the topmost tubes by the open end and rotated it. Still no blood. If Quentin had used one of these to clock Celeste, he could've wiped it down. That was the smart thing to do. But would he have cleaned out the insides? I peered through both open ends. If any blood had seeped through the air holes, I couldn't see it.

One by one, I repeated the process, setting the examined tubes on the straw.

At the bottom of the box, two of the tubes still had the heavy metal end caps that once kept the rats inside. Afraid the caps might hold relevant evidence, I looked at the nearby tools. Selecting a pair of wire cutters, I used the blade to roll each tube so I could see their exteriors from all sides. Again, nothing screamed "evidence."

Something white inside one of the tubes caught the light. Was there a rat trapped there? How long had it been since Playtime switched from metal tubes to PVC? Chewing the inside of my cheek, I debated picking it up. But how could I not? Gingerly lifting it, I shone the light into the holes. Something white definitely blocked the openings, but it wasn't furry. Thank goodness. Turning it over, I focused the beam again. Same thing. Hoping I wasn't tampering with the murder weapon, I wrenched off one end and studied the interior.

A rolled sheet of paper lined the tube.

Using my gloved index finger, I dragged the sheet out. Mouth dry, I set down the metal pieces and unrolled the piece of notepaper. On it was a list of numbers written in ink with an angular hand. Each of the five lines of numbers included twenty-three digits and ended with two letters. What on earth?

A footfall came from somewhere inside the barn followed by muffled voices. Time was up.

I opened the camera function on my cell and took pictures of the page, wincing at the flash and click accompanying each shot. Quickly rerolling the sheet, I slid it back inside, replaced the end cap, and returned the tube to the crate. Wishing I could dump the remaining tubes into the box all at once, I lifted each one by the end and quietly placed it inside.

Breathing hard, I moved to the tarp and peered around the edge.

Quentin and a sandy-haired man stood near the barn doors. The Rat Wrangler wore his usual T-shirt, jeans, and boots, while the other man looked office ready in a pair of pressed slacks, a button-down shirt, and loafers. Whoever he was, the man wasn't here to train his dog. Not dressed like that.

What was Quentin doing here on his day off? Too far away to hear what they were saying, it was clear the second man was angry. Though the Rat Wrangler was taller than the other man by at least four inches and much burlier, he looked cowed. Stepping away from the tarp, my mind raced. I couldn't stay hidden here. The odds of Quentin checking in on the rats were too high.

His work space was on the same side of the barn as the smaller door I'd noted from the front of the barn. Maybe I could get there from here? I crept away from the tarp. Once I thought it was safe, I shielded the bulb with my hand and turned on my flashlight, moving past the crate and into the shadows. In the barn behind me, one of the men swore, followed by an angry voice. It didn't sound like Quentin's.

"Too risky? Too risky? I'll show you what risk is."

Words indistinct, Quentin's lower rumble followed.

Hoping their argument would mask my movements, I reached the stack of bales lining the back wall. No orange safety fence blocked off the bales the way it did in the public areas of the barn. Shining the beam around, I looked for a way out. A floor-to-ceiling gap between two stacks drew me. The dark space was maybe ten inches wide. I reached my arm between the columns, touching nothing but air. Turning sideways, I wedged myself into the opening, hoping I wouldn't wind up stuck or crushed under a tumbling pile of straw. The flashlight shone on a narrow corridor between the bales and a plank wall. Wriggling until I made it through to the other side, I fought the urge to sneeze while studying my surroundings. For some reason, Playtime hadn't stacked the bales flush against the wall. A passageway remained behind them. Light seeped in at the front of the building. Hoping it was from the door, I edged toward it.

Less worried now about my flashlight beam being spotted by the men in the main part of the barn, I sidled forward, staying close to the stacked bales. Various pieces of rusted and rotted farm equipment leaned against the wood wall, blocking my way. Carefully moving broken shovels and rakes and stepping over detritus, I continued on. Maybe this secret junk pile explained the gap; someone had been too lazy to move the discarded items.

I froze and refocused the light. So this was the resting place for Playtime's abandoned equipment. I ran the beam across the haphazard piles of wood and steel, but saw no signs of blood. Not daring to linger, I stepped around the next obstacle and continued on. If the murder weapon had been hidden here, I'd need access to the space when no one was around.

Or smarter still, I could call the Sheriff's Department and tell them about the hidden dumping area.

CHAPTER 15

The light at the front of the building haloed around a stack of bales obstructing the door. Several fence poles leaned across the narrow path. Once again, I shined my flashlight, searching for signs of blood. Nothing. I repositioned the pieces of wood and continued heading to the door. When I reached my goal, I studied the bales. Gripping the wire tied around the bottom one, I pulled. The column shifted about two inches. I lowered my weight and tugged. The stack slid maybe half an inch. Hands aching where the wire dug into my gloved fingers, I shook them out, then tried again. The stack moved another inch on one side. Not enough. I wedged myself between the bales and the door, put my back against the stack, and shoved.

The topmost bales shifted, but the lower ones didn't budge. The last thing I needed was to knock over the entire stack. Sweat dampened my back as I crammed myself around the column of bales, crouched, and yanked on the lower ones. When I stood, the stack was still cockeyed and I'd only moved it another half inch. Gritting my teeth, I wrenched the bottom bale toward me. The entire stack shifted away from the door. Yes! I'd cleared enough space to open it maybe six inches.

I rounded the bales and squeezed the door's thumb latch. The mechanism refused to budge. Using both hands, I pressed as hard as I could. Finally, the latch clicked and I hauled on the balky door. Hinges squealed, freezing me in place. I waited for the sounds of footsteps or shouts from Quentin or the sandy-haired man, but all I heard was my thumping heart. Squinting at the bright sunlight, I eased the door open a couple more inches. The area in front of the barn was empty. I slipped through the gap and gently closed the door.

Straw clung to me. Ducking around the far side of the barn, I pulled off my gloves and swiped at my clothes. My knit top acted like Velcro, holding the amber fragments in place. I started picking them off, then heard footsteps crunch on gravel. I edged my way to the building's corner and peeked at the front. The sandy-haired man strode from the barn. I darted back out of sight. A minute later, I looked again. Sandy-hair was headed to the parking lot. Quentin must still be inside the barn.

A hawk launched from a nearby live oak. I jumped. Ordering myself to calm down, I leaned against the barn and watched the powerful raptor cut through the air, catch a thermal, and spiral upward. Wishing I could make an equally smooth departure, I refocused on my straw-speckled clothes.

My back itched. I reached over my shoulder. More straw. I brushed it off as best I could, then pulled stragglers from my hair. My phone vibrated. I checked the screen, then answered, keeping my voice low. "Hi, Mom."

"Hi, sweetie. Glad I caught you."

Hoping my appearance would pass for normal, I looked around the front corner of the barn again. Coast clear, I stepped from my hiding spot and walked toward the agility fields. "You've been dating Mr. Calabrese? How long?"

"Two months now. Actually, we're engaged."

"You're engaged? I know you said things were getting serious, but that's fast, Mom. Really fast. Are you sure about this?"

"Of course. I've known Bruno for years. It's not like we just met."

"You bought deli meats from the man. It's not like you were friends or palled around together. How long have you been dating? A couple months?"

"Yes, but—"

"And you're talking about marrying him?"

"Honey, I've been single for thirty-one years. I think I know when I've met the right man. Be happy for me."

"I am, I just . . . Are you sure about this?"

"Yes. And we're planning to get married Christmas Day."

"That's only three months away."

"I know, and I want you to be there."

"Why the rush? Should I be expecting a little sister or brother?"

"Molly! Don't be difficult. The simple truth is, neither of us is getting any younger. And it'll ensure that you're here for the holiday."

I ignored her implication that only something this momentous would get me back to Massachusetts. "Wow. This is big."

"You'll come?"

"Of course I'll come." Oh God. December was when the man who killed my husband was supposed to go on trial. My next trip home promised to be an emotional roller coaster. "Congratulations, Mom."

She giggled like a teenager. My mom never giggled. Double wow.

"I've got to scoot. Bruno's taking me out tonight."

"Lucky you."

"You're right." She giggled again. "Love you."

"Love you, too." I tucked my cell inside my pocket. It was difficult picturing my hard-driving, independent mother marrying anyone—let alone the cleaver-wielding deli man, Mr. Calabrese.

A meaty hand grabbed my arm.

Startled, I turned. Quentin scowled down at me. Had he spotted me leaving the barn? Or worse, seen me inside? I tried to pull free. "Let go."

His viselike grip tightened. "Give it back."

Not what I was expecting. "Let go of me. Now. As a former cop, I can assure you this is assault."

His frown deepened, but he released me. Retreating a step, he crossed his arms.

"That's better. Now, give what back?"

The smell of sweat came off him in waves. "You know."

"No, I don't."

He looked past me toward the parking lot, then leaned down and hissed, "The tube."

Doing my best to look and sound self-righteous, I met his gaze. "What tube?"

"Dammit. You know exactly what I'm talking about."

Resisting the urge to step backward, I widened my stance, readying myself for a possible attack. "I didn't take anything of yours. Let alone some tube."

"I had twenty-four metal tubes, now there's only twenty-three." He thrust a finger near my face. "You were snooping around yesterday and here you are again today. And you've got straw in your hair and on your clothes. Which means you were in the barn. What'd you do with my tube?"

My cleanup job hadn't been as thorough as I'd hoped. "I don't have your stupid tube."

Sweat beaded his forehead. "You have to."

Did the missing piece of pipe hold the list of numbers I'd found? Impossible. Quentin was still inside the barn when I snuck out. No way someone else got in there to take it. Maybe he used a second tube to hide more numbers, one that had already been removed before I searched the crate? How many tubes had I examined? Too many to bother counting at the time. "When did you see it last?"

"Why?"

"Knowing that will help you narrow the window."

"What window?"

I bit back a sigh. "For when it disappeared."

"Oh." His frown deepened. "Don't know. I just noticed it."

Hoping to shake more information loose, I said, "Why were you counting the old tubes? It's not like you use the metal ones anymore."

"That's none of your business."

I cocked my head. His face had gone pale, and he had a slight tremble to his hands. Quentin wasn't just angry, he was scared. "What's going on? What's so important about a missing piece of pipe?"

"You . . ." He thrust his index finger toward my face again. "Stay out of the barn. If I catch you in my area . . ." He opened and closed his mouth, then turned and stomped back to the barn.

I watched him disappear inside. If the missing metal tube was the murder weapon, his fear made sense. But why would he kill Celeste? She'd ruffled a lot of folks' feathers, but I'd heard no murmurs about run-ins with Quentin.

If the missing tube wasn't the weapon, maybe there was

something secreted inside it. Quentin obviously liked hiding things in them. I pulled out my cell and scanned through the photos I'd taken. One picture appeared crisper than the rest, each number clearly legible. But the list still meant nothing to me. Every line had too many digits for social security or credit card numbers. Maybe Ava would have some idea what they meant.

After walking the grounds and peeking behind buildings, glancing inside sheds, and examining the rings and unoccupied field, I still hadn't come up with a likelier murder weapon than one of Quentin's metal rat tubes.

I popped into the office before leaving. "Hey."

Simone looked up from her laptop. Today she wore her hair loose, curls reaching her shoulders. With her perfect posture, she made her jeans and Playtime polo shirt look elegant. "You're going to look around now?"

"Actually, I'm just finishing up."

"Oh." She looked past me, toward the agility fields. "You talk to any of the students?"

"Nope. This was strictly a looking-no-talking visit. Though, I've got to say, today's group seems more on the ball than yesterday's."

She puffed out her cheeks. "Some of our regulars are return-ing. Thank goodness."

Though I was curious about what "other" trouble had driven folks away from classes, this wasn't the time to ask. "Thanks for letting me poke around."

"No problem."

Before pulling out of the lot, I fished Detective DeFelice's busi-ness card from my wallet and called.

"DeFelice."

Surprised to get straight through to her, I blurted out, "Hi. This is Molly Madison. You interviewed me at Playtime Academy for Dogs two weeks ago. My dog found Celeste Simmons's body."

"Sure. What's on your mind, Ms. Madison?"

I told her about the cache of old tools and broken fence posts hidden behind the hay bales at Playtime. "The lighting wasn't great, so I've got no idea if there was blood on anything, but I thought you should know."

"Thanks. And you say this area is inside the barn?"

"You can get to it from the area where the rats are kept."

"We'll send a team out."

I disconnected, then sighed. Simone wasn't going to be happy about the Sheriff's Department making a return appearance at Playtime.

I arrived back in Pier Point just after two o'clock. Before going home, I stopped in the grocery store and loaded up on diet root beer, frozen burritos, and a few other necessities. While in the dog food aisle, I saw Joel, the guy from the Camarillo agility club who had the Australian shepherd.

He grinned and ambled over, toting a thirty-five-pound bag of dog chow. "How're you doing?"

"Okay."

"Good." His expression downshifted to concerned. "You hear about Felicity's arrest?"

"Yep. But she's out now."

His eyes widened. "Glad to hear it. She and Royal are insepara-ble. Her poor dog must've been going nuts while she was locked up."

The conversation shifted from Royal to our dogs. I finally managed to nudge the topic back to Celeste's murder. "I take it you knew her?"

He set down the bag of dog chow. "A little of that woman went a long way. And I've gotta say, I never understood how she did so well in competition. For a former athlete, her dog handling was pretty sloppy."

"Really? I never got to see her run. Just heard that she received good scores."

"Yeah. That's only because she and Buster were fast. But when I watched them compete, it was more like Celeste was racing after him rather than the two running as a team. I always thought most of the credit for her wins belonged to Buster."

"Interesting. That must've pissed off some people."

"You mean besides Felicity?" He shrugged. "I heard what happened at Playtime the day Celeste was killed. Everybody says those two were going at it."

"I was there and saw the show. And I've got to say, I never once thought Felicity was a threat to Celeste."

"Really? Huh." He stared at the cans of dog food, but it was clear he wasn't seeing them. "I didn't care for her. I don't think anyone did. But I never thought anyone actually hated her. Except . . ."

"What?"

"She said something to me about a month ago. But she'd been drinking . . ."

"And?" I waited, hoping the silence would push him to keep talking.

"I was at Shorebirds. A bar near the harbor."

I nodded.

"I didn't see Celeste when I first sat down, but she must've been there for a while already. She came over and grabbed the stool next to mine. The woman was slurring and almost fell over. I had to grab and steady her."

"What'd she say?"

Joel rubbed the stubble along his jaw. "That her husband was an idiot. He'd made some stupid decision that could cost him his business." His gaze drilled in on me. "We didn't have the kind of relationship where she'd normally share a confidence like that. I was sure Celeste would regret anything she told me when she sobered up—and take it out on me. Hoping to shut her down, I said some useless platitudes, but she kept going. Took me awhile to realize it—the booze had softened her edges—but she was furious with him."

"She say anything else?"

"Just that if Del thought she was going to bail him out again, it'd be over her dead body."

I raised my eyebrows.

Joel's Adam's apple bobbed. "I didn't . . . I mean, I'm sure she didn't mean it that way . . ."

"Uh-huh." A few minutes later, we said an awkward goodbye.

People said "over my dead body" all the time and didn't wind up murder victims. Still . . . I shook myself, then focused on the task at hand. I hoisted two large bags of dog chow into my cart. Taking in Noodle had really ramped up the pace of consumption. I also grabbed four boxes of dog treats: two for my pups, one for Ava's, and one for J. D.'s.

Parking in the driveway, I went in through the front door and deposited the bags on the kitchen counter. After putting away the groceries, I opened the slider. The dogs raced to greet me. "Hey, kiddos. I missed you, too."

I stepped outside and ran them through the basic training commands again. We were wrapping up with a game of fetch when my phone rang. I checked the screen. David Smythe. Sending the ball flying one last time, I answered and strode inside the house, closing the screen behind me. "Hi."

"Hello. This is David Smythe. I'm calling for Molly Madison."

"Speaking. Thank you for calling back."

"Yes. You had a question about Kodiak Sun? Do you mind telling me how you're involved with the dog?" Concern laced his voice. "Has something happened to him?"

"No. He's doing fine. Great, actually. Unfortunately, his owner, Celeste Simmons, has died. You knew her, I assume?"

A staticky pause, then Smythe continued. "Yes. I don't understand. When we last spoke, she was in good health. At least that's what she said."

Oh dear. I'd imagined them to be acquaintances, not friends who kept in touch. "I'm sorry to have to tell you, Celeste was murdered."

"Dear Lord. Was it her husband?"

Interesting leap. "I don't know. A woman was arrested, but the evidence against her is circumstantial. I doubt the charges will stand. But her husband hasn't seemed too broken up about her death."

"Well, he wouldn't, would he?"

"Meaning?"

"Celeste's been the man's meal ticket for years. As long as he's got her money, he won't miss her."

Wow. "Why in the world would she stay with him?"

"She never said."

Thinking back to what Joel had told me, I had to ask. "Did she happen to say anything that made you think her husband's business was in trouble?"

"No."

"How do—I mean how did—you two know each other?"

"Many years ago, we met at a gymnastics competition. The woman was amazing. Watching her, I could believe she actually flew." He cleared his throat. "We got to chatting afterwards and made a point of catching up with one another at meets. Even after both of our gymnastics careers ended, we kept in touch. Very casually. Over the years. Holiday and birthday cards. That sort of thing. She called me after becoming involved with dog agility. In previous conversations, I'd told her how I trained and competed with dogs, primarily boxers. She wanted to buy another boxer for agility. She thought I could educate her about what to look for. As luck would have it, when she called, I'd just come to the decision I needed to find a new home for Dervish. I mean Kodiak Sun."

"Right. Dervish was the dog's nickname."

"That's correct."

"Do you mind if I ask why? I mean, why you gave him up?"

"I have an old back injury. It flared up to the point where running or even walking with him became impossible."

"I'm sorry to hear that." Something was off. I chewed over what Smythe had said so far. My pulse quickened. "Did you say Celeste got in touch with you after she became involved in dog agility?"

"That's right."

According to Felicity, Buster was the first dog Celeste had trained. Unless she competed in agility before moving here and lied about it. That could explain her quick success in the sport. "When did Celeste buy Dervish—or Kodiak Sun, if you prefer—from you?"

"That should be included in his paperwork."

"It is, but I want to clarify the date. There's some confusion on that topic."

"Should be clear enough. Let me check my calendar." A few moments later, he spoke again. "She flew out here earlier this year and purchased him. Back in January."

"Eight months ago."

"Correct."

"Okay, I'm still confused. Celeste has been competing locally with a boxer she called Buster for over a year now. How is that possible if she only bought him eight months ago?"

"She changed his name from Dervish to Buster?"

"Apparently."

"How odd. That bit of news aside, I think I see the confusion. Dervish—or Buster, as you call him—wasn't Celeste's first agility dog. When she called me for advice, she already had a boxer. It's possible she called that fellow Buster as well. Unusual, but possible. Anyway, the poor beast wasn't doing what she wanted. She thought she'd been sold a lemon. I suggested, since she was new to agility, that she buy Dervish. She seemed fond of boxers— which Dervish obviously is—and he was already completely trained and had shown great success at trials and competitions."

After thanking Smythe for his time, I hung up.

Celeste had substituted a better-trained dog for the original Buster? If Felicity had known, she would have told the world, not killed Celeste. I'd follow up with Felicity later. I grabbed my purse and went outside to kiss each dog goodbye.

First things first. I needed to check out Del's business. Celeste drunkenly complaining to Joel about its pending failure was hardly proof of anything. I needed to do some digging.

CHAPTER 16

I slowed as I neared Del's Sportswear. Located in one of Ventura's industrial areas, the factory was surrounded by a chain-link fence topped with razor wire. Sections of stucco had fallen off, leaving the exterior looking like it had leprosy. Though the windows were located behind safety grates, several were cracked or broken. The place looked abandoned, but a dozen cars were parked near the rear of the building. To my surprise, the front gate was open. I drove in and parked in a weed-pocked slot near an exterior door marked "Office."

When I walked inside, a woman in her sixties turned from her computer screen and frowned at me over her glasses. Her spiky red hair was the same shade as her lipstick. She gave me a world-weary look, stubbed out a cigarette, and shrugged. "Smoking's not allowed inside, but I'm the only one in the office, so who am I hurting?"

"Not me." I closed the distance between the door and her desk. "Is Del here?"

"Mr. Big Shot barely drops by these days."

Trying to keep things conversational, I cocked my head. "Why's that?"

"You from the Chamber?"

"No."

Her frown deepened. "The bank?"

"No." Maybe a bit of honesty might help. "I took in his wife's dog."

A smile transformed her face. "You got Buster? You lucky thing. He's such a beautiful dog. Smart, too. Del brought him to work one day. Buster and me had the best time together. He reminded me of my little Soloman. Bless his soul."

"Soloman?"

"My schnauzer. Buster didn't look anything like my little guy, but the attitude was the same, you know? I still miss him. But I'm not sure that getting another dog is the best move right now." She shook her head. "So Del actually gave away the dog?"

"Yep."

"That man." She lit another cigarette, then offered me the pack.

"No, thanks." I scanned the desk for a name plate, then added "Maureen."

She took a deep drag. "Don't get me wrong, I didn't care for that wife of his, but at least she was a dog person."

"Anyone who loves dogs is usually okay in my book."

"Usually." She exhaled a jet of smoke, then smirked.

"So why is Del not coming to work anymore?"

"Pfft. Look at the place. When things were going good, he took the profits and didn't bother investing in the business. Now we barely got enough orders coming in to keep the doors open.

We're operating at twenty percent of our usual crew. And the building's falling apart."

I sat on the wooden chair opposite the desk. "What's going on?"

Suspicion narrowed her eyes. "Why you want to know? Sure you're not from the bank?"

I held up three fingers and gave my best "I'm innocent" smile. "Scout's honor. I'm just nosy."

The smirk returned. "Nothing wrong with having a healthy curiosity. Mr. Big Shot used to give me guff about paying too much attention to his business. But I always figured, his business was my business. If he screwed up, my job was in danger. And did he ever screw up."

"What happened?"

"It all has to do with some dye. In a fabric we used. We didn't make the stuff or dye the material, but Mr. Big Shot bought a ton of it. Said he got a real deal. Pfft. The stuff—it's called aza or azu . . . Turns out it can cause cancer. And a whole bunch of allergic reactions."

"That's terrible."

"You're telling me. Del had to lay off most of the staff. I keep expecting to get the ax every day."

"I'm sorry to hear this. Hopefully he'll keep you on."

"Fingers crossed."

I stood. "Thanks for your time. I'll be sure to give Buster a pat from you."

"You do that."

When I climbed into my 4Runner, I sat for a moment before starting the engine. Del was in financial trouble, but even if his business failed, he'd still have a roof over his head. Could the man really have been desperate enough to hire someone to bump off his wife?

I drove home to collect the dogs. I still wanted to find out what Celeste and Felicity argued about. Dropping by without warning gave me a better shot at getting an answer. Dropping by with the dogs would make it nearly impossible for her to kick me out once I broached the topic.

Piling them all into the SUV, I headed to her place in Camarillo. If nothing else, Royal would be thrilled to see his pals.

The afternoon was growing cool. Felicity tucked her knees inside her baggy blue pullover as she absorbed what I'd learned from my conversation with David Smythe. She picked up her mug of tea and drank. Though the back deck was still getting some sun, I was grateful I'd thrown on a sweatshirt.

While I waited to hear Felicity's thoughts, I watched the dogs. Noodle lounged in Royal's elevated pet bed with no complaint from the boxer. The other dogs scampered around the yard as each sought to control the fate of a muddy tennis ball. When Felicity sighed, I turned to face her.

"This totally makes sense. Well, maybe not totally. But Celeste started training with the club in August. Over a year ago. And she did terribly. Didn't communicate well with her dog. Didn't clearly signal intent. And was sloppy on the blinds. I'll give her credit, though. She wasn't a quitter. She kept at it until around Christmas, then said she was taking a month off. To bond with her dog." Felicity rolled her eyes. "I didn't suspect a thing. Bonding with your dog is super important. God, I'm an idiot."

"Or Celeste played on your instincts as a dog lover."

"Maybe." She took another sip of tea, then set down her mug. "When she returned to club activities, Celeste was like an agility Jedi. Don't get me wrong, she was still sloppy on the course. But it no longer made a difference. The damn dog did great no matter how she screwed up." Felicity's gaze bore into me. "Did she know the new dog was a match for Buster before she bought him?"

"According to Smythe, she flew out to make the purchase."

"Oh my God. So she saw the resemblance. I wonder if that's when she decided to pass him off as Buster?"

The dogs stopped playing and charged the fence, barking and interrupting our conversation. A squirrel looked down at them and chattered before skedaddling. I couldn't help but smile. "Wow, guys. Good team effort."

Felicity ignored my conversation with the dogs. "What do you think?"

"It's possible."

She freed her knees from her sweater and sat up straight. "What happened to the first Buster?"

"No clue." I stood and crossed the lawn to retrieve the ball the dogs had battled over pre-squirrel. After I tossed it to the far side of the yard, Sky, Harlow, and Royal ran for it. Noodle yawned, looking like a curly-haired pasha on his throne.

Felicity ran a hand through her hair. "This is insane. Celeste bought an identical dog—or close enough to fool people—and pretended she was the one who trained him. Why?"

"That's the big question." I returned to my chair and sat. "People hire trainers all the time. There's no shame in it."

"I know, right? They even pay professional handlers to run their dogs at competitions. Why would Celeste try to pass off a matching dog just so she could pretend to be a master trainer?"

"Maybe having that rep was more important than the reality."

"No wonder she was never willing to share any of her training secrets with me."

"I've got to say, it all seems pretty hollow. Getting the wins and great reputation based on a lie. Who would want that?"

"Not me."

"Any thoughts on what Joel told me? Did Del's financial problems cause trouble at home?"

"Celeste would never admit something like that to me. She wanted everyone to envy her. And people don't envy failure."

In spite of our discussion and her recent incarceration, Felicity looked at ease. I hated to spoil the moment, but I'd come here to get information—not just give. "I've been looking into the murder. Like you wanted. I've gone to Playtime twice and poked around. I already think there are a few other potential suspects."

She set down her mug and leaned forward. "Who?"

"I don't want to get into that at this point. It's all theoretical. But before I narrow the suspect pool, I need to know what you and Celeste fought about."

Felicity closed her eyes for a moment. "I was expecting this. And you're right." She rubbed her temples. "But if I tell you, you'll hate me."

The sadness in her voice stopped me from disagreeing. "Maybe. But if you don't tell me, you could wind up in prison. I need to know."

"I'm gonna pour myself a glass of wine first." She stood. "Can I get you one?"

"I'll pass."

Dreading what Felicity was about to say, I walked onto the lawn. Scrounging another ball from the tall grass, I tossed it to the dogs. The question reflected in their faces was clear: Which ball to track? Pandemonium followed. Harlow kept the old ball clenched in her jaw while Sky and Royal raced for the new one.

Felicity trudged onto the deck, carrying a wineglass and bottle. Shifting her mug, she set down the glass and gave herself a heavy pour. She lifted it and drank. "I wish I didn't have to tell you this." Eyes damp, she clutched the glass to her chest and took a shuddering breath. "Three weeks ago, I attended an agility class at Playtime. In the evening. Celeste was there. So was Joel—the guy with the Australian shepherd you ran into at the store. Along with a few other folks from the club in Camarillo. After class, some of us hung out in the parking lot talking. I've had a thing for Joel ever since I met him, so I stayed, hoping he might show some interest." She drank more wine. "He didn't. But I stayed until after he left. By then, it was dark. You've been on that road—there are no streetlights."

I'd driven the road from Playtime once at night. The day Celeste was killed and I'd been allowed to take Buster home with me. Focused as I'd been on the woman's death and keeping her dog calm, I hadn't noticed the absence of light stanchions. "And that's important because . . . ?"

She covered her face. "I hit him. The missing golden retriever. I hit the dog."

The tea in my gut rebelled. I covered my mouth. Once the nausea had retreated, I said, "You mean Freddy?"

Felicity nodded.

"Oh no. Was he . . . ?"

She didn't seem to hear my question. "Coyotes were howling and I thought I saw a bunch of them on the right side of the road. Then something big dashed from the grove on that side. It was only an impression. Before I felt a thump. He flew up into the path of my headlights. That's when I saw him and knew it was a dog. He landed in the irrigation ditch. I pulled over right away but was afraid to get out because the coyotes followed him into the ditch."

My mouth went dry. "You left him there?"

"Royal was yipping and whining. And I was freaking out. I should've gotten out of my Jeep, I know. Instead, I pulled back on the road and drove away." Closing her eyes, she emptied her glass then set it down. "I think about that poor dog every day."

If I'd been in Felicity's shoes, would I have had the nerve to climb out and face a pack of hungry coyotes? I hoped so. "You didn't tell his owner what happened?"

"How could I? I hit Freddy, then did nothing to save him from the coyotes. After that, there was no way I could look that man in the eye and tell him what I'd done."

"But you must've seen all those flyers. Hopkins needs to know what happened."

"I couldn't. I can't." She picked up the bottle and refilled her glass. "That's what Celeste and I fought about."

I straightened. "You told her what happened?"

"God, no. I'd never trust her with something like that."

"Then what?"

Felicity chugged half her glass. Blurry-eyed, she rubbed her face. "She saw the whole thing. Apparently, she pulled out of the lot behind me. But Buster's crate needed some sort of adjustment, so when she reached the road, Celeste parked. And had a clear view of what happened. That horrible woman threatened to tell everyone at agility how I'd killed Freddy. I . . . I . . . Agility and Royal are my world. How could I show my face again if everyone knew?"

Awful as this was, it didn't answer my question. I did my best to keep my voice level. "What does this have to do with the fight at Playtime?"

"When you headed to the crating area that day, Celeste pulled me aside. She wasn't happy about the amount of time you helped me shave on the course. Said she'd tell Mr. Hopkins I'd killed his dog if I didn't pull out of the next agility meet."

"She blackmailed you to drop out?"

"Yes." Felicity wiped her damp cheeks with both hands. "You must think I'm a monster, letting that poor man wonder what happened to his dog. And worse, staying in my Jeep rather than jumping out and trying to protect Freddy." She picked up her glass again and drank.

"I hated Celeste for threatening me. And I wished her dead that day. But I didn't kill her."

"I believe you." But did I believe her because it was easier? If Celeste blackmailed Felicity because of her improved run times, and Felicity killed Celeste over the blackmail, that would mean the tips I gave her sparked whatever fight followed.

A whisper of hope lighted her face. "You'll keep looking into it?"

"Yep." What Felicity had done was horrible. An accident, sure. But doing nothing to save the dog after hitting him? That wasn't. And letting Freddy's owner sweat and worry for three weeks? No excuse fixed that. Yet Celeste taking advantage of the tragedy was also wrong. I rose and called my dogs. "I know that wasn't easy for you to share. I do. But I think you should tell your lawyer, too."

"I can't have people knowing . . ."

"He can't tell anyone without your permission. And your story will inform him about Celeste's character. It could be important. If her need to win meant she'd do that to you, who else might she have threatened?"

Felicity's mouth dropped open.

"Think about it. If you come up with some names, call me."

Tuckered out from running around Felicity's yard, Harlow and

Sky curled up on their respective seats, while a refreshed Noodle stuck his muzzle out the back window. As I pulled away from the curb, I checked the time. I had ninety minutes until I needed to get Sky to Izzy's. Barely enough time to drive out to Playtime and back again. But this couldn't wait.

After an uneventful drive, I rapped on the open door of Simone's office. When she saw me, she didn't even try to smile. "Why're you here?"

"Just wanted to ask where Mr. Hopkins's house is. You said his property is adjacent to Playtime."

A small V formed between her eyebrows. "Why do you want to see Mr. Hopkins?"

"I need to tell him what happened to his dog."

Simone jumped to her feet. "You found Freddy?"

I shook my head. "No. But I discovered what happened."

"What?"

"Sorry. I need to talk to Mr. Hopkins about that."

She chewed the inside of her cheek, then said, "Right. Sure." Simone joined me at the door and pointed past the parking lot. "Head back down the driveway. When you get to the road, turn left. Hopkins's place is the first driveway on the left. You can't see the house so it looks like a small road. It's maybe a five-minute drive through the avocado grove before you'll get there."

"Five minutes?"

"It's a rough road. You'll want to go slow."

"Oh. Thanks." I walked back to my 4Runner, dreading the upcoming conversation.

Too soon, I found the gravel lane Simone had described and turned. Leathery-leafed avocado trees cast shadows across the road. Harlow perked up and stuck her nose out the front window. The 4Runner hit a pothole and the dogs scrambled to keep their seats. I slowed to a crawl, then continued along the rutted drive.

When I finally spied the two-story hacienda-style home, five minutes had passed—just as Simone had predicted. I parked on a shaded portion of a gravel pull-out, leaving the dogs in the vehicle. Water from an ornate fountain splashed in front of the house. The lovely sound failed to raise my mood. Crunching my way to the entrance, I pressed the decorative brass button set into the wall on the left of the wooden door. A deep series of bongs sounded.

Two minutes later, a white-haired man answered, dressed in a plaid flannel shirt, blue jeans, and cowboy boots. An annoyed expression flickered across his face. Not a good sign. "Mr. Hopkins?"

"I don't buy anything at the door. Didn't you see the 'No Soliciting' sign?" He pointed to the placard posted on a stake a few feet from the porch.

"I'm not selling anything. I just . . ." This was going to be awful. "I talked with someone today who admitted they hit your dog with their car. I'm sorry. He's dead."

The man's jaw tightened and he rocked back on his heels. "Freddy's gone? Then where's his body?"

"Coyotes attacked after he was hit."

A deep frown creased his face. "Who are you?"

"My name's Molly Madison."

"And 'your friend' did this? Is that code for you killing my dog?"

My stomach plunged past my knees. "No. I . . . just found out. The person who did it was afraid to tell you. But I felt you should know."

"Damn right I should know. Freddy was family. And now

you expect that one-thousand-dollar reward? For your 'friend' killing my dog?"

"No. I—"

"Shame on you—or anyone else—who hurt him. Now, git."

I swallowed the lump in my throat, managing a hoarse, "Sorry for your loss." Vision blurry, I turned and headed back across the gravel. I was reaching for the car door handle when Hopkins's voice stopped me.

"Ms. Madison?"

Expecting another volley of abuse, I faced the grieving man.

"Sorry. I'm upset. I don't believe you killed my dog. If you had, it makes no sense for you to come forward now." He cleared his throat. "You're not gonna tell me who did it?"

I shook my head. "They feel awful about it. Would identifying them make this better for you?"

"It'd give me someone to punch." Hopkins scrubbed his face with a bony hand. "Guess you think that's a good reason not to tell me." He pinched the bridge of his nose and closed his eyes. "I appreciate you coming by. I . . . Thank you."

"Take care." I climbed into my 4Runner and started the engine. I still thought Felicity should talk to him. It wouldn't fix anything, but it was better to deal with things than to let them fester.

Speaking of festering . . .

When I reached the main road, I pulled over and grabbed my cell. I scrolled to Miguel's contact information and texted: **I'm ready to talk. When and where?**

I pulled back onto the road. Instead of heading to my house, I drove straight to Izzy's. Even though traffic was light, it was past eight when I unlocked her front door. Expecting another tongue-lashing about my tardiness, I gave Sky a kiss on her forehead before turning the knob. Stepping into the chilly entryway, I waited. Nothing. "Hello?" Still nothing. Part of me regretted Izzy's absence. I wanted to see if her bad behavior toward Sky was a one-time thing. If it wasn't, she had no business keeping the Frenchie.

"Guess you've got the place to yourself for now." I unhooked Sky's leash and draped it over the banister. "See you tomorrow."

CHAPTER 17

Thursday morning, I picked up Buster, then walked the dogs to Izzy's to collect Sky. I still couldn't believe my mother was getting remarried. I needed to check in with my lawyer and see if the trial for the man who killed my husband was still set for December. If it was within ten days of Christmas, there was no point making two separate trips to Massachusetts. Hopefully J. D. would be able to look after Harlow and Noodle.

As the joyous reunion with the Frenchie played out—like it did every day—I shook my head and smiled. A flutter of worry about Sky ran through me. When the celebration slowed, I crouched and ran my hands along her sides and legs. The Frenchie neither yipped nor whimpered. No sore spots or bruises. Good.

Once again, we cut between the houses to the beach. More birds than usual congregated on the sand. Harlow and Buster barked, scattering several groups of sandpipers. Wind gusted off the water while I stared at the horizon. A decent series of swells surged toward shore. The half-dozen surfers started paddling. I pictured J. D. trapped inside his home. "He'll be back in the water soon, right, Buster?"

At the sound of his name, the boxer pranced and woofed.

When we turned up the alley at the end of our walk, I spied someone sitting on my front porch. Miguel. Ignoring him, I urged the dogs to the opposite side of the street and knocked at J. D.'s. He answered fully dressed, hair combed. Wow. Talk about a change for the better.

"Hey. Thanks for taking this guy out." He crouched and rubbed Buster's ears. "Uh, something seems off with your boyfriend. You guys have a fight?" He thrust his chin toward my porch.

I turned to look at Miguel. His gaze lasered in on J. D., mouth forming a grim line.

"What's his deal?" J. D. straightened and took the leash from my hand.

"We broke up."

"You didn't say anything."

"I meant to . . ."

"But I was in the middle of a freak-out?" The half smile softened his words.

"Yep."

"You need me to talk to the guy?"

"Nah. I knew he was coming over. I've got it under control." I appreciated J. D.'s words even though, with his phobia, marching across the alley to talk with Miguel was likely impossible right now.

He straightened and urged the boxer inside. "You change your mind, let me know."

"You got it. Thanks."

I turned. Miguel's gaze softened into the puppy dog eyes I knew so well. Steeling myself, I crossed to my house. As much as I wanted to rip off his head, I forced myself to keep my voice level. "You're early."

"I know." He unfolded himself and stood.

"Let me get the dogs settled, then I'll come back out and we can talk."

"Oh." The fact I wasn't inviting him to follow me inside seemed to rock him. "Okay."

I took the dogs through the house to the backyard. After unhooking leashes and checking their water, I gave each a kiss. "I promise to brush you later." Closing the slider, I leaned my forehead against it, while gathering myself. Then I crossed to the front door and stepped outside. "Let's take a walk."

"Sure." Miguel stood again and gestured for me to lead the way.

We walked to the cul-de-sac overlooking the beach.

"So you got another dog?"

"What?"

"The bulldog."

"Oh. No, I'm dog-sitting." Feeling closed off and defensive, I didn't even want to share Sky's name with him. When we reached the road's end, I turned my back to the ocean and leaned against the seawall. "I'm here. You wanted to talk. So talk."

Miguel puffed out his cheeks and propped himself against the wall, leaving a six-inch gap between us. "My wife, Sloan, is sick. Early on, while she was locked up, she showed signs of mania. Turned out she's bipolar. The docs thought she'd been using the pills and alcohol to smooth out her mood swings. Self-medicating. Illegally."

"Sorry to hear that."

"When I learned the pill popping, stealing, and raiding our bank account had all been out of her control, I couldn't abandon her. By then she'd already been sentenced and was going to spend years in prison. She needed me more than ever. I was her lifeline to the world. To her old life." He turned to face me. "You need to understand, she and I have been together since high school. We started dating in tenth grade. She'd always been volatile, but that was part of the excitement of being with her. I never suspected there was a medical problem." He crossed his arms and looked at me expectantly.

"While I'm sorry for your wife and her having to cope with this condition, I'm not seeing how that absolves you. I mean, great—you've been the good guy to her. But you weren't the good guy with me. I told you about Stefan's cheating." Heat rushed up my neck and face. "How it made me feel. And rather than having the guts to get into an uncomfortable conversation with me and admit you're married, you lied and made me a participant in your cheating."

Miguel's eyes went wide. He took a step back. "I didn't lie."

I snorted. "You certainly didn't tell the truth."

Ten more minutes of Miguel talking did nothing to change my mind, but my anger drained away. "Look, like I said before, I'm sorry about your wife. But that's the problem: She's your wife. I'm not spending time with a married man. It's over." I moved away from the wall. "Besides, she's going to be out in a year or so. That's when she'll need you most."

He started to speak, but I waved him off. Feeling a mix of self-righteousness, exhaustion, and loss, I made my way home.

My mom had been widowed when I was six. That meant she'd flown solo for thirty years. Granted, she'd finally found someone to love, but I couldn't help wondering if I'd be by myself for as long as she'd been.

The next day, I had my two dogs and Sky leashed and ready to go by eight. Based on J. D.'s severe case of bed head, I suspected he'd been sleeping when I knocked to collect Buster. True, it was earlier than usual, but I needed to move and stay busy. Wordlessly, he retrieved the boxer's leash and handed him over.

I changed up our routine and headed to Pier Point's "Restaurant Row" to start. We passed the brew house. Its sidewalk smell of stale beer slowed our progress as the dogs investigated. The Thai restaurant also caught their attention, but the surf wear store and board shop proved less interesting to their sensitive noses. The street terminated at a cul-de-sac abutting the beach, and we crossed the sand to the water. Huge homes fronted the water here, windows shuttered or covered with blinds. Seasonal homes? Or owned by late risers?

Even at this hour, the north end of the beach was too populated to let the dogs run free. While they barked at birds, I kept an eye on Sky, making sure her stubby legs were up to the challenge of a longer walk.

I returned Buster to a much more alert-looking J. D.

"Thanks, Molly." He crouched to rub the boxer's coat. "I was kind of out of it when you picked this guy up, so I apologize for not asking earlier."

"Asking what?"

"How are you? I mean, after seeing Miguel yesterday?"

"I'm all right."

"Not to pry—okay, I'm totally prying—but what happened?"

I was surprised to find I felt okay talking about this with him. "The guy's married."

"No." J. D. straightened.

"Yep."

"Wow. You must've been pissed when you found out."

"I was. But now . . ."

"What? You're over it already?"

"Kind of. I mean, I will never be able to trust him again . . ." I shook my head. "But he's in a pretty sad situation."

J. D. raised his eyebrows. "You're saying that Miguel cheating on both you and his wife is a sad situation—for him?"

"Sounds weird, I know. But his wife's in prison."

"Oh." The fire in his eyes dimmed but didn't completely die. "That kind of makes it worse."

"Yep."

"If you need to talk—or just drink heavily—I'm here."

"Thanks." I crossed the alley and let the dogs into my backyard. The three hit the water bowls. Once they were done, I brushed their coats. Content and tired, they sprawled and napped. I kept busy until it was time to head to Ava's by mopping the great room and kitchen floors, and wiping nose prints off the cupboards, refrigerator, and sliding glass door. The dogs were still dozing when I left.

The wind had picked up. Wishing I'd pulled my hair into a ponytail, I shoved it out of my eyes. Hank the cyclist was pedaling toward his home. "Already done for the day?"

"Getting a bit too gusty. I'll probably go out for a second ride later."

Though he lived only two doors down, all I knew about the man was he loved to bicycle. This was about as deep as any of our interactions went. "Have a good one."

"You, too."

At Ava's I knocked once and the door immediately swung open. The girl smiled up at me. Dressed again in jeans, she wore a red-checked blouse and her hair was gathered in one braid instead of two. Good for her. Trying new things was important. Something it wouldn't hurt me to practice myself.

"*Buenas dias, Molly. Por favor, ven a mi casa.*"

I recognized the word *casa* and her waving me inside clarified the rest. "*Gracias.*"

Butterscotch scrambled over to greet me. After giving her some love, the three of us headed through the house to the backyard.

"Sounds like your Spanish is coming along."

"*Sí.* It's fun because Lincoln's learning Spanish, too. We've started quizzing each other once a day."

"Sounds like you've found the perfect friend."

"Right? He's not interested in Butterscotch the way most people are, but he loves chess, math, engineering, and now Spanish." Her grin broadened, revealing the gap from her missing incisor.

"Glad to hear it. Now, why don't you run Butterscotch through her paces for me?" I gave her the box of dog treats I'd bought the other day and waited while Ava pulled a few out. After pocketing them, she worked the Basset-Retriever. Butterscotch stayed focused on her as the girl gave a series of commands.

We'd already cut our training sessions from daily to twice a week. But if Ava was making new age-appropriate friends, it might be time to reduce our lessons to once a week. One of my goals in taking on her dog's training had been to help her learn to interact with others successfully, not to hold her back.

The idea of seeing Ava only once a week added to the sense of loss that had dogged me since waking. But just because I didn't want to do it didn't mean I shouldn't anyway.

Ava ran over to me, cheeks flushed. "How'd we do?"

"Perfect. Let's toss her the ball."

Ava hurled the squeaky ball to the other side of the yard. Her arm was growing strong and her aim more accurate.

"Hey, I want to show you something." I pulled out my cell and opened the photo I'd taken of the list I found inside the old rat tube. "Look at this, will you?" I handed her my phone. "The numbers are too long to be from social security cards or driver's licenses. Also too long for credit cards. I'm stumped. What do they mean?"

"Can you ask the person who wrote them down?"

"No. He doesn't know I found the list or that I took a picture of it."

Ava nodded and returned her attention to the screen.

"The sheet of paper had been hidden, so I think the numbers are important. I just don't know why."

"Can you send it to me? That way I can spend more time with it. See if I can come up with something. And maybe, if you don't mind, I can ask Lincoln what he thinks?"

"Go ahead. Three brains are better than two." Especially when two of them belonged to prodigies. "How'd the pulley project with Lincoln go?"

"Great. We built a fixed pulley system using a single rope, then constructed a wood box for ferrying supplies. We attached the box to the rope with a large S-hook."

"But did you have a good time?"

Ava's brow furrowed as she considered my question. I got it. For her, all learning was fun.

"Yes. But you haven't heard one of the best parts yet."

I couldn't help but smile. "Go on."

"When our pulley and box were done, we hoisted two sodas

and a plate of cookies into the tree house." Butterscotch scampered over and she threw a ball across the yard. "I got to pull the rope and raise the sodas to the top while Lincoln waited in the tree house. Because I was his guest. Then I climbed the ladder and Lincoln came down to pull up the plate of cookies."

"Good job. What kind of cookies?"

Ava looked around, then whispered, "Chocolate chip."

Jemma had a strict "no sweets" policy. I leaned down and whispered back, "Were they good?"

"Yes!"

"You two have any other projects in mind?"

"We want to make a block and tackle pulley next. So we can lift heavier things. There's an old coffee table Lincoln's dad says he can use if we're able to get it into the tree house. After we finished our snack, we went inside and researched how to make one."

It sounded like Ava had stumbled across the perfect pal. "How's a block and tackle pulley different than what you guys have already done?"

"This one will have a two-wheel pulley. With two wheels, you can lift the weight with half the force."

"Wow. That's pretty cool."

"I know. And the other best part?"

"What?"

She gave an unexpectedly shy glance. "When I got there, Lincoln wasn't mad at me. Even though I've beaten him the last few times we played chess."

I guessed that meant other kids—and possibly adults—didn't accept Ava's victories as graciously. "Lincoln sounds okay to me."

"He is." When I returned home, I decided that while Ava and Lincoln turned their big brains to the list of numbers, I'd do some cybersleuthing about Quentin. I couldn't remember his last name but, fortunately, Playtime's website helpfully provided it: Cooke. Opening my Trackers account, I went to work.

It turned out Quentin had a terrible credit history. The guy was paying the minimum monthly balance on four credit cards, plus his Ford F-150 pickup was in danger of being repossessed. He owned no real property. Had no rental history I could find. Was he crashing with friends or a girlfriend? Or maybe he still lived with his parents? On the plus side, his police record only consisted of a five-year-old drunk and disorderly charge where the court gave him community service and probation.

Still, when someone owed money to a lot of people or institutions, they were often more open to trying stupid things to get creditors off their backs. Was the list of numbers I'd found part of that? And were Quentin's financial problems linked to the mysterious "other" problem Playtime had been experiencing? And what risk had the sandy-haired man been talking about?

After ninety minutes, I took a break to clear my head. "Come on, pups. Time for another walk." Once everyone was leashed, I led them over to J. D.'s and knocked.

He answered, Buster at his side. The boxer's tail started swinging. "A little early, isn't it?"

"Yep. I was doing some research and needed a break."

"No problem. Let me grab this guy's leash."

I checked the time. When J. D. returned, I said, "I think I'll take them to Hillside Park. Should have him back to you in an hour, hour-and-a-half."

His eyes grew sad, but he forced a smile. "Have fun."

As I drove to the park, I wondered whether I was going too easy on J. D. Before his setback, he had set the pace for what he was ready to do. I'd never pushed. But should I push him now? Urge him to get outside again?

I pulled into the parking lot and the dogs began to bark. They knew where we were. After unloading them, I stuffed a bottle of water inside my knapsack. We headed up our favorite trail. Less popular than the others—maybe due to its sharp ascent—the narrow track cut through the chapparal-covered hill to the west of the park's grassy bowl. When we reached the first switchback, Harlow began to bark, then the others chimed in. I looked around for the cause. A rabbit stood frozen alongside the trail. I waved my arm and the frightened thing took off into the scrub. "Good job, everyone."

By the time we were halfway up the hill, I still hadn't seen any other hikers and let the dogs off their leads. Harlow scampered forward, ears flopping and tags jingling. Buster gave me a "Really?" sort of look, then took off after her. Noodle and Sky stayed by my side.

I still hadn't called off tonight's training session with Lupe and her Dalmatian. If I went, there was no way she wouldn't bring up her brother. True, she was on my side, but I still didn't want to talk about it with her. Funny, since I'd had no problem talking to J. D. But then, Miguel wasn't J. D.'s brother.

When we reached the crest, I pulled the four nested water bowls from my pack, filled them, and called Buster and Harlow back. While the dogs lapped, I checked my phone. The hilltop had reception. Taking the coward's way out, I sent Lupe a text saying I couldn't come by tonight but that I'd be there next week if that worked for her. A minute later, she responded with a thumbs-up emoji.

Releashing the dogs, we headed back down the trail. The drive home was slow, but I wasn't in a rush. After returning Buster to J. D., I parked in the garage, then led the dogs through the yard to the house. While they napped, I opened my laptop and dove back into Quentin's life. This time I explored his social networks. A big Reddit guy, some Facebook—mostly photos of his rats—and an active Twitter presence. I scrolled through his feed, looking for recurring topics. Largely apolitical, he was a raging misogynist with a cruel sense of humor.

I pulled out my cell and looked at the photographed list of numbers again. Opening another window on my laptop, I typed "23-digit number" into the search box. The top result read, "Such a number is a 1 followed by 22 zeros—also known as ten sextillion." Interesting, but not what I was looking for. Deciding to leave the number stuff to Ava and her friend, I resumed prying into Quentin's life.

My cell rang. J. D.'s name appeared on the screen. I grabbed it. "What's up?"

"You know, you don't always have to answer on the first ring when I call."

"I—"

"I'm just busting your chops. Want to come over for dinner? I made spaghetti. Something I'm actually good at. But I'm still not used to cooking for one and I've got way too much."

I checked the time and was surprised to see it was almost six o'clock. I'd been down the Quentin Cooke rabbit hole—or should I say rat hole?—longer than I'd realized. "Sure. I should walk Sky home first. Is that a problem?"

"No worries. I'll keep everything warm until you get here."

I collected the Frenchie and headed out. J. D.'s invitation was a real win-win: I didn't need to cook dinner, and I wouldn't be home if Lupe checked on my lack of availability tonight.

For the second night in a row, I saw no sign of the dark-haired man standing opposite Izzy's house. Though he didn't feel like a threat to me, my cop brain couldn't help thinking his lurking about signaled trouble. I unlocked the door and led Sky inside. Crouching to unhook her leash, I once again heard the angry tap-tap-tap of Izzy's heels on the marble floor as she approached. I straightened and faced her. "You're home early."

"And you're dropping off the dog early." Her bitter tone matched the twist of her lips.

Trying not to show my anger, I took a deep breath before answering. "We never set a time for returning Sky. You just said I needed to have her back by seven-thirty."

Izzy made an elaborate show of checking her watch. "And it's now half-past six. Looks like someone's trying to get paid without doing the work."

If I wasn't so worried about Sky, I would've quit right then. I managed to keep my voice level as I said, "Perhaps you should've made your expectations clearer."

"Don't get smart with me." Her cheeks flushed a violent red. "I'm the one who pays you. From now on, you bring the damn dog home between seven and seven-thirty. Are we clear now?"

I glanced down at Sky, then swallowed my fury. "Sure thing."

CHAPTER 18

In spite of Izzy's bad behavior, my appetite hadn't dulled. Chalk it up to all the walking and cleaning I'd done today. When J. D. opened his front door, the scent of oregano and garlic wafted out to greet me. My mouth began to water. "Wow. The food smells amazing."

"Well, get in here. I've got a bottle of merlot breathing. Want a glass?"

"Sure." J. D.'s parents had a great wine "library," as they called it; I'd be a fool to decline anything he offered. I followed him down the hall into the airy kitchen. "What can I do to help?"

"Put the salad on the table. And"—he pointed at the Wolf six-burner—"if you can grab the garlic bread from the oven, that'd be great. Might need to use a mitt. They're in the right-hand drawer."

I brought the bamboo bowl brimming with red and green lettuce, tomatoes, and purple sprouts into the dining room. J. D. had laid the place settings at one corner of the long table. I positioned the salad between them. As soon as I returned to the kitchen and opened the oven, my stomach rumbled. I unwrapped the foil from the garlic bread and transferred the already sliced loaf to the plate provided.

J. D. carried the spaghetti and marinara sauce to the table. I trailed behind him as if the aroma had hooked me by the nose, and I sat down. He poured us each a glass of wine.

"Damn, you know how to put a meal together."

"Thanks." He passed me the pasta, and I served myself. The next few minutes were filled with chewing and savoring. "I had no idea you could cook like this."

"My repertoire is limited, but the things I do make, I do right."

"Hear, hear." I lifted my glass. "Thanks for sharing." We clinked and drank. I told him about my mother's upcoming wedding and my plan to go to Massachusetts for that and the trial.

"And your mom's been single for how long?"

"Just over thirty years."

"Wow. Well, good for her."

"What do you mean?"

"Obviously, I've never met her, but when people are alone for a long time, they can get set in their ways. I think it's great she's taking a chance on love again."

"I guess."

"You guess?"

"It's all happening so fast. But she did sound happy."

J. D. leaned back in his chair. "Would you say your mom's a smart woman?"

"Of course."

"Then trust her on this. I'm sure she knows what she's doing."

"You're right." I picked up my glass, but didn't bring it to my lips. "I know it's still three months off, but would you be able to look after my dogs while I'm gone?"

"Of course. I might not be able to walk them, but I can work that out when the time comes."

"Thanks."

He picked up his glass and swirled the garnet liquid. "Do you know the man she's marrying?"

"Only to say 'hi' to. We used to shop at his deli when I was a kid. He was always nice to me, but that's pretty much the extent of our interactions. Right before I moved to California, Mom told me his wife had died."

Conversation meandered to dogs and training, to my progress on Celeste's case. When his plate was clean, J. D. set down his fork. "You think this Rat Wrangler's the killer?"

I leaned back in my chair, amazed by how much food I'd put away. "He's a leading contender, but I can't ignore Celeste's husband, Del Kaminsky. According to what Joel DeCarolis told me—"

"Who?"

"The guy from the agility club in Camarillo."

"Right. The one with the Australian shepherd."

"Exactly. He and Del's secretary both told me her husband's company is in deep financial trouble. And according to Joel, Celeste was unwilling to bail him out. Del could've killed her for the money."

"I thought the husband was in Hawaii when she died."

"He was. But that doesn't mean he didn't pay someone else to do it for him."

"Hmm. How does what Smythe told you about selling Buster the Second to Celeste fit in?" At the sound of his name, the boxer sat up, eyes hopeful. J. D. looked down at him. "Huh-uh, bud. You already ate." He rolled his glass between his palms. "If someone figured out Celeste was passing off this guy as her previous dog and pretending she'd trained him, I'm betting they would've been angry."

"True. If they knew. Oh my God. Ava was right."

"She usually is. But right about what?" J. D. set down his glass and rested his elbows on the table.

"When I told her how Celeste kept besting Felicity in agility, even though they had the same breed of dog and Celeste had been doing the sport for a much shorter time, Ava suggested that maybe she cheated."

"Out of the mouths of babes."

"Yeah, I just couldn't see how. It never occurred to me Celeste substituted a better-trained dog for her own."

"That's some epic cheating. I mean, the woman flew all the way to England to buy a second purebred just so she could win a few agility ribbons? That's crazy."

I shrugged. "A lot of people take their dog sports pretty seriously."

"For all the time you spend training, you'd never do something like that."

"No. I don't really see the point. Don't get me wrong, I love it when Harlow and I win. But part of that is because she loves it. Loves the applause. Loves the challenge. I'm usually just grateful I didn't screw up her run. So while I do love the wins, it's not about the awards."

"And there's the difference."

Talking with J. D. had a way of helping me articulate things I'd never given much thought. I grinned at him.

He downed the last of his wine. "You still doing okay? With the whole Miguel thing?"

"I am."

"Good." He rose. "Want to sit outside?"

"Sure."

He picked up the bottle of merlot and led the way to the open-air atrium. I sank into the lounge chair on the right and looked up at the night sky.

"Top you off?" He held up the wine.

"Thanks."

He poured, then set the bottle between us on the tile-topped table. "So you've got two solid suspects. Besides Felicity."

"Then there's the fact that Simone alluded to some other problem at Playtime which has been driving away students."

"But you don't know what the problem is, so it might be whatever Quentin's up to?"

"Right again. I'm thinking I should go back and lean on Simone. Or maybe try to get one of the trainers to talk. If fewer people are coming to class, their jobs are in danger. I might find someone who's willing to tell me what's going on." I lifted my glass and sipped. "Also, I've learned Celeste treated some of her gymnasts badly. The information is several years old, but if she was cruel then, it's likely she was cruel to her current students, too."

"Wow. How're you gonna narrow down who done it? You've got some serious options. A shady Rat Wrangler—a job I didn't even know existed before tonight. A husband with a failing business. And the guy doesn't seem to even care that his wife is dead. Oh, and maybe an angry gymnast. Have I got that right?"

"There's also the sandy-haired man who was yelling at Quentin."

"Right. The man who told Quentin he didn't know what risk meant?"

"The very one."

"And you've got your crack team of eight-year-olds working on the list of numbers you found hidden in a rat tube."

"Correct. Though, I've got to admit, I've never asked how old Lincoln is."

After the previous night's generous servings of food and wine, I slept late. When I finally woke, I threw on a pair of shorts and a long-sleeve tee and trotted downstairs. I let the dogs out and got their breakfast together. While they busied themselves eating, I headed to Izzy's to collect the Frenchie. Once again, there was no sign of the dark-haired man. It looked like he only hung out across the street in the evening.

The short trip home turned exciting for Sky when she got to sniff a Chihuahua walking in the opposite direction with a trim, silver-haired woman.

"I don't usually let Hercules get too close to other dogs. Most of the ones in this neighborhood are so big. But your little princess isn't intimidating. What's her name?"

"Sky."

"Hello, Sky." The woman held out her free hand. "I'm Elinore."

"Molly." We shook.

She nodded at the Frenchie. "I haven't seen you out walking her before."

"I'm providing doggy day care but got a late start today."

"Oh." Her brow furrowed. "Does Sky belong to that horrible woman?"

"Uh . . ." Slamming my employer didn't seem a smart move.

"Sky belongs to Izzy Harmon. They live in the glass and concrete three-story." I pointed back the way we'd come.

"That's the one." Elinore sniffed. "I wouldn't trust her anywhere near my Hercules."

"Have you seen Izzy mistreat Sky?"

"Not exactly. But the way she jerks the leash and yells at this poor girl . . ." Elinore shook her head. "The woman is obviously no dog lover."

"Huh. Thanks for the information."

When I let Sky into the backyard, Harlow and Noodle raced to greet her. I tossed a tennis ball into the mix and pandemonium ensued. I pondered what Elinore had told me while I sipped my coffee. Not abuse per se, but the more I learned, the more convinced I was that Sky shouldn't be in Izzy's "care."

I put my mug in the dishwasher, then crossed the alley to pick up Buster. Hair combed and looking chipper, J. D. answered the door. "I was thinking about your 'case' after you left last night. Specifically, about the Rat Wrangler."

"And?"

"The way he hid the list of numbers . . . the guy's up to no good. I mean, if he's not doing something shifty, why all the rigamarole with the rat tube?"

"Good point."

"I keep coming back to the fact that he needs money. So maybe he's stealing from the business or the customers, I don't know. Or maybe the numbers are some kind of code. Like, what if he's dealing drugs out of the barn and the list is a way of tracking customers? Or the money they owe? From what you said, the guy is in debt up to his eyeballs. Drugs or theft would both bring in some green."

"True."

"But the bigger question is: Why does Quentin need money?"

"I . . . like you just said, he's in debt."

"But"—he paused and raised his eyebrows—"why is Quentin in debt? You said he's got no mortgage or property taxes to pay. No rent. He's got a job. How come he's falling behind on his bills?"

"That's a great question."

"One you'll be looking into?"

"Count on it. Thanks."

J. D. handed me the boxer's lead. Buster and Harlow wagged and circled each other. "We'll be back in about an hour." I set off for the beach.

Could Quentin be dealing drugs? My time at the training facility had been limited, and I had no idea whether any people dropped by to meet with the Rat Wrangler but didn't stay for classes. I doubted Simone would welcome me running a long-term stakeout of Playtime's barn.

This late on a Saturday, the beach was too crowded to let the dogs run free. I jogged on the hard-packed sand. Not Noodle's favorite activity, but the big dog had no trouble keeping up. In deference to Sky's stubby legs, I periodically slowed to a walk before picking up the pace again. When we reached the play area, I turned and we strolled back along the sand.

My cell rang. I switched the leashes to my left hand and checked the screen: Ava. "Hey there. What's up?"

"Do you know that the lowest twenty-three-digit number is ten sextillion?"

"Yep."

"You do?"

"I understand your surprised tone but, remember, I know how to use a search engine."

"Oh, okay. Lincoln and I spent a lot of time looking at the numbers you sent me. In a lot of different ways. To see if the numbers were being used to hide the real data. We explored the idea of Godel's numbers or whether they're some sort of cipher."

It was like the kid was speaking a foreign language. "And?"

"We weren't able to make anything work."

I tried to keep the disappointment out of my voice. "Well, thank you for trying. And please thank Lincoln for me."

"We do have a theory, though."

"Really?" Hope flared in my chest.

"They're credit card numbers."

"But they're too long."

"I know. Do you have a credit card you can look at?"

"Sure." I told the dogs to sit, dug my wallet from my pocket, and slid my Visa card free. "Got it. What do you want me to do?"

"The card number is sixteen digits, right?"

"Right."

"Which means we're seven digits and two letters short."

"Right again."

"What if the expiration date is included as a two-digit month and two-digit year? That makes four more numbers."

"Bringing us to twenty."

"Then add the three-digit security code from the back."

Whoa. This kid was smart. "Twenty-three numbers. Well done. What about the two letters at the end?"

"Lincoln thinks they're initials. For whoever the card belongs to."

"So Quentin's stealing credit card numbers?"

"Who's Quentin?"

"Not important. But why just the initials—why not the whole name?"

"If the name had been written out, you probably would've figured this out without me and Lincoln."

I chuckled. "Good point. Thanks, Ava."

"We had fun. Lincoln and I are thinking about developing a cipher of our own."

Of course they were. "Good luck with that."

"It'll take hard work and patience, not luck."

"You're right again." Hanging up, I switched over to my photo album and stared at the list of numbers. Rather than copying actual credit card receipts, Quentin had jotted down the necessary information. Did he sometimes help in the office, taking payments? That would give him access to the card information. I reread all the initials. There was no CS. Did that mean Celeste's death was unrelated?

Harlow barked at a seagull foolish enough to land within six feet of her. "You're bored. I get it, girl." We resumed walking as my thoughts whirled. If Quentin knew the person whose card information he was stealing, he'd only need to note their initials to remember which name went with each card number. Rather than being a victim of his scam, had Celeste seen Quentin copying the information? Or maybe hiding the list? She'd proven herself willing to confront and blackmail others. Maybe she'd done the same with Quentin? And wound up dead because of it.

Was this enough to take to the Sheriff's Department? Probably not. I needed Simone to confirm that customers were complaining about theft of their credit card information.

That meant another trip to Playtime.

Before returning home from our walk, I dropped off Buster. The smell of cinnamon and apples filled the air when J. D. opened the door. While he crouched and petted his dog, I inhaled deeply. "What are you cooking now?"

"Apple pie." He stood and urged the boxer inside. "Cooking yesterday was so relaxing, I figured I'd do some baking today. Keep the flow going."

"By any chance do you think you're making too much of today's item, too?"

"Pretty sure I am." He grinned. "If they turn out right, I'll let you know."

"Yay."

I crossed the alley to the side gate and let the dogs into the backyard. While they found spots to settle in the sunshine, I went into the house to look up the schedule at Playtime. As I sat at the kitchen counter staring at my computer, part of me missed having a purring cat curled in my lap.

The training facility had a full schedule today: agility, barn hunt, and obedience classes. Barn hunt wasn't until late afternoon. Since Simone taught that class, I'd have a better shot at talking to her if I went earlier. And since I had to drive there anyway, I enrolled Noodle in the class. It'd be fun for him and— as an added bonus—Simone couldn't ignore a paying customer. I just hoped Detective DeFelice hadn't told her I was the one who'd tipped off the Sheriff's Department about the abandoned tools hidden inside the barn.

I'd never taken Noodle anywhere without bringing Harlow, too. But there was no reason to drag the Golden along—especially when she'd need to spend most of the day inside the car or a crate. Besides, she and Sky could keep each other company. Sky was sleeping, so I gave Harlow an extra helping of love before topping off the water bowls. "Be good. Come, Noodle."

I hooked on the big dog's leash. The Frenchie continued snorting, legs twitching as she dreamed. Harlow raised her head, then rolled on her back, letting the sun warm her belly. Pleasantly surprised she didn't seem to mind being left behind, I scratched her stomach, then led the Saint Berdoodle into the garage.

As I drove, Noodle stuck his nose out the back window, sampling the air and moving from the left side to the right as his nose saw fit. Drool occasionally broke free from his flews. Fortunately, once we'd got out into the county area, no one was behind us on the road to get splattered. When I reached the two-lane road leading to Playtime, Noodle woofed. "That's right. You've been here before."

Something was off. I studied our surroundings. Then it clicked. "Oh." The "missing dog" flyers had been removed. A wave of sadness passed through me. After several deep breaths, I refocused on what I was going to say to Simone.

After turning right onto Playtime's driveway, we bumped our way over the ruts up to the gravel area at the top of the incline. The lot was almost full. I circled until I found a spot. Of course, it was one of the farthest from the crating area. Noodle stuck his head out the back window, drool dripping down the door's exterior. "Stay."

I hoisted my cart from the rear of the 4Runner, then arranged the crate, tarp, and knapsack on top and rolled them to the area beneath the trees. Setting up Noodle's space took a few minutes. A cocker spaniel in the adjacent crate watched my progress with sincere brown eyes.

I filled the Saint Berdoodle's water bowl, then headed to the car. Noodle sniffed tree trunks and scrub on the way back, leaving his mark in a few spots. When we reached his crate, he refilled his tank at the water bowl. Chin dripping, he looked up at me, tail sweeping the dirt.

"Good job." I kissed his forehead and settled him inside his crate. The cocker spaniel roused himself to gaze at the big dog. Apparently unimpressed, he rested his chin on his paws. "I'll be back in a few."

CHAPTER 19

The air smelled of eucalyptus, dry grass, and dog. One dirt arena and one grass field were in use. In the first arena, under Cowboy Ben's watchful eye, fifteen handlers walked the agility course in preparation for their runs. I spied a bright-looking border collie approaching the ring with a broad-shouldered woman. Didn't she know the dog stayed crated while the handler learned the course? When she turned to the right, I glimpsed her face. Stacy Marinkovic. The one time we'd met, she hadn't seemed to enjoy agility. I was surprised to see she was still working with her dead daughter's dog. Unlike last time, the dog looked like he'd been groomed.

The grass field held an obedience class. More than a dozen students and their dogs were lined up along the center. The instructor was a curvy blonde dressed in jeans and a snug snap-front shirt. Between the rings and the barn, a blue pop-up canopy shaded the check-in area. Simone sat behind a card table talking to a heavyset man. A gray-muzzled German shepherd stayed tight beside his right leg. The man looked over his shoulder as I walked up behind him. He nodded, then his eyes widened.

"You're the one with the Saint Berdoodle. Is he coming to class today?"

"That's the plan." I pointed at the crating area. "Noodle's hanging out over there right now."

"Good. I'd love to see him work again. His nose is amazing."

I noted his elbow brace. Right. This was the guy who'd had the quickest run during our first—and last—time doing barn hunt. At least until Noodle took a turn. "Thanks. We're hoping for a less eventful class today."

"Aren't we all." He nodded to Simone, then spoke to Desi. "Want to watch the other dogs work?" The shepherd wagged his tail. "Heel." They walked toward the rings.

Simone glared at me, jaw tightening. A small V appeared between her arched brows.

Was I supposed to pretend Celeste's dead body hadn't derailed that class? Or did she blame me for the return visit of the Sheriff's Department earlier in the week?

I glanced at the class list in front of her. Talk about an opportunity. I tried to recall what initials had been included with the list of credit card numbers I'd found. "SK" was one. And there was "Kraus, Susan" on Simone's attendance sheet. Wasn't there a "PT," too? While Simone picked up a pen and checked the box beside my name, I scanned the printout. There he was: "Thibideaux, Paul." "Roberts, Chester" caught my eye. I was pretty sure there'd been a "CR" as well.

"I see you paid online and signed your waiver last time you were here. You're all set."

I lifted my gaze. Fortunately, Simone's focus remained resolutely fixed on the attendance sheet. I took the opportunity to read and memorize as many names as I could. "I take it the Sheriff's Department has released the crime scene?"

"Not exactly. We can use the arena inside the barn, but not the area in the back—where the bales are—or the north side of the barn." She pursed her lips.

Guessing the north side included the Rat Wrangler's area, I said, "Is that a problem?"

"No. We're doing our best to keep things running with their restrictions. But a heads-up would've been nice. They just showed up Wednesday afternoon and told us we had to stay out of the barn. Fortunately, we had time to move the scheduled obedience class to the outdoor ring before most of the students showed up. But people noticed what was going on. How could they not? A bunch of cop cars outside the barn and officers inside moving bales. When they left, they took a bunch of old equipment."

"Did they find something related to the murder?"

"Like they'd tell me." She tapped her pen against the tabletop. "And as if that wasn't bad enough, one of their officers was supposed to come out yesterday and remove the tape and give us the official okay to use the entire barn."

"No one showed?"

"Or called. I had to call them. Again. They *say* they'll be by today. I just hope it's not during class."

I glanced around the area to make sure no one else was within earshot. "I wanted to ask you about Playtime's problem—"

"Don't." She tilted her head toward the class area. "We've got a lot of people here today."

"I can see that. I just have a couple questions."

She stood. "I've already said too much to you."

Irritation flashed through me. "Tough. A woman's dead. And you're going to listen to what I have to say. Playtime's losing business because of complaints about stolen credit card information, isn't it?"

Her mouth dropped open. "How did you . . . .?" She did a quick visual sweep of the area, then lowered her voice. "I can't talk to you about that."

I moved around the table into her space. "I think you need to. I've got evidence that points to the likely person responsible. Or at the very least, an accomplice. But I need confirmation from you that the thefts are actually happening."

"Who is it? Who's trying to ruin us?"

A confirmation, but not a declarative statement. "Huh-uh. That's for me to tell the Sheriff's Department."

"I . . . I don't know." Simone knotted her hands. "I can't confirm anything. I'd need to speak to Mr. Hopkins first."

Talk about bad news. The fire inside me struggled to stay lit. I doubted Hopkins held any warm fuzzy feelings for the woman who'd broken the news about his dog. "Is that absolutely necessary?"

"He's Playtime's owner."

If I was going to get shot down, there was no need to put it off. "Can you call him now?"

Simone's sigh could've filled a stadium. "I can try." She pulled out her cell, scrolled, and hit the call icon.

Nerves tightening, I waited.

"Mr. Hopkins. Hi, it's Simone." She chewed her lip and made eye contact with me while her boss spoke.

I nodded, trying to imbue the gesture with all the encouragement I could muster.

"I did. I'm still waiting for them to come out."

Another pause while Hopkins spoke.

"I will." She cleared her throat. "I'm calling because I have a woman here who says she has evidence about . . ." She gave a furtive glance over her shoulder, then resumed talking, voice low. "The person who's been messing with the business." She closed her eyes as a muffled voice raged. "I understand. She's here right now and wants to meet with you."

Again his angry tone reached me, though I couldn't decipher the words. Simone winced, then handed her cell to me.

"Hello?"

"You know how to get to my place?" Rage infused his gravelly voice.

"Yep."

"Be here in ten minutes."

"You got it." The line went dead. I handed back the phone.

"I don't think I've ever heard him that mad," Simone said. "You're on your own talking to him. I need to stay at Playtime."

"Lucky you." I hurried back to the crating area and released Noodle. If I was going to visit a furious man, I wanted the big dog at my side. I let the Saint Berdoodle water a few trees, then loaded him into the 4Runner. Before pulling out, I took a moment to write down all the names I remembered from Simone's attendance list. There was no guarantee Hopkins would prove helpful. I checked my phone. I had less than seven minutes to get to his house. I'd have to compare the names to the list I'd photographed later.

This time I parked in the circular drive between the fountain and the hacienda-style home. I climbed out and opened the back door. "Come, Noodle." If Hopkins didn't want a drooling dog inside his home, we could have our conversation on the front porch. I crunched across the gravel while Noodle padded at my side.

When I pushed the brass doorbell, three deep bongs sounded. Noodle sat, looking up at me as if this was the most interesting thing he'd done in days. "I forget sometimes how bright you are. I've been falling behind on challenging you."

Noodle drooled on the tinted concrete.

The arched door opened. Hopkins looked down at me. His eyes narrowed. "You."

"That's right. Me."

"Is that how you found out about Freddy's death? Investigating the credit card thefts?"

I waggled my free hand. "Not exactly. I discovered the information while looking into Celeste Simmons's death. Then stumbled across the other."

"Might as well come inside."

"I should warn you, the dog drools."

To my surprise, he cracked a smile. "I can see that."

I followed him down a wide entryway hall. He walked with a slight limp, cowboy boots clacking an uneven rhythm on the tiles. At a wide arched doorway on the right, he turned. The room was high ceilinged and filled with natural light. Built-in floor-to-ceiling bookshelves lined two of the walls. The third featured a large picture window overlooking a dell filled with rows of avocado trees. "Wow. Your view is stunning."

"And practical. This here's a working farm. That window gives me a chance to keep an eye on the trees. Make sure their leaves look healthy." He gestured toward one of two cushy chestnut-colored sofas. "Have a seat."

I sat where directed and surveyed the room. Tile floor, leather sofas. This was the home of a dog owner. Or it had been. Poor Freddy. My eyes stung.

"Noodle, sit." The Saint Berdoodle sank onto his haunches. I turned my attention back to my host. "Thank you for agreeing to meet with me. I'm hoping you'll tell me which Playtime customers have contacted your business to complain. Specifically about someone using their credit card number."

He waved away my words. "We'll get to that. First things first. Who ran over my dog and left him to the 'yotes?"

Not a good start. "I understand you wanting to know, but I can't tell you that. I gave my word."

"You gave your word? Then came to tell me my dog was dead?"

I spread my hands wide. "Please don't take my refusal to answer for a lack of feeling. I agree: You should know who did this. But it's not my story to tell. That said, I couldn't leave you . . . waiting for a dog who wasn't coming home." He opened his mouth and I held up my hand to stop him. "I hope someday the person responsible will contact you. I tried to convince them it was the right thing to do. Maybe I'm kidding myself, but I think they will . . . in time."

Hopkins leaned back against the cushion, seeming to shrink in size. "Well, crap. I was hoping you'd feel differently."

"I'm not going to break my word. Which I think you'll appreciate—at least with regard to the credit card problem at Playtime. If you can give me the names of the people who complained, I can take that, along with the list of credit card numbers I found. That'll give the Sheriff's Department both the victims and potential marks. And I won't talk about it to anyone except them. You have my word."

"Your word's kind of a double-edged sword. I like the idea of it working to protect my business, but I want to know who killed my Freddy."

"Seems we're at an impasse." I leaned back, doing my best to appear unruffled.

Hopkins's frown deepened. "At least tell me who the credit card thief is."

Not sure I was making the right choice, I nodded. "I'll give you the name, but I need you to understand that nothing has been proven yet. That's up to the cops."

"You're telling me not to go after the steaming turd until there's an actual arrest?"

"At least until then."

He harrumphed. "All right."

"I was in the barn at Playtime and found a list of numbers hidden inside a metal tube. One of the old ones the Rat Wrangler used before you guys changed over to PVC pipe."

"Quentin's doing this to me?"

"There may be another man involved. I saw the two of them arguing, but don't know if it's relevant. Nor do I have a name for the other man. With your list of angry clients, the Sheriff's Department will take the problem seriously. Then, when I tell them I've got a list of potential victims, they'll see an easy bust on the horizon."

He rose, knee creaking, and pulled a cell phone from his rear pocket. "Excuse me for a moment." He left the room, boot heels echoing on the tile.

I shifted forward to pet Noodle. His curly coat felt silky and comforting. He pressed his head into my hand. "You're such a sweet fellow."

When Hopkins returned, he handed me a page torn from a notepad. "These are the folks who complained recently."

"How long have complaints been coming in?"

"Close to six months."

I scanned the sheet. Celeste's wasn't among the eight names.

What did that mean? A couple names jumped out at me: "Chester Roberts," "Paul Thibideaux." "Huh?"

"What is it?"

"Hang on." Opening the photo on my phone, I enlarged the image. "Wow."

"What's going on?"

I looked up. Hopkins had remained standing. "Six of the names on your list match the initials on mine."

"That's good, right?"

"I don't know. If Quentin's already using the card numbers, why is he hiding the list in an old rat tube?"

"Who knows with that boy?"

I waggled the note. "You okay with me taking this to the cops?"

He waved his hand. "Go ahead." Looking weary, he added, "I can't believe Quentin betrayed my trust."

His tone hinted at more than an employee-employer relationship. "Have you known him a long time?"

"I've known his parents forever. The boy was always an odd one. Playing with rodents and the like. But he seemed like a hard worker."

The boy? Quentin was almost in his thirties. "When did he start working at Playtime?"

"Year and a half ago. He'd gotten himself into some sort of mess. His parents weren't too specific." Hopkins shook his head. "They asked if I could give the boy some work. They thought getting him away from the knuckleheads he lifted weights with was the answer. Figured if he had a job that kept him busy, he'd stay out of trouble. Apparently, they were wrong."

"Though I'll only talk about this with the cops, if I give this information to them and they think it's solid, they're going to investigate. Will that be a problem for you?" The man had already lost his dog; I didn't want to make matters worse.

"Doesn't matter. The boy messed with my business. He needs to learn from his mistakes. If his parents don't like it? Too damn bad."

CHAPTER 20

I pulled over at the end of Hopkins's long driveway, unsure whether to head to the coast or return to Playtime. Though the training center had a Moorpark address, it was actually in an unincorporated part of the county—just as the Rat Wrangler had told me when I found Celeste's body. Though Detective DeFelice had responded swiftly to my call three days earlier, I doubted I'd get her or her partner to come to me over a list of numbers. If I wanted to show the list to her, that meant driving all the way to Government Center in Ventura. I probably had a better chance of getting a patrol officer to listen to my story. I looked over my shoulder at Noodle. "What do you think, boy? I don't like the idea of letting Quentin out of our sight that long. If we go back for barn hunt, we can keep an eye on him. Think we could get one of the deputies we met before to come out?"

Noodle drooled.

"Right. It's worth a try." I searched for the Ventura Sheriff's Department business line, then tapped the number into my cell.

A crisp voice answered. "Good afternoon. Ventura County Sheriff's Department. How may I direct your call?"

Wow. No one at my old police department ever answered the phone with such enthusiasm. "Hi. Is Deputy Alvarez or Deputy Wallace available?"

"Is there a problem?"

"No. I want to follow up about a prior call."

"Of course. Please hold."

A jaunty tune filled the line, followed by a less jaunty one. Finally, the efficient voice returned. "Deputy Alvarez is on patrol. I can patch you through."

"Thank you."

A couple beeps were followed by static, then, "Alvarez."

"Hi. This is Molly Madison. We met at Playtime Academy for Dogs a week and a half ago."

A heavy sigh filled the line. "Uh-huh."

"You and Deputy Wallace were the first officers on the scene."

"Look, I'm gonna get out there as soon as I can to take down the tape."

"That's not why I'm calling."

"Who are you again?"

I repeated my name.

"Like the president's wife?"

"Uh, James Madison's wife was Dolley."

"You sure?"

Weird conversational detour. "Yep. I'm the woman with the Saint Berdoodle. The big dog who found Celeste Simmons's body."

"Right. I remember you. Sorry to be so abrupt. The manager at Playtime's been on my case about releasing the crime scene. She doesn't seem to get that we've got higher priorities. Look, I'm not trying to blow you off, but Detectives Stern and DeFelice have been assigned that case."

"I'm not calling about the murder."

"They having another problem there?"

"Yep." I explained about the complaints Playtime had received regarding illicit credit card use and the hidden list of numbers I'd found.

"And you think this Rat Wrangler guy might be copying credit card info?"

"Exactly. It might be related to the murder—or it might not. I don't even know whether the list is still inside the tube. Quentin could've removed it by now. But I can send you a photo of it along with the names the owner gave me."

Alvarez recited her cell number and promised to come by Playtime to check it out. "And tell that woman I'll take down the crime scene tape then."

"You got it." After disconnecting, I snapped a picture of Hopkins's list of names and sent it and the numbers to Alvarez. I glanced at Noodle in the rearview. "Looks like you're going to get to do some barn hunt after all."

When we returned, Simone wasn't at the table under the blue canopy. Neither was her attendance sheet. I scanned the nearby fields. Still no sign of her. I walked Noodle to the office. For a change, the door was shut. I knocked and waited. No answer. I looked at the Saint Berdoodle. "You think she's ducking me?"

Noodle wagged his tail.

With an hour to kill before our class, I headed to the first arena. The agility students were still hard at work. Spotting Thor, the border collie, I led Noodle to him and let the two dogs sniff each other. Tails immediately began wagging. Though Stacy Marinkovic stood beside the collie, she didn't notice me or the

Saint Berdoodle. Odd. Most dog people paid close attention when another dog approached theirs. As a new dog owner, maybe Stacy didn't understand that not all canine interactions went smoothly.

"Hi."

Stacy pulled her gaze from the ring and stared blankly at me.

"Molly Madison. We met week before last."

"Oh." Recognition flared in her eyes. "You're a friend of Felicity's."

The idea of being labeled Felicity's friend no longer sat well. Not after what I'd learned about the missing golden retriever's death. "We're more like acquaintances."

She cocked her head. "But I heard you were helping her. Trying to prove she didn't kill Celeste."

"True. But I'm doing that because I don't think she did it."

Stacy's gaze sharpened. "Why not?"

Huh. She was the first person who hadn't automatically agreed Felicity was innocent. Did Stacy know something I didn't? "Her motive's thin and I doubt she could've hauled Celeste to the top of the stack of bales. Something like that would've taken a lot of upper body strength. More than I think Felicity has. Don't get me wrong, she's not weak, but lifting a dead body all the way up there? We're talking about a whole other kind of strong."

"You don't think maybe Celeste climbed up, then got killed?"

"Nope. And I'm sure the crime scene techs don't think so, either."

Her brows drew together. "Why not?"

"Head wounds bleed a lot. There wasn't enough blood on the top bale."

"Oh."

This conversation had to be painful for a woman who'd recently lost her daughter. I gestured toward the ring. "How's the agility training going?"

She shrugged. "Not great. I mean, Thor's great, but I'm a mess." She knotted her hands together in front of her chest. "You never met my Ramona. That girl moved like a gazelle. Every step precise, graceful. She and Thor ran like a matched set, neither one hesitating or tiring. I'll never be like that. This poor guy probably deserves a better handler. But I can't bear to let him go."

"Hey, Thor's getting to run the course, take on the obstacles. Trust me, your dog is having fun. That's what matters. He doesn't care how good your score is."

"I guess." She frowned down at the collie.

A lanky older gentleman entered the ring with a Rhodesian ridgeback. "Whoa. I've never seen that breed do agility. Have you?"

Stacy shrugged again, reminding me a little of Ava. "What breed is it?"

"Ridgeback. They don't like crowds. Or running in the heat. At least it's a cool day."

The silver-haired man conferred with Cowboy Ben. Moving a few feet away, he signaled his dog and took off with an awkward gait.

"Oh. I get it." He had some sort of leg injury, running with one leg straight, the other bending to take the impact. From what I knew, ridgebacks were unlikely to go fast—unless they felt like it. A perfect dog partner if a handler couldn't run well.

The two made it through the course at a sedate pace, with zero errors.

"Even Harold runs his dog better than I do." Stacy chewed her lower lip. "And he's got a bum knee and hip."

The woman wasn't enjoying herself. Maybe Stacy just needed permission to stop. "You know, agility's not for everyone."

Her mouth dropped open.

"I'm not saying you should quit. But if you're not having fun,

Thor's going to sense that. If you can decide the score doesn't matter and just do this for your dog, fine. But if you're going to be miserable because you're not doing as well as your daughter did, then maybe you should find something else you and he can do together."

She frowned and crossed her arms over her chest. "No one's ever told me I shouldn't continue doing Ramona's sport."

"It's up to you. But if it's making you unhappy, what's the point?"

"To feel close to my daughter."

I might be crossing a line, but Stacy needed a dose of reality. "Is it working?"

Again, her jaw sagged. This time her eyes grew damp. "No."

"Do you have any activities you like doing?" In spite of her pallor, the woman looked athletic. "Maybe hiking or running? Something you already enjoy that Thor can join in on? If you do, try that. Then, if Thor's not getting enough exercise or stimulation, you can always hire a handler to do agility with him." Noting Stacy's furrowed brow, I said, "Look, I know it's none of my business, but it doesn't seem like forcing yourself to do something you don't like is a good way to feel connected to your daughter."

She tilted her head down, seeming to stare at her feet. Long after the silence between us had grown awkward, she said, "I swim and kayak." She finally met my gaze again. "One or the other, every day. In the ocean."

"Oh." That explained Stacy's physique. "Border collies are supersmart. Maybe you could take him with you in the kayak."

"Sounds like a recipe for capsizing to me."

"Stacy and Thor," Cowboy Ben yelled. "You're up."

Looking flustered, Stacy told the collie to come and trotted to the course entrance. She unhooked Thor's leash, then leaned in as the instructor spoke. She nodded once, then glanced back at me.

The last thing Stacy needed was to be focusing on me. I pointed toward the instructor.

Stacy turned to face him again.

When they broke apart, she trudged a few yards away from the dog, looking defeated before she'd begun. This was unlikely to go well.

Their run wasn't a disaster, but it wasn't pretty, either. Stacy set up Thor well for the first jump but, once he landed, ran him the wrong way toward the next obstacle. Catching her error before the dog entered the exit end of the tunnel, she redirected him, her face bright red.

By the time Thor soared over the panel jump at the end of their run, Stacy looked dejected, seeming not to notice the collie happily capering around her.

Thinking I was the last person Stacy would want to see when she left the ring, I told Noodle to heel and we headed for the barn. Simone stood inside next to Quentin, the two conferring quietly about something. I hoped Hopkins hadn't said anything to her yet about my suspicions. I didn't want Simone inadvertently warning the Rat Wrangler.

The man with the elbow brace entered the barn with his German shepherd. He walked over to us and the dogs greeted each other. Large for his breed, I imagined Desi didn't often meet another dog that was bigger than him.

"Well, that was a bit of a mess. I gotta give Ben credit—the man stays patient with everyone."

I nodded. "I imagine that's a big part of why he's good at what he does."

He held out his hand. "My name's Chester, by the way."

"Molly." We shook. Was this the Chester from Hopkins's list? I resisted asking him about fraudulent credit card charges. Instead, we talked dogs and training.

More students entered and Simone moved through the new arrivals. Clipboard in hand, she greeted people and checked off names, somehow managing to steer clear of me and Chester. Finally, Simone stepped into the barn hunt arena. "I think everyone here today has attended at least one barn hunt class, right?"

People nodded.

"Okay. Today we'll go smallest dogs to largest."

Chester groaned, then muttered so only I could hear, "Looks like you and me are going last."

I gave him a "Whaddya gonna do" shrug, while wondering if Simone was doing this to let me know she didn't want me here.

"There will only be one rat on the course for today. Let's get started. Quentin, bring in the tubes."

The muscle-bound man lifted the cardboard box sitting on a nearby bale and set it on the ground. After wiping his hands on the front of his T-shirt, he held a foot-long piece of pipe aloft. "This here's the empty." He gave it a shake and set it on the ground. "This is the one with rat bedding, but no rat." He unscrewed the end cap and held up the tube so everyone could see. After placing it a foot from the other tube, he raised the remaining one. "And this here holds the rat." He set it in between the other two tubes.

"Line up to my right," Simone said. "Smallest dogs to largest. Each handler will get a chance to let their dog sniff the tubes."

Noodle and I moved to the end of the line.

Today's class was larger than the previous one I'd attended.

With a dozen dogs and handlers, it took more than twenty minutes for each dog to smell the tubes. Noodle and I went last, after Chester and Desi. Like the German shepherd, the Saint Berdoodle immediately zeroed in on the tube with the rat. Instead of pawing it like Desi had, he barked. "Good boy."

When I led him back to the group, I caught the Rat Wrangler glaring at me.

"Okay, put them in place." Simone nodded at Quentin. He picked up the tubes and began setting them on the course. "When your dog finds the correct tube and alerts, you need to yell 'Rat' and hand the tube to our wrangler. When you pick it up, be sure to hold it level. We want to keep the little fellow safe and comfortable. Got it?"

More nods from the group.

"Each dog must go through at least one tunnel to complete the course. If your dog finds the rat before going through a tunnel, you'll need to command him or her through before leaving the arena. If you don't, your run won't count. Got it? And remember, all dogs run naked." Simone checked the list on her clipboard. "Edgar Deluca? You and Pip are up first."

A stocky man with a wispy mustache and shaved head stepped forward, a tan teddy-bear-faced Pomeranian trotting alongside. He crouched and removed the dog's baby blue harness.

"Remember, once your dog starts, only use hand gestures and vocal commands to urge them on. You can touch the dog if you're praising or giving him a treat after he finds the rat." She walked deeper into the arena and pointed to a white tube sitting on top of a three-bale-high stack. "The rat is inside this tube. When your dog finds it, watch for his alert. As you just saw, some will nose it, some paw at it, others bark. When your turn comes, the dog and handler should enter the ring at the same time. No leading the dog." She nodded at Edgar. "Go when ready."

Edgar and Pip entered. The tiny Pom scampered around the bales, sniffing and panting with Edgar calling, "Go, go, go." When the dog hesitated at the hay tunnel, he urged, "In, baby. In."

I felt bad that the little dog had to scale the bales, but with Edgar's encouragement, the Pom made it to the top and sat down on the tube. Interesting alert.

After his run, Simone gave him an approving smile. "Good job, you two." She turned to the rest of the class. "At the Novice Barn Hunt level, you'd normally have two minutes to find the tubes. But since this is a class, not a competition, there's no time limit."

To keep Noodle from getting bored while we waited for our turn, I took him outside. We circled the barn several times, then walked to the now-empty arena and fields. He had a good time sniffing everything within reach. When we went back to the barn, a fifty-something woman with close-cropped black hair was urging a Yorkie through the hay tunnel. I glanced at the line of waiting handlers and dogs. Good, this was the last of the small ones. We only had the medium and large dogs to go.

In between taking Noodle outside for frequent breaks, I watched several handlers' techniques as they worked their dogs. When Chester and Desi's turn came, I led Noodle back inside. Chester and the German shepherd moved to the arena entrance, then he removed Desi's collar.

"Go when ready," Simone said.

"Desi, in." Side by side, the two entered. The rangy shepherd kept his nose to the straw-covered floor, swiftly locating the empty tube and the one with used bedding, then moving on. He climbed the bale stack with ease and pawed the tube. Chester rushed over to pet and praise the dog, then called out "Rat!" and carefully lifted the tube. He waited for Quentin to enter the arena and take it.

A gentle murmur among the students pulled my attention away. Several heads were turned toward the open barn door. A black-and-white Sheriff's Department SUV had pulled into the lot. Deputy Alvarez climbed out.

CHAPTER 21

Unsure if I should go out to meet the deputy, I decided to stay put and see how Alvarez wanted to handle this.

As if feeling the group's attention being siphoned away, Simone turned and peered outside. Her entire body appeared to clench. The woman wanted Playtime's problems solved, but not within sight of paying customers.

Quentin's reaction was almost comical. The color drained from his already pasty face. His head swiveled back and forth, shaggy hair looking more mop-like than usual. Dropping the rat tube, he barreled toward the open doors, pushing people aside. Voices rose in alarm and a middle-aged woman fell. Quentin tripped over the cocker spaniel I'd seen in the crating area. Her handler cried out. Regaining his footing, he bolted outside, heading left and down the brushy slope.

"What the hell?" Chester murmured.

His confusion was mirrored on the other class members'

faces. Two young women were the first to move, helping the older woman to her feet and brushing straw from her clothes.

Simone's gaze lasered in on me. One by one, the group followed her lead and turned away from the Good Samaritans. So much for keeping a low profile. I looked down at the Saint Berdoodle. "Heel, Noodle." We walked outside to meet the deputy.

Alvarez crossed the open area in front of the barn and jerked her thumb toward the dust cloud marking Quentin's escape. "Who's that numbskull?"

"The Rat Wrangler." Noodle busied himself by sniffing the deputy's boots.

Alvarez smiled at the dog before taking off her shades. "He thinks he can outrun the Sheriff's Department?"

"Who knows? Want me to show you where I found the list?"

"That's why I'm here. But I need to get permission to search. Is the owner on-site?"

"No. But the manager is."

"Oh. Her."

Right. Simone had been pestering Alvarez to release the crime scene. And I'd not gotten the chance to tell her the deputy would be coming out today to do just that.

Simone didn't wait for me to bring the deputy inside, joining us out front. Noodle shifted his attention to her high-tops. "Deputy Alvarez. You here to clear the crime scene?"

Alvarez cocked her eyebrow at me.

I shrugged. "I tried to tell her, but she was avoiding me."

Now looking puzzled, Simone crossed her arms over her chest. "What's going on?"

After Alvarez and I had brought her up to speed, Simone said,

"You can search anything you want. Just let me dismiss the class first." The deputy agreed and Simone walked into the barn.

Though everyone except for Noodle and me had already had one run, she promised all attendees a future barn hunt class at half price. While the group filed out, I saw her talking to the woman Quentin had knocked over. The conversation ended with a hug. Once the barn was empty, I told Noodle to heel and led the deputy to the Rat Wrangler's alcove. Noodle looked up at me and drooled. "Right. No crime scene for you. Sit. Stay." Once I was confident the Saint Berdoodle wouldn't budge, I pulled the tarp aside.

Light filtered in from the main section of the barn, sending dozens of rats scurrying inside their cages. I pointed at the wooden crate. "There it is. I found the list in a tube at the bottom. There were two tubes that had end caps on them. The list was in one of those."

Alvarez looked up. "Can we get more light in here?"

"Give me a second." Simone found the correct switch. A bright fluorescent light came on overhead.

After pulling on gloves, the deputy began removing the perforated metal pipes from the crate.

"Like I said, it was at the bottom."

Alvarez gave me a look. I was over-helping.

As more tubes were taken from the crate, my pulse quickened. Quentin wasn't carrying anything when he took off, but he could've already removed the list.

Finally, the deputy held a piece of pipe up to the light. "I think this is it." She unscrewed the end cap and extracted a rolled piece of paper. After studying it, she slid the sheet inside an evidence bag and flattened it. Pulling out her cell phone, Alvarez held the screen beside the note. "I got a different set of numbers here."

"Is it the same setup? Twenty-three digits followed by initials?"

"Uh-huh." Alvarez looked at Simone. "Seems your employee's been a busy fellow." She opened the remaining tube and pulled out a second rolled piece of paper. Pulling it taut, she grinned. "And this one's the list you photographed." She slid the sheet into a second evidence bag and straightened. "This guy have access to payment information?"

Simone looked shell-shocked. "Yes. He helps in the office when things get busy."

"I'm gonna need his address and any contact info you have."

"Sure. Let me get that from the file cabinet." Shoulders slumped, Simone hurried off.

When she was out of earshot, I said, "One more thing . . ."

The deputy looked up at me.

"See the gap between those two stacks of bales?" I pointed at my escape route from the other day. "If you step between them, you can access a gap that runs along the exterior wall. All the way to the front of the barn. The space is full of old tools, pieces of wood, and piping. I told Detective DeFelice about the area. I don't know if you were involved in the search, but back then, I didn't realize how important Quentin having easy access to the space might be."

Alvarez stood and shined her flashlight beam into the gap.

"Great place to hide a murder weapon," I said.

"Maybe. Far as I know, the lab results aren't back yet on the equipment we took." She pursed her lips, then ushered me from the Rat Wrangler's den.

I told Noodle to come. We stepped outside again. Sunset stained the sky, turning the scattered clouds overhead pink.

Simone jogged back to join us and handed an orange sticky note to the deputy.

"I'm gonna call this in. Stay out of the barn. Both of you," Alvarez said. She gave us a curt nod before striding to her vehicle.

Simone turned to me. "I can't believe Quentin's the one . . . Does Mr. Hopkins know?"

I nodded.

"That poor man. He's had to deal with so much lately. First his dog, now a friend of the family stealing from him." She tugged one of her curls. "Oh God. Is Celeste . . . I mean, did she find out what Quentin was doing? And he killed her? Over a bunch of credit card numbers?"

Noodle whined. Simone's tone had worried him. "I don't know. Maybe." I crouched to pet the big dog. "He looks like a strong guy. Strong enough to haul a dead body up an eight-foot-high stack of bales. And I recently heard that Celeste wasn't above blackmailing people."

"What?"

"I can't say more about it. But it makes me wonder if . . ."

"If she tried to blackmail Quentin." Simone shuddered. "I can't believe I've been working alongside a murderer."

"Slow down. We don't know that. Earlier, I told the deputy I saw Quentin with a man in Playtime's barn. He obviously wasn't a student. Didn't have a dog and wore impractical leather loafers. It looked like he was chewing out Quentin. And your Rat Wrangler looked scared. Maybe that guy had something to do with Celeste's death."

"I guess. That description doesn't sound like anyone who comes here. Student or vendor." Simone knotted her hands in front of her. "Sorry, but you were right. I was avoiding you when you came back from Mr. Hopkins's place. He doesn't want me to let the trouble we've been having affect the business. Or the students' impression of us and our reputation. But the only way I can do that is to pretend it's not happening. Which I can't do if I'm discussing credit card theft with you. Let the deputy know I'm in the office, okay?"

"Sure."

She turned and trudged away.

I still didn't understand what Quentin was doing. At least some of the credit card numbers were already being used—based on the customer complaints Playtime had received. Why hide the list in his work area?

I spent the next fifteen minutes working with Noodle on the "watch me," "take it," and "find it" commands. By the time Deputy Alvarez returned from her vehicle, the sky had darkened and stars pocked the sky. She cocked her head and watched as the Saint Berdoodle located the treat I'd hidden.

"That's one smart dog."

"Yeah. He's amazing." I called him to my side and offered him another treat.

"Deputies are already on the lookout for our missing Rat Wrangler. And the techs are on their way. So are Detectives DeFelice and Stern. Rather than making you wait for them, I've written up what you told me over the phone and what happened when I arrived. Give it a look." She handed me her notepad. "Let me know if anything's missing."

I moved closer to the exterior light on the barn. The deputy's writing was neat and easy to read. Alvarez was thorough; no detail had been omitted. "Looks good." I handed back the pad. "You think the murder is connected to this?"

"Maybe. Maybe not."

I'd hoped for more candor but, to her, I was just a civilian. "Guess I'm done here."

"The detectives will probably be in touch with you in the next couple days."

"Okay." It felt weird leaving without talking to DeFelice or Stern, but Alvarez had made it clear my presence was no longer necessary. "Come, Noodle." I started for the parking lot, then turned back. "Simone said to tell you she's in the office." We continued to my 4Runner. I loaded Noodle into the back seat. To my surprise, Stacy Marinkovic was in the lot, too, settling Thor inside a crate in the cargo area of her CRV. I cracked a window for Noodle and walked over to join her.

She looked up, her expression hard to read in the dark.

"Hi. I thought agility ended a couple hours ago."

"It did. Ben gave me a few pointers afterward. Then Thor and I took a walk around the grounds."

The trees dotting the landscape were now inky silhouettes, but this would be a lovely place for a sunset stroll. "Nice night for a walk."

Stacy thrust her chin toward the black-and-white SUV. "Why is a cop here? Does it have to do with Celeste's death?"

"I don't know. Someone's been stealing credit card information. Whether or not it's connected to the murder, that's for the cops to figure out. But it might affect you. Have you noticed any suspicious charges on your card?"

Stacy shook her head. "I . . . Who knows? I haven't been on top of things like I used to be. Not since . . ."

When she didn't try to bring that sentence to completion, I took the reins again. "Right. Well, you might want to take a look at your latest bill. Make sure your information's safe."

"Thanks, I will."

Time to ask what I really wanted to know. "When we were

talking earlier, you seemed surprised I thought Felicity was innocent. Any particular reason?"

Stacy retreated a step and crossed her arms. "Well, she and
Celeste didn't like each other. Felicity really resented how much
better Celeste scored at agility—especially since the woman
probably wouldn't have discovered the sport if Felicity hadn't told
her about it."

"But did she ever do or say anything that would make you
think she wanted Celeste dead?"

Stacy shrugged. "Nothing specific."

I let the silence stretch.

"I know you're new here, but a lot of people hated Celeste.
She was a terrible person."

"I've heard that. But when I first met you, weren't you hanging
out with her? Why spend time together if you didn't like her?"

"I wasn't 'hanging out' with Celeste. She was talking to a couple dog handlers, making fun of Thor's dirty coat. She likes—I
mean liked—needling people. Getting under their skin. For her,
a bad reaction was better than being ignored." Stacy retreated
another step. "I didn't bring any food along for Thor and need to
get him home."

"I've got some kibble in my car."

"Thanks, but if I head out now, we'll be home by his usual
dinnertime." Brushing past me, she climbed behind the wheel.

So Celeste wasn't just mean; she needed to play the expert.
Grandstand for attention. That would explain pretending she'd
been the one to train Buster. Headlights blazed in the empty lot
as Stacy gunned the engine. Her CRV lurched across the gravel
to the driveway.

I climbed into my 4Runner and stared at the steering wheel.

Stacy's dislike of Celeste seemed to pale in comparison to Felicity's, but was still worth investigating, even though the woman had only started agility recently. How much nastiness could Celeste have directed her way in that short time? Maybe Celeste had been cruel to Stacy's daughter.

That made no sense. According to Stacy, her daughter had been an agility whiz. What if the girl hadn't been as wonderful at the sport as her mother claimed?

When we returned home, Harlow and Sky eagerly greeted me and Noodle, then made it clear they were ready for dinner. I mixed the usual wet and dry food combo and set their bowls out on the deck. My cell burred. I pulled it from my pocket. A text from J. D.

Want some apple pie?

My salivary glands responded before I typed: YES!

J.D.: Come over now?

Molly: Soon as I take Sky home.

After they hoovered up their chow, I leashed Sky. With apple pie beckoning, I loaded her into the car and drove her home. When I pulled to the curb, my headlights shone on the tall, dark-haired man standing opposite Izzy's. Being safely inside my 4Runner helped in the bravery department. I rolled down the passenger window. Sky stuck her head out and snorted, then barked. I grabbed her collar and called out, "You live around here?"

The man bolted down the side street.

I looked at the Frenchie. "Was it something I said?"

Once Sky was inside, I drove home and went up to my bedroom. I changed into a drool-free pullover and jeans. Feeling funny about mooching off J. D. again, I grabbed the last container of my homemade salsa and headed across the street.

J. D. opened the door and grinned down at me. "What've you got there?"

"That salsa you liked so much. Obviously not for tonight. Just be sure to store it in the fridge." I handed over the container, then crouched to pet Buster. The boxer's tail went nuts.

"I set things up in the atrium and have the firepit going. We can eat our pie out there."

"Sounds good to me." I followed him down the wide hallway.

"You have had dinner, right?"

"Does eating a granola bar in the car count?"

He shook his head and tsked.

"But hey, apple pie—that's like having fresh fruit for dinner."

"Tell yourself that—if it's what you need to believe."

In the kitchen, the aroma of apples, cinnamon, and nutmeg practically made me swoon. J. D. stopped to put the salsa inside the refrigerator. Picking up a plate in each hand, he led the way to the atrium.

As soon as I sat, my stomach rumbled. "This smells delicious."

"Gotta say, I'm pretty happy about how it turned out."

I picked up my fork, cutting through crust and golden apple and took a bite. "Wow. This is amazing."

"Probably because I used apples from the farmer's market."

Was J. D. doing well enough to go out again? "You went to the farmer's market?"

He shook his head. "My shopper went for me."

In spite of his agoraphobia, J. D. was fortunate. With a rich family, he could pay others to do what he currently couldn't. I took another bite. "Whatever the cause, this is great."

We ate and talked about the case. After his last bite, J. D. mashed his fork against the plate to collect the remaining crumbs. "And the Rat Wrangler just ran away when he saw the cop car?"

"Pretty much. Speaking of which, he's the first guy I watched run away today." I told him about seeing the same man loitering near Izzy's place when I returned Sky at night.

"But not every night?"

"No. More like four nights out of five. And he's not smoking or talking on his phone. He just stands there."

"Unless you try to talk to him."

"Apparently. But should I tell Izzy? I don't want to alarm her needlessly. It might have nothing to do with her. Just because I don't like her, it doesn't mean that man's out to get her. But if it does . . ."

"You'll regret not warning her."

"Right."

"So you'll talk to her tomorrow. Problem solved. Now back to the other thing. If they charge this rat guy with Celeste's murder, does that mean you're off the case?"

"Yep. Everyone will know Felicity didn't do it."

"You sound disappointed."

I considered his comment. "I will be. Not by her being proved innocent, but because I've been having fun sticking my nose into other people's business."

"Well, you can keep sticking your nose into mine," he said with a grin.

I cocked an eyebrow at him. "You think what I've been doing with you is the same as sticking my nose into your business? You have no idea."

"Oh yeah?" His grin widened.

"If I was sticking my nose where I shouldn't, I'd know your credit score, shoe size, the name of your first girlfriend, and your GPA."

He stretched out his legs and crossed them at the ankles. "Eight hundred twelve, fourteen wide, Annabelle, and three point seven two."

"Three point seven two?"

"Uh-huh."

"I'm impressed."

"Huh. Thought you'd be more impressed by my massive shoe size."

I chuckled.

"Maybe you should look into getting an investigator's license here."

"No, I'm done with all that."

"You don't seem to be."

CHAPTER 22

Izzy was gone by the time I picked up Sky the next morning. After a beach walk, I returned Buster, dried off Harlow, and groomed the other two dogs. Then I went inside and fortified myself with a mug of tepid coffee and sat at my kitchen counter to call her.

"Izzy Harmon."

The woman's irritated tone set my teeth on edge. "Hi. It's Molly." Silence. "Molly Madison. Your dog-sitter."

"What's Sky done now?"

Thrown off guard by her reaction, I needed a moment to get back on track. "Nothing. I just wanted to tell you that when I return Sky in the evening, I keep seeing a man standing across the street from your place. Not every night, but enough times that I thought you should know."

"What does he look like?"

Not the response I'd expected. "Close to six feet tall. Slim. Dark hair. Usually wearing a peacoat."

"Kyle."

"Kyle?"

"My ex. You need to be careful."

"Is he dangerous?"

She snorted. "Not to you or me. He wants Sky."

"Why? I mean, she's adorable, but there must be more to it."

"Oh, he claims she's his. It's nonsense. Everything that man says is nonsense."

"I—"

"I've got to go. Don't let Kyle get anywhere near the dog." The line went dead.

Well, that explained a lot. I wondered how long ago the ex had left? If he'd been the one caring for and spending time with Sky, that would explain the dog's sudden bout of chewing.

Must've been an ugly breakup. Otherwise, why not let her ex have Sky? Izzy didn't seem to even like the dog. The fact that Kyle was hanging out across the street at night while I returned the Frenchie demonstrated a greater interest in her than Izzy had ever shown. But until I knew for sure whether Izzy mistreated Sky, there was nothing I could do about it.

I spun on the stool and tried to focus on my case. Though it seemed like Quentin was on track to be arrested for Celeste's death, my gut still had trouble believing he'd killed her. The man was unpleasant and a thief, but a murderer? That didn't leave me with too many suspects—other than Del Kaminsky, Felicity, or a homicidal gymnast.

I'd talk to Del first.

Remembering the man's size, I leashed up the dogs. If he threatened me, Harlow would bark like crazy and Noodle would protect me with his life. While Sky's various woofs and snorts wouldn't threaten the gentlest soul, she'd cheer her friends on. I got the bigger dogs settled in the back and Sky in the passenger seat, then drove the six blocks to Del's white two-story cube of a home. I walked the dogs up the front path and told them to sit before ringing the bell. A minute later, the door jerked open.

Unshaven, dressed in a wrinkled aloha shirt and gym shorts, Del once again smelled of booze. His square jaw tightened as he frowned down at me. "You."

"Yep. Can we talk?"

"I've got nothing to say to you." He started to close the door.

"You may want to reconsider."

The door stopped moving. "Why?"

"I'm guessing you gave the detectives a rock-solid alibi for the time of your wife's murder."

"That's right." His unruly eyebrows lowered.

"A strong alibi's great, but husbands—and wives—have been known to pay other people to off their spouses for them. I'm pretty sure if I tell the cops they need to speak with Joel DeCarolis, they'll give you another look. Once they hear what he has to say."

"Who the hell is Joel DeWhatever?"

"An acquaintance of Celeste's. She told him your business was going under. And that she'd bail you out, and I quote, 'Over my dead body.'"

His face turned a startling shade of red. "So what? Doesn't make me a killer."

"No, but getting your hands on Celeste's money could either save your company or take away some of the sting of losing it. I know you were in Hawaii when she died, but you didn't need to personally kill her." I shrugged. "The thing is, whether you're guilty or not, if the cops focus on you, it'll make your life extremely uncomfortable." Something I'd learned from personal experience.

He pulled the door open all the way. "What do you want?"

"For you to answer a few questions."

He crossed his beefy arms over his chest. "Like?"

"Did your recent financial setback upset Celeste?"

"What do you think? Of course it did."

"Is it true she was unwilling to help bail you out?"

"This is none of your business."

"I know. But you can tell me—or you can tell the cops."

"Like they're not going to get there eventually."

"Maybe they won't—if I can prove someone else killed Celeste first."

His jaw unclenched while he uncrossed his arms. "She was pissed. Didn't want anyone to know. Like my business losses would reflect badly on her." He gave his head a shake. "The woman hated to admit any failure. Even mine. She insisted I keep the factory running with a skeleton crew. For appearances' sake."

"What about now? Will you keep it going?"

"No. We could've weathered the hit if it was just lost sales, but the company's reputation is shot. I figure I'll shut it down, sell what remaining assets I can, and try to enjoy all my new free time. Fortunately, Celeste made a good living." He gestured at the house. "This place is paid for."

If Del was to be believed, he was dealing well with losing his business. Almost as well as he seemed to be dealing with his wife's death. "How about all the fights? One of your neighbors told me you and Celeste had frequent, loud arguments."

"Who said that?"

"Doesn't matter."

"The hell it doesn't."

No way would I tell him it was Felicity from his old neighborhood. "Too bad."

He huffed out a breath. "They weren't about anything important. Just over stupid stuff."

"Like?"

"Like not putting a coaster under my beer. She'd also lose it if I left the toilet seat up. Or missed the wastebasket when I tossed my used floss. Crap like that. The woman was a control freak. Wanted everything 'just so.' I'm more live and let live."

Del was either an accomplished liar or genuinely unmoved by his wife's murder.

"We done here?"

I nodded. The door slammed shut.

I loaded up the dogs and drove home. Was Del a viable suspect? Angry as he'd gotten at my questions, none of the dogs reacted. He had seemed neither threatened nor threatening. But maybe he was a gifted actor. Or a sociopath. If Del wasn't behind his wife's murder, who did that leave? Stacy Marinkovic's willingness to blame Felicity for Celeste's death didn't sit right. It made me wonder if she had an ulterior motive. What if Ramona wasn't the agility whiz her mother claimed? Watching someone make fun of your sick child's skill set would send most mothers over the edge. While waiting at a stoplight, I texted Felicity and asked:

How good was Ramona with Thor in competition?

When I got home, I waited until we were inside before unleashing the dogs. "Good job, you guys. Thanks for keeping me company." I checked SimNastics' website to see if they were open on Sundays. They were. I headed out, leaving the dogs in the great room, Sky curled on the sofa, and Noodle and Harlow sprawled on their pillows.

Located in a semi-industrial part of nearby Ventura, the gym shared a warehouse-like building with a tile showroom. The parking lot was jammed. Either the 10:00 a.m. class at the gym was popular or the neighboring store was doing a banner business. I finally found a space in the lot of a mattress store a little farther down the block.

My phone burred as I walked to SimNastics. I read the text from Felicity: Ramona was excellent. Double Qs, blue ribbons. Had a real future in the sport.

So much for that theory. I sighed. If only the girl had actually had a future.

I opened the glass door. The smell of sweat, hairspray, and camphor permeated the inside of SimNastics' half of the building. A small anteroom had been carved out with wooden partitions that stopped at least three feet from the ceiling. The sounds of feet thumping, equipment squeaking, grunts, and shouts of encouragement filled the front office. The blade-thin brunette sitting behind the utilitarian metal desk shoved a bag of cookies into a drawer. I wondered how she was able to answer phones and get her work done with all the noise.

"Help you?" Dark circles rimmed her eyes. Her complexion looked sallow. Either the young woman was ill or in deep mourning for Celeste.

"Hi. I was hoping I could look around. Check out the facility?"

She gave me a head-to-toe inspection. The doubt on her face told me she knew I was no gymnast. "Why?"

"My sister's moving to the area and her daughter's into gymnastics. She asked me to check this place out."

"Oh. Sure. Go on back. Just don't disturb any of the athletes." She rummaged in the center drawer, then held out a brochure. "This will tell you about the available programs along with our fee schedule."

"Thanks." I stepped through the narrow doorway into a cavernous space. To the left, a group of women in their thirties and forties sat on folding chairs. One or two seemed to be following the gymnasts' actions, but most were involved in conversation. Moving to the opposite side of the gym, I leaned against the wall. The big room was cold. I jammed my hands deep into my pockets as I surveyed the scene. Sixteen girls were scattered about—stretching, tumbling, working on or waiting for the equipment. A twentysomething woman dressed in a maroon tracksuit supervised.

She approached a girl chalking her hands beside the mat leading to the vault table. As she spoke, the girl nodded. The gymnast walked to the end of the mat. My best guess said she was now more than eighty feet from her target. The girl took off at a run. When she hit the springboard, she flew into a handstand on the vault, followed by some sort of complicated twist, landing with both hands raised in the air. I felt like cheering. The instructor merely waggled her hand from side to side.

Tough audience.

Several huge mats took up the majority of the floor space. A young girl with chalk on her thighs worked on her routine, while another did backflips on the adjacent mat. Three girls watched from the sidelines. Most of the gymnasts appeared to be between ten and fifteen, though one or two looked older. A few were average to tall in height, but most were petite whippet-like girls with prominent rib cages and powerful leg muscles.

I watched a sprite dressed in a blue-and-green leotard fly through the air on the uneven bars. Tiny as she was, the bars still squeaked and bowed each time she swung up and over. I thought back to what Shondra Davis had told me about Celeste pushing her too hard, driving her to the point of injury.

On the chalk-spattered balance beam, a girl did a split followed by a flip and two back handsprings. The thumps when her feet connected with the beam demonstrated the power behind each move. All on a narrow piece of wood.

One of the older girls stood at the edge of the beam's mat, head cocked and staring at me. I smiled and nodded. After casting a glance toward the front office doorway, the girl draped a towel around her neck and strode over. "Can I help you with something?"

"I'm just checking out the place for my niece. Her family's thinking about moving to Pier Point. You like training here?"

The girl cocked her head. "Of course. What's her specialty?"

"Her specialty?"

"Her main strength. Is it the parallel bars or the beam? The vault? Floor? This is a very competitive program. The traveling team is already solid. Unless your niece can fill a gap or strengthen our overall performance, she won't make the cut."

I gazed past her at the girl on the beam. "Is everyone here on the team?"

"No. But they're trying to get on it. That's why girls join this gym. At least the ones who are serious about gymnastics."

"So a person can still train here even if they're not on the team?"

"Sure. But if your niece is having you check out programs before moving here, it sounds like she's serious. Where's she train now?"

Coming up with a lie was way too much work. Ignoring her question, I said, "What do you think of the woman who used to run the gym?"

"Why do you care? She's dead." She put on a mournful face.

"Was she a good teacher?"

"She was very talented. Driven."

"I've heard that. I've also heard she was . . . unkind to some of her students."

The girl put her right thumb to her mouth and began gnawing on the nail. I noted all her nails were bitten down to the quick. "I don't think I'm supposed to talk about that. And why does it matter? She won't be teaching your niece."

"True. But I'm trying to get a feel for the culture here. Did Celeste act badly with the students?"

She shook her head, ponytail whipping back and forth.

"Okay. Do you know what's going to happen to this place now?"

"What do you mean?"

"Is someone else going to manage it? Teach classes? Or is Celeste's husband going to sell it—along with the other branches?"

"I . . . I've got no idea. Either way, he'll have a tough time finding someone who can motivate like Celeste did. Mindy's okay." She glanced at the woman in the maroon tracksuit. "But Celeste not only knew her stuff, she wasn't afraid to push us to achieve." The girl jerked her head toward the far wall. "Our team's won more competitions than any other in the state."

"Huh." I walked to the end of the gym, the girl following along. Rosettes and ribbons covered the giant corkboard mounted there. Group photos ringed the board. I studied the pictures at eye level.

"That's our team after we took state." She pointed at a photo on the left side of the board.

I peered at the image, then down at the girl. "You were on that team." I guessed she was sixteen or seventeen now but looked far younger in the picture. "How long ago was this taken?"

"Six years. I've been on every travel team since I turned ten. Except for when I sprained my ankle."

She was one of the youngest-looking athletes in the picture. Some of the older girls might not be doing gymnastics anymore. Or at least they were no longer part of Celeste's crew. If this girl was unwilling to give me her unvarnished opinion of Celeste, maybe I could track down one who would. "Do all the girls in this photo still train here?"

"Some are off to college. Some couldn't come back after injuries. Like Shelby." The girl pointed out a petite blonde on the far end of the picture. Her fingertip drifted to a tall girl in the center, expression clouding over. "That girl died. And her best friend . . ." The finger shifted to the left. "She had to go to a special program for behavioral problems." Taking a deep breath, she lifted her chin. "You've got to be tough if you want to succeed in gymnastics."

I leaned in and studied the photo. Was that the receptionist? Yep. "What sort of behavioral problems?"

The gymnast shrugged and gnawed on another nail.

"The girl who died, it wasn't . . . I mean, she didn't hurt herself doing gymnastics, did she?"

"We *all* hurt ourselves. It's part of being the best. But no one *dies* because of it."

"Right." I glanced back at the uneven parallel bars, remembering what Shondra had told me. "Did Celeste push some girls too hard?"

"Sometimes." The girl eyed the group of women chatting with one another.

"Did that cause some girls to get hurt?"

"Sometimes."

A gymnast who suffered a career-ending injury might hold her trainer responsible. But would that person hate Celeste enough to murder her?

The girl chewed on another fingernail, then muttered, "Na-na-na."

"What?"

"Nothing. I've got to go. It's my turn on the beam." She scurried away.

I walked toward the entrance, stopping near the women. If these were mothers of students, would they admit they paid for their daughters to be bullied and pushed past their limits? Unlikely. Still, I propped myself against the wall and listened. The conversation drifted from their own exercise regimes to great deals on hair bands and gym wear for their daughters.

A pixie of a girl who looked like she was twelve kept darting glances my way. One of the women noticed and turned to stare at me. I nodded before shifting my gaze back to the gymnasts.

The woman rose and marched over to stand directly in front of me. "What are you doing here? None of these girls are yours."

Not in the mood to spin more stories, I said, "I'm investigating some matters surrounding Celeste's murder."

Her mouth dropped open, then she snapped it shut and hissed, "Here? In front of the girls?"

What did that even mean? "I'm just looking around. Getting familiar with her business."

"Well, I don't think you should do that while the girls are here. They're all traumatized by her death."

I looked at the lithe, muscular bodies flying through the air, then back at the woman. "Yeah, they look all broken up about it."

She sniffed. "They're redirecting their grief into their sport. That's what Celeste would want."

Her sanctimonious remark and tone struck a nerve. "I'm betting what Celeste would want is to be alive. But sure, what you said."

The woman's eyes grew wide. She took a quick breath and pointed at me, obviously ready to launch into a lecture. One I didn't want.

"I'll see myself out." I stepped through the doorway to the small lobby, disappointed not to see the receptionist. She might have some stories to tell about Celeste. My two cups of morning coffee pressured my bladder. I followed a sign for the bathrooms down a poorly lit hall to the women's room. The door was locked.

"Occupied," someone called out.

I stepped back to wait. The sound of retching followed. The receptionist was sick after all. Not wanting to use a bathroom reeking of vomit, I told myself I didn't need to pee that badly. I could come back another time to question her.

When I walked outside, the pixie who'd been staring at me earlier was waiting by the entrance. "Are you the new owner?"

"No."

The girl's face fell.

"Has the place been sold?"

"I don't know. None of us do. Reggie says she doesn't know anything about what's going on and won't even try to find out."

A cold breeze tousled my hair. I resisted the urge to pull my jacket closed while the pixie faced me shiver-free, wearing nothing but a leotard. "Who's Reggie?"

"Receptionist."

"And she doesn't know if the place has been sold?"

"She doesn't know about anything. Not even if the team's entry for the next meet was submitted in time."

"Oh. And Reggie can't look up the paperwork? Or make a phone call?"

"Not her. All she wants to do is stuff her face and puke it up."

Yikes. I flashed on the bag of cookies hastily shoved out of sight. So, not sick. At least not in the way I'd thought. "Sorry I can't help you. But maybe you can help me."

Her brown eyes narrowed. "How?"

"You know a girl named Shelby? Used to train here?"

"Sure. But she hasn't been here in months."

"You know her last name?"

She squinched up her face in concentration. "Talbot. Shelby Talbot. Why do you want to know?"

"Just nosy, I guess. Thanks."

The girl frowned, then scampered back inside.

As I climbed into my 4Runner, the conversation I'd had with Ava the day before yesterday popped into my brain. What if Celeste's killer threw a length of rope over a beam inside the barn and hauled her dead body to the top of the hay? Like a pulley. Ava said pulleys could make objects easier to lift. That would mean whoever killed her didn't have to be unusually strong. Celeste had been muscular, but still petite—the same as the gymnasts inside. I needed to ask Ava how much strength it would take for a person to lift something weighing a hundred to one hundred and ten pounds using a pulley.

CHAPTER 23

I sat behind the wheel, wondering whether the angry mother would storm out and try to chase me from the parking lot. Keeping one eye on the door, I turned on my cell and scrolled through my contacts to Ava's name. Hoping I could get the information I needed without her asking why, I tapped the call icon.

"Hi, Molly. What's up?"

"What's up?" was a new colloquialism she'd recently embraced. I couldn't help but smile. "I've got a question for you about pulleys."

"Are you okay with me putting you on speaker? I'm at Lincoln's. He's the pulley expert."

"Sure, go ahead."

A new voice said, "I wouldn't call myself an expert. I'm well grounded in the subject and have a strong understanding of the underlying physics involved, but—"

"Say hi," Ava hissed.

"Oh. Hi, Molly."

So her new friend was even more socially awkward than Ava had once been. "Hi, Lincoln."

Ava spoke again. "What do you want to know?"

"You told me that a two-wheel pulley makes it possible to lift something with half the normal force. Have I got that right?"

"That's correct," Lincoln said. "Physics dictates a certain amount of force is needed to lift an object. The heavier the item, the greater the force you need. Understand?"

Having never studied physics, I took him at his word. "I'm following. At least so far. What I'm wondering is, would throwing a rope over a beam to hoist up something require significantly less effort than pulling the object up with your hands?"

"In this hypothetical," he said, "what level of effort is considered 'significant'?"

"You're right. That was way too vague. Let's say the item weighs around one hundred pounds." A pang of guilt hit my gut. Referring to Celeste as an "item" was all kinds of wrong. But talking dead bodies with a pair of children was worse—no matter how gifted they were. "What percent of that weight would be offset by using a rope over a beam?"

"Well, technically, that's not a pulley."

"No?"

"No. You need to run the rope, cable, or chain over a wheel for it to be a pulley. That's true even for a simple pulley."

"Oh. Well, would using a rope without a wheel make it easier to lift something? Easier than doing it by hand, I mean."

"Even with a simple pulley, you need to exert a force equal to the weight of the load. If you want to lift it, that is. The added friction caused by dragging a rope across a beam would increase the effort needed. Making the total force required larger than the load weight. You wouldn't have that problem with a complex pulley. They're all about load distribution. Of course, a block and tackle pulley will require a longer rope than a simple pulley."

I tried to keep the disappointment from my voice. "Got it. That's helpful. Thanks."

To my surprise, he continued. "However, it *is* easier to apply force in a downward direction than in an upward one. Like in your rope and beam scenario. Also, that sort of primitive hoist does allow you to lift an item vertically—unlike pulling with your hands or using a winch—which is designed for moving things horizontally. So if you want to lift the item straight up, a rope tossed over a beam would be beneficial—if an actual pulley isn't available. Provided you can apply enough force on the rope."

My idea might have some merit after all. "Great information. Thanks so much, guys."

"Anytime, Molly," Ava said. "See you Wednesday."

"Say 'hi' to Butterscotch for me."

Before I disconnected I heard Lincoln saying, "Does she think your dog understands the word 'hi'?"

Oh, to be a fly on the wall for that conversation.

I set the phone on the passenger seat and started the engine. If the killer used a rope to haul Celeste's body to the top of the stack of bales, it would require enough upper body strength to lift at least a hundred pounds. Which meant, if the killer was a man, he'd only need to be average in the strength department. But if the killer was a woman, she probably worked out. Hard. Either lifting weights or taking part in a sport requiring upper body strength. Like gymnastics. I opened a search for Shelby Talbot on my cell. I found her Snapchat, Twitter, and Instagram accounts, but no phone number.

A group of girls dressed in jewel-toned leotards exited the building, followed by a flock of moms. Time for me to go. Better to continue researching at home anyway. Shelby was probably still in her teens and living with her parents. I'd check them out through my Trackers account.

Before shifting the car into drive and exiting the lot, I once again noted the leading body type among the gymnasts was both muscular and petite. Would one of these four-foot-ten sprites be able to haul one hundred pounds of deadweight up a stack of hay bales?

When I entered the house, all three dogs trotted to greet me, tails wagging. I crouched to hug them and receive their kisses. "You guys. You always make me feel loved and missed." Harlow cocked her head as if digesting what I'd said, while Sky snorted and pranced, and a glob of saliva traveled from the Saint Berdoodle's flews to the floor.

I took them into the backyard, where we romped about for a wonderful twenty minutes. When Noodle began to flag, I brought them inside and refreshed their water bowls. Once they'd settled on their pillows, I opened my laptop and logged on to the Trackers site. Fortunately, Talbot wasn't a common name. At least not in Pier Point. Only one couple in town had that name: Beryl and Jeremy. I was betting they were Shelby's parents.

The next twenty minutes were spent diving down digital rabbit holes and collecting data points. The Talbots had been married for twenty-two years and had an excellent credit rating, no bankruptcies, divorces, or arrests. He was a tax attorney, she a chiropractor. On paper, they looked like upstanding people. Hopefully they were and had taught their daughter to do the right thing. I needed at least one of Celeste's recent students to tell the truth about how she'd treated her gymnasts.

I tried the two phone numbers I found for the family. The first went to Jeremy's voice mail and the second to Beryl's. I didn't leave a message. Their address was only a few blocks away. Seemed unlikely either would be working on a Sunday. It might be worth dropping by. It was always harder to shut the door in someone's face than to hang up on them.

After changing into clean jeans and a sweater, I pulled on my new red windbreaker. At the jingle of my house keys, the dogs lifted their heads. "We'll go to the beach later."

Locking the door behind me, I headed toward the water then turned north. A damp breeze blew off the ocean. I zipped my jacket and tucked my hands inside the pockets. There was a nip in the air, but the leaves on the trees in the postage-stamp yards I passed remained green. I'd heard there was some strain of maple that grew locally and changed color, but none appeared to be in the yards of my neighbors. As much as I loved my new hometown, a part of me missed being in Massachusetts to see the autumn leaves.

The Talbots' street wound up being farther than I'd thought. Twelve blocks later, I reached the two-story Mediterranean overlooking the beach. A Juliet balcony sat above the arched front door. Over the garage, two windows broke up the façade. Forest green umbrellas hinted at a rooftop deck. On either side of the front door, large urns planted with chrysanthemums burst with shades of rust and gold.

I knocked and waited. No one answered. I tried again. It looked like I'd need to come back another time. I turned away, then heard the door open behind me. A girl, about sixteen or seventeen years old, leaned against the frame. Just over five feet tall and weighing in at an estimated one hundred pounds, she stared at me with dilated eyes.

Someone getting high while Mom and Dad were out?

She wore pink sweatpants and a black tank top with a matching black sling immobilizing her right arm. "Hi? My parents don't do any sales at the door?" She made it sound like a question.

"Good for them. I'm not selling anything. Are you Shelby Talbot?"

"Yes?"

"My name's Molly Madison. I've been looking into the murder of Celeste Simmons. I was hoping to talk to you about her gymnastics program."

Beneath wispy blond bangs, her forehead furrowed. "Why?"

"Mostly for background information. To help me get a better feel for the woman."

"Oh, sure. But I don't go to her gym anymore."

"I know. Could you tell—"

"Sorry. My leg's a lot stronger now but standing with my weight on it gets uncomfortable pretty fast. Mind coming in?"

"That'd be great." This girl was too trusting for her own good. Or maybe too stoned.

She limped her way across a tiled entryway to a ground floor sitting area. My boots sank into the deep pile carpet. With her injuries, it seemed unlikely Shelby was the one who had climbed to the top of the hay bales at Playtime and dragged a dead Celeste up after her.

A huge picture window framed the ocean view. On the adjacent wall, flames danced in the fireplace. The dish of potpourri on a side table added a hint of apple and cinnamon to the air. On the cherrywood coffee table, a can of soda sat on a coaster next to a physiology textbook and an open bag of corn chips.

"Can I get you something to drink?"

"No, thanks." I settled in the burgundy armchair perpendicular to the sofa.

Shelby lowered herself onto the seat cushion, picked up the soda, and propped her right leg on the table. "Mom hates when I do that." She nodded toward her elevated foot. "But it feels better this way. I tore my ACL." She tapped her right knee. "The ligament completely separated from the bone. Plus I dislocated my shoulder at the same time."

"Ouch." Was it too intrusive to ask why she was still wearing a sling six months later? Probably. Instead I said, "The injury was gymnastics related?"

"Oh yeah." Anger briefly flashed in her eyes.

"Did it happen during practice at SimNastics or at a competition?"

"Competition." She frowned. "I knew I shouldn't have gone to the meet. I'd tweaked my knee earlier in the week. Celeste told me to put a brace on it and suck it up. She didn't want me to no-show since I was the strongest vaulter on the team."

Sounded a lot like what Shondra Davis had told me about hurting herself while training with Celeste. "But you competed anyway?"

"Unfortunately." She gave a single-shoulder shrug. "I didn't want to let Celeste—or the team—down. Big mistake. As soon as I started running toward the vault, I knew something was wrong."

The silence stretched. I leaned forward. "What happened?"

Shelby looked surprised, like she'd forgotten I was there. "When I hit the springboard, I heard a pop. My adrenaline was pumping so hard, I didn't feel any pain. Not then. But my launch didn't have its usual lift." She drifted off again.

"What does that mean? To a non-gymnast?"

"Oh. I didn't fly high enough. Couldn't fully extend my arms before I hit the vaulting table. I did manage to push off it with both hands instead of smacking my head. But my right arm kind of collapsed on me. I landed on the mat and my knee gave out. That's when the pain came. It hurt so bad. But the worst part was the fear. I couldn't make my leg move the way I wanted."

I looked at her sweatpant-covered leg. "You needed surgery?"

"Yeah. Grade three tear. Then a brace and crutches. Still have two to three more months of rehab ahead of me."

"Sorry to hear that."

"At least I can use my leg again. For the first couple days after, I was furious. At myself. At Celeste. At my knee for failing me. Then a funny thing happened." She stared at the fireplace.

"What?"

Seeming not to hear me, she kept her gaze on the flames. The silence between us grew heavy.

"Shelby?"

She turned her attention back to me. "Sorry. Spaced out there. Last week I lost my balance on the stairs and fell. Tumbled all the way to the landing and reinjured my shoulder. Had to have another surgery. I'm on pain meds again. They make me kind of loopy."

"That's . . . Wow. Talk about unlucky. I'm sorry." So, stoned, but with a doctor's approval.

"Anyway, when I came home after the first surgery, friends started dropping by. Friends I couldn't spare time to see when I was competing. I started catching up on schoolwork. I'd forgotten how much I loved science. Somewhere along the way, I realized I'm happier not doing gymnastics. It's weird. Since I was six, being a gymnast has been practically my whole identity." She lifted the can and drank again. "I'm back in school, too."

I raised my eyebrows.

"A couple years ago I started homeschooling so I could train more. Now I have a social life." She dimpled. "And a girlfriend. I'm rethinking my future. Maybe I'll go to med school someday."

"I know someone you might want to talk to. Her name's Shondra Davis. She's another of Celeste's former students. Maybe eight or nine years older than you. Injury sidelined her gymnastics career and she's a doctor now."

"Really? Talking to her would be great." Shelby helped herself to a chip and offered me the bag.

"No, thanks."

"If I was still in training now, no way could I eat this."

"I guess you had to eat healthy in order to compete."

"Pretty much. If I gained half a pound, Celeste would freak out."

"Really? Would a small change like that make a difference in your performance?"

"No. And it's not like the weight was gonna stay—not with all the exercise I got. But that didn't matter to Celeste. She even told a few of the girls she thought weren't thin enough not to drink water before a competition."

"Why?"

"So they wouldn't look bloated."

My jaw sagged. Celeste said that to children? "That's terrible."

"It was. She regularly humiliated them at practice. Some started purging after eating. To stop her calling them chubby. She'd also pinch the fleshy part on their hips and waist, then tsk and sigh."

Shondra had told me something similar. I shook my head.

"A few got obsessive about losing weight. Me, I'd rather go hungry than take a bunch of laxatives or stick my fingers down my throat."

Starving yourself didn't seem like a healthy choice, either. "People die from eating disorders."

Shelby bit her lower lip and seemed to drift off again. Finally, she lifted her chin and said, "I know."

"Did Celeste encourage them to do . . . that?"

"Not exactly. But . . . Na-na-na." She singsonged the repeating syllable, then straightened, refocusing on me. "You know?"

"No."

She sighed. "You're talking about a bunch of girls who were already working out countless hours every day. Burning fuel. And someone's telling them it's not enough. That they needed to be thinner. I'm not saying she drew anyone a map, but . . ."

"You think she's responsible."

"Pretty much. Of course, people will say I'm biased."

I looked at her sling. "You're probably right. I don't mean to pry . . ." Total lie. "But you're the second gymnast I've heard use the phrase 'na-na-na' when talking about Celeste. What's it mean?"

Shelby took another chip. "This will sound awful, but the girls who lost themselves in their eating disorder—at least the ones I knew—they weren't top tier at the gym. I think they figured if they dropped more weight, they'd improve. But the truth was, they weren't good enough to begin with. I'm not saying great gymnasts don't get caught up in the body dysmorphia thing. They do. That just wasn't the case with the people I knew at SimNastics."

"And na-na-na?"

She looked at the flickering flames again.

Just hearing about Celeste's behavior made me want to hit something. If someone had actually starved themselves at her direction—no matter how oblique the guidance—it might motivate them to bash in her head. "Can you give me the name of anyone who had to stop competing because of an eating disorder?"

"Reggie Ouradnic."

"She live here in town?"

"I think so. I mean I think she's back now. Things got so bad for her, I heard she had to go to some special clinic. I'm not really connected to that group anymore, so all my info's, like, six months old."

I pictured the young receptionist at SimNastics. "Was there more than one Reggie who practiced at Celeste's gym in Ventura?"

"Not that I know."

"She may be working the front desk at the gym."

"Really?" The girl's gaze sharpened. "That seems like a bad idea. She should move on with her life."

"Sometimes that's easier said than done." I thanked Shelby for her time and told her I'd let myself out. When I reached the front path, I stared at the ocean and took a deep breath. Two gymnasts now had muttered "na-na-na" when I asked how Celeste treated her students. And both of them had failed to answer my question about what the phrase meant.

Looked like I was heading back to SimNastics.

CHAPTER 24

Two blocks from the gym, my phone vibrated inside the cup holder. I glanced at the screen and answered. "Hi, Simone. What's up?"

"They arrested Quentin."

I checked my rearview and side mirrors, then pulled to the curb. "For Celeste's murder?"

"No. He's only been charged with the credit card thefts. Even though they found blood on the floor of his area inside the barn. Fresh straw had been scattered on top of it to hide the stain. Who'd do that besides him?"

"Sounds pretty damning. Why no murder charge?"

"Apparently, Quentin was seen by several students during the window when the cops think Celeste was killed. I mean, the entire time. No gaps."

"Solid alibi. And he doesn't seem like he's got the money or leverage to get someone to kill Celeste for him."

"Whoa. I hadn't even thought of that. This has all been so . . . distressing. Not to mention bad for business."

A vague uneasiness niggled. While Simone shared more details, I tried to pin down what it was, but couldn't identify its source. When she paused, I said, "I'm surprised the deputies tracked him down so quickly. Or did Quentin turn himself in?"

"Neither. His parents called the cops. Said they spotted him sleeping in his car a couple houses down from theirs. Not exactly the Great Escape. Don't get me wrong, I'm glad he's been arrested. But I can't believe his own parents turned him in."

"The dynamics of other people's families can be baffling. Plus, maybe they know something about their son that we don't."

"I suppose. I heard as soon as the deputies brought him in, Quentin completely caved."

Remembering how closemouthed Deputy Alvarez had been with me, I realized what was bugging me. "How do you know all this?"

"Mr. Hopkins. He heard it from Quentin's parents. They were his first call. I'm guessing Quentin doesn't know it was his folks who turned him in. Anyway, they feel terrible. Not about calling the cops on him, but about what he did—since Mr. Hopkins gave him a job as a favor to them. The Cookes called Mr. Hopkins to tell him what happened and offer restitution to all our affected students."

"Wow."

"Yeah. Turns out Quentin's run up a huge gambling debt. With no hope of paying it off. The guy he owed told him he could steal credit card data from us or take the broken bone and missing body parts repayment route."

"A real rock and a hard place situation."

"Yeah. Of course Quentin took the easy—and by that I mean backstabbing—way out."

"I get it. You trusted him."

"This whole thing makes me question my judgment." A deep sigh filled the line. "According to what Mr. Hopkins told me, after Celeste was murdered and the cops showed up, Quentin wanted to stop. But the boss guy wouldn't let him."

"That explains what the sandy-haired man was doing at Playtime and why Quentin looked frightened."

"Maybe. Either way, Quentin followed orders and stole more info from our clients and passed it on. Oh, and the cops found two more lists of credit card numbers in an old tube inside a rat cage."

I stared through the windshield at a vintage truck rumbling past, its cherry red paint gleaming in the sunshine. "I don't get it. If Quentin gave the information to his boss, why were those lists still inside the metal tubes?"

"He told the cops—and his parents—that he kept copies of the information. Like an insurance policy. Lucky for us he did. He can't wiggle his way out of this. And, in spite of what Quentin's parents have offered, Mr. Hopkins is furious. He's pressing charges."

"I imagine your students will, too."

"It's going to be a real mess, but I think Playtime will weather the storm. Sorry I wasn't as cooperative with you as I could've been."

"Don't worry about it. But you realize the killer's still out there, right?"

"Yeah. I mean, I'm relieved they got Quentin and that the thefts will stop. I didn't want to think I'd been working side by side with a murderer, but . . ."

"It would've been simpler if he'd been responsible for both crimes."

"Exactly."

After thanking her for sharing the news, I disconnected. It looked like my case was still active. I waited for a gap in the traffic, then pulled away from the curb.

When I arrived at SimNastics for my second visit of the day, fewer cars were in the lot. I parked in the second aisle and checked the time: quarter-past two. Since no one was entering or leaving the building, a class was probably in session.

Inside the reception area, the same sorts of squeaks, thumps, and grunts as before floated over the room divider. Reggie sat behind the desk, looking worse than she had that morning.

When she noticed me, she squared her shoulders and made a wan attempt at a smile. "You're back. Did your sister have some questions?"

Time to come clean. I spread my hands wide and said, "Sorry, but I wasn't exactly honest with you when I came by before."

Her forehead scrunched. "Huh?"

"I wasn't scoping out the place for my niece. I came here to ask the girls how Celeste treated her gymnasts."

"Oh." She looked down at the desk and began straightening a stack of envelopes.

"I've heard your boss could be cruel to the athletes. Pushed some too hard, berated others, called them fat. I heard you were one of those she singled out."

The young woman's face crumpled and tears began to spill. "Who told you?"

"It's not important. Her cruelty is."

She wiped her face with her sleeve. "God, I hated her. And I hated myself, too."

"I don't want to make things worse by digging around in a painful subject. Are you comfortable telling me more about it?"

She shook her head.

The last thing I wanted was to inadvertently spur on her eating disorder. "Okay. No problem. Can you at least tell me if the phrase 'na-na-na' means anything to you?"

Her mouth dropped open and she began to sob. Jumping to her feet, Reggie raced around the desk and ran for the bathroom. I followed. The door slammed shut, followed by the lock clicking. Fortunately, this time no sounds of retching came from inside. Unfortunately, her sobs continued unabated. Afraid to leave her alone when she was this upset—and worried she might try to duck out on me—I waited outside the restroom.

When Reggie finally emerged, she was red-eyed, but no longer crying. She took a shaky breath and said, "There's a Tiny Tumblers class starting soon. Mind if we talk outside?"

"Not at all." I led the way to the parking lot. In the short time I'd been inside, clouds had swooped in, blocking the sun. I repressed a shiver. "I'm sorry if the term 'na-na-na' is insulting or something. I don't know what it means—other than being a line from a song. Are you okay with telling me?"

She nodded, then blew her nose on a wad of toilet paper. "God, it started so long ago. Seven, no eight years now. We were best friends. The three of us. I think we came together because we wanted to be great gymnasts." Her gaze followed a string of cars pulling into the lot. "I mean, every girl who starts at Sim-Nastics dreams of that. But the three of us didn't fit the mold. We were a couple years older when we started and were taller and bigger than the other girls. We felt at a disadvantage."

Unsure how this was answering my questions, I prodded, "And?"

Car doors slammed, then several mothers accompanied their girls across the parking lot. Reggie nodded at them as they passed. Once they'd disappeared inside, she continued. "We all tried to make our bodies fit the ideal. Soon I was either starving myself or bingeing and purging. After a couple years, Ro developed some throat problem—from all the vomiting—and her parents took her to a psychiatrist who specialized in eating disorders. They pulled her out of the gymnastics program and moved somewhere up north. That left just me and Mona."

"Mona?" An unsettled feeling needled beneath my breastbone, telling me I'd missed something. Something big.

"She couldn't stand purging. She was the first of our trio to just stop eating. I remember how impressed I was at her self-control. And how thin she became. But she couldn't stop. Eventually she grew too weak to practice, let alone compete."

"So, na-na-na?"

"That was the three of us—since all our names ended in N-A: Regina, Rowena, Ramona. Celeste would kind of singsong it for everyone to hear. To let us know it was time for our weigh-in."

My throat tightened. "That's awful. And Mona was short for Ramona?"

"Uh-huh."

"And *her* last name was?"

"Marinkovic. Why?"

I didn't fight the shiver this time. "That means Ramona didn't die from cancer."

Reggie took a step back. "No. Did someone tell you she had?"

"Yep."

"Well, they lied." Her mouth twisted like she'd bitten a lemon. "The anorexia killed her. Mona's mom hospitalized her a couple times. Each stay, she'd gain some weight. Enough so they'd let her go home. But then she'd stop eating again. She couldn't seem to find her way back to who she'd once been." She lifted her teary eyes to meet my gaze. "It's not an easy thing to do once you're hooked. Eventually Mona's organs started shutting down. I thought her mom would go completely mental." She straightened her shoulders. "I don't want to do that to my parents. Break their hearts, destroy them. I'm trying to do better. But it's hard."

"Maybe working here isn't the best idea."

"It reminds me of what I lost." She crossed her spindly arms over her chest. "That helps me focus. Though I still fail sometimes."

"I don't think you need to come here to remember your friend or how much the loss of her hurts. I hope you'll at least think about finding some other job, okay?"

"Okay." She wiped her nose again before heading back inside the building.

As soon as I got behind the wheel of my 4Runner, I called Felicity. The phone rang repeatedly. "Come on, pick up."

On the sixth ring, she answered. "Hi, Molly. I heard the good news about Quentin's arrest."

Word traveled fast in the dog lover community. "Yeah, but it's not for the murder."

"Oh." The joy drained from her voice. "I thought that meant—"

"Don't worry. I'm still looking into Celeste's death. We'll figure out who's responsible. I don't know if this is relevant, but I stumbled across something today and have to ask: Why'd you tell me Stacy Marinkovic's daughter died of cancer?"

"I . . . That's what everyone said. Are you saying she didn't?"

"Did you know she used to attend classes at Celeste's gym?"

"No. I mean, I heard she was active in some other sport—besides agility—before she got sick."

"Do you remember who told you Ramona had cancer?"

"Sorry, no. But if it wasn't cancer, what was it?"

"I've got to go." I hung up and called Simone. The line rang until her voice mail answered. "Hi, it's me, Molly Madison. How late are the classes running this afternoon? Call me." I hung up, a sense of urgency thrumming inside me. Unsure if I was over-reacting, I pulled out of the lot again and headed for Playtime.

CHAPTER 25

I pulled into a vacant spot in Playtime's gravel lot. Only a third full. Most of the classes must be done for the day. I hopped out and spied a deep blue CRV a few cars over. It looked identical to Stacy Marinkovic's. Cupping my hands around my eyes, I peered into the cargo area. No Thor, but an empty dog crate was visible.

The outdoor fields and arenas were empty. I raced to the barn. Warm light spilled between the open doors. An obedience class was going on inside with Simone and Cowboy Ben instructing. I scanned the students' faces but didn't see Stacy.

Not wanting to disturb the class, I edged my way past the group. Quentin's work area was now taped off. The tarps that had separated it from the rest of the barn were gone, as were the cages. Simone must have relocated the rats until the Sheriff's Department finished its investigation. At the rear of the building, I stared up. An exposed beam extended above the stack of bales where Celeste's body had been left. My rope and beam theory—courtesy of Ava and Lincoln—might be true: The killer could've used a length of rope to haul the body to the top of the bales to hide it.

If it hadn't been for Noodle's keen sense of smell, how long would it have taken before someone found Celeste?

I managed to return outside without disturbing the class and circled the barn. Still no sign of Stacy. Day was quickly surrendering to night. Until three months ago, I'd been a lifelong Bay Stater; the chill in the air didn't account for the shivers racking my spine. I jammed my hands inside my pockets, wishing I'd brought the dogs along.

Where could Stacy and Thor be? Remembering her comment about taking the border collie for a sunset walk around Playtime's grounds, I strode along the property's fence line. An owl hooted and I jumped. "Get a grip."

In spite of telling myself to calm down, every time my foot snapped a twig or crunched a leaf, my heart juddered. Ten stress-filled minutes later, I spotted a faint beam of light heading my way. Stacy? A dog charged ahead.

Thor. I stopped and waited. The border collie bounded up to me and nosed my calf. I crouched to stroke his coarse coat. Tongue hanging out, he rolled onto his back. After rubbing him and giving him a final pat, I straightened. "Nice night for a walk."

The gathering darkness made it hard to read Stacy's expression. "I like the quiet."

"Sure." There was no easy way to say what I needed to. I took a deep breath and dove in. "Why'd you tell people your daughter died from cancer?"

"What? I never did."

Her outraged tone made me flinch. "But everyone thought that."

She straightened her broad shoulders. "If people chose to gossip about Ramona's health—rather than asking what was wrong—how is that my problem?"

"You're right. But Celeste bullied your daughter. Told her not to drink water before competing. Weighed her in front of the other girls at the gym. Why wouldn't you want everyone to know what that woman did?"

A cloud shifted, unmasking the moon. Stacy's face shone with tears. "Because I didn't know." She covered her mouth and choked out a sob. At her anguished tone, Thor drew close and leaned against her leg. She wiped her nose with her sleeve. "I had no idea why my beautiful, talented daughter was starving herself to death. I thought I'd failed her. But how? I loved Ramona more than anything. Her dad died before she was born and Ramona became my entire world. I loved her more than I'd ever loved anyone. Wasn't that enough?" She raised her hand, palm up, as if offering something, but she held nothing. "I started thinking maybe I loved her too much. That I was somehow smothering her with my love. I . . . I hated myself for failing her."

The tingling sensation beneath my breastbone was back. "But you found out. Eventually, right? Did one of the gymnasts tell you?"

Stacy shook her head. "No one said a word to me. Not even those 'friends' of hers at the gym. Two weeks after my daughter died, I found her journal. I didn't even know Ramona kept one. I was going through her drawers. Not to get rid of anything—I still can't bear the thought of doing that. I was trying to spark happier memories. Instead I found . . . it." Her gaze bore into mine. "I read every word she wrote. Do you know what that horrible woman said to my daughter?" Her wild eyes seemed to expect an answer.

"No."

"She called Ramona a cow. Said she'd never make it as a gymnast if she couldn't control what she ate. Celeste fat-shamed my girl. Convinced Ramona there was something wrong with her body. Something disgraceful about her.

"My daughter was a beautiful, athletic girl. Then that horrible woman got her claws into her. Ramona starved herself until she looked like a war refugee. Celeste made my daughter feel like a failure. Worthless. Ugly. Eventually, she became too weak to compete in the sport she loved." Stacy wiped her eyes. "I had Ramona hospitalized twice—for her own good. But each time after she got out, she'd starve herself again. That monster, Celeste, killed my daughter."

Though my heart was racing, I kept my voice low and calm. "Finding her journal . . . Is that when you started bringing Thor to agility class?"

"Celeste wouldn't take my calls. Refused to see me when I stopped by her gym. I even tried waiting outside her home. But she drove straight into the garage and closed the door. I wasn't able to catch her."

Amazed Celeste hadn't filed a complaint with the police, I considered the possible reasons. Maybe she'd kept her mouth shut because she feared what Stacy might tell the cops about how she treated her athletes? While not illegal, that news might have tanked her business. "What were you hoping to accomplish by talking to her?"

"I wanted to look her in the eye. Tell that monster what she'd done to my beautiful girl."

There was no way Celeste didn't know how she'd hurt Ramona—or her two friends. Needing answers, I played along. "And did you?"

"Even here at Playtime, it took several tries before I was able to get her alone." She scrubbed her hand across her face. "Finally, I was able to catch her and say my piece." Her brow furrowed. "You know what she said?"

I shook my head.

"She claimed everything she did was designed to make her girls tough. To make them the best. She called my Ramona weak."

The scene unfolded inside my mind. "And you hit her."

Stacy stared off at the nearby hills. After a shake of her head, she straightened and took a ragged breath. "We were in a little area inside the barn where the rats are kept. I . . . I . . ." She scrubbed one hand across her face. Collecting herself, she continued. "That evil woman. It was clear she didn't give a damn about Ramona." A shudder shook her frame. She cleared her throat. "There was a crate full of metal pipes. I picked one up and struck her. She went down. I hit her again. And again."

I studied her. She had the upper body strength to haul tiny Celeste to the top of the stack of bales. "Where's the weapon?"

"The pipe? I took it home. I wasn't thinking clearly. Don't get me wrong, I'm glad I killed her, but taking the murder weapon home with me?" She shook her head. "I've been trying to put it back in that damn crate ever since. But someone's always been around. I couldn't get in there without being seen. And now there's crime scene tape blocking off the area."

A murderer afraid of violating a crime scene? This woman wasn't a criminal by nature. She'd been pushed. After her devastating loss, I wanted Stacy to at least feel a modicum of control now. "Have you thought about what happens next?"

"It's clear you know how horrible Celeste was. She deserved what she got. The only regret I have is that I didn't learn what she'd done to my daughter sooner. But I don't want to go to jail.

Can't her death go unsolved?" She looked at me with pleading eyes. "Become one of those 'cold cases' like you see on TV?"

As terrible as I felt for her, I couldn't let someone else take the blame for Celeste's death. "If you turned yourself in to the Sheriff's Department, that would help Felicity."

Her jaw sagged. "You don't think they'll clear her without me admitting what I did?"

"It doesn't look good. And would you want to take that risk with her life?"

Stacy turned off the flashlight function on her cell. "I don't think I have the courage to do it."

My stomach clenched. I didn't want to force this woman to confess.

"Would you make the call for me?"

Relief flooded through me. Stacy was a good person. A good person who'd lost her way. "Sure." I pulled out my cell and scrolled to Deputy Alvarez's number. While I waited for the deputy to answer, Stacy thrust Thor's leash into my free hand.

"Take care of him. For me and Ramona."

I opened my mouth as a voice spoke in my ear.

"Alvarez."

"Deputy. Hi. This is Molly Madison. I'm at Playtime Academy for Dogs with Stacy Marinkovic. She just confessed to murdering Celeste Simmons."

"Can you speak freely?" Tension infused the deputy's voice.

"Yep."

"Are you in danger?"

I looked at Stacy's slumped shoulders. "No."

"Are you in a crowd or alone with her?"

"Alone."

"I'll call it in. Move her to a more populated area if you can. I'm on my way. Should be there in ten to fifteen minutes."

I disconnected and lifted my gaze to meet Stacy's. "Let's get closer to the barn." She nodded and I led, Thor at my side, Stacy trailing a half step behind the dog. Uncomfortable having her where I couldn't see her, I stopped and waited until she passed me. When we reached the open doors to the barn, I raised my free hand and caught Simone's eye.

When she noticed, her forehead creased. She said something to Cowboy Ben and hurried outside. Her gaze traveled from me to Stacy. Turning away, Stacy shuffled toward the shadows along the side of the barn.

"What's going on?" Simone said.

"The Sheriff's Department should be here soon. I thought you might want to dismiss class early."

She pulled a lock free from her ponytail. "Why are they coming back?"

"Stacy admitted she killed Celeste."

Her mouth sagged open. She turned to the woman leaning against the corner of the barn. "I can't . . . I mean, that's . . . Oh my God."

"It'll probably be better for Playtime if those people aren't here." I nodded at the class behind her.

"Right." Looking shell-shocked, she tottered back inside the barn.

By the time the first black-and-white SUV rolled up the driveway, all the students had driven off.

Alvarez climbed out and shined a high-powered flashlight in our direction. After a moment, she strode across the dirt. Keeping her gaze glued on Stacy, she still managed a small nod in my direction. "Stacy Marinkovic?"

Stacy finally lifted her head. "Uh-huh."

"I need to have a word in private." Alvarez pointed at her vehicle. Without argument, Stacy trudged to the SUV. The deputy followed, hand on her sidearm. She seated Stacy in the back seat.

A few minutes later, two more cars had pulled onto the dirt apron: another black-and-white and a dark sedan. A uniformed deputy climbed from the SUV. A man and a woman emerged from the nondescript car. Detective Stern wore a brown suit, DeFelice a blue one. All three surveyed the area before approaching Alvarez's vehicle. After a brief conversation with Alvarez, the detectives led Stacy to the office. The second deputy conferred with Alvarez, then followed the detectives.

Alvarez joined me and Simone by the open barn doors. "Hope you don't mind. Detectives DeFelice and Stern just commandeered your work space."

"Not a problem." Simone tugged on a curl.

Alvarez turned to me. "I'm going to write up your statement and the situation when I arrived, then have you read it over."

"Okay."

The deputy headed for her vehicle.

Simone shook her head. "I'm not sure what I should do. Normally, I'd go to the office. What should I do?"

"Maybe call Mr. Hopkins and let him know what's going on?"

"Right. Good." She pulled her cell from her pocket and walked a few feet away.

I led Thor to the empty crating area, where he watered a few trees, then we strolled back to the barn. The ever-efficient Alvarez soon returned and handed me her notepad.

After a quick read-through, I said, "Looks good. Accurate."

She took back the offered pad. "The detectives want to talk to you before you head home."

"Okay." No surprise there. "I didn't get a chance to say it earlier, but thanks for the quick response."

"Sure." Alvarez chewed her lip. "I've got to say, this is the first time I've ever felt sorry for a killer."

"I hear you."

By the time Alvarez led me to the office, forty-five minutes had passed. The other deputy opened the door, but both stayed outside. When I entered, Detective DeFelice stood. She gestured me toward the folding chair I'd sat in only thirteen days earlier. Once again her partner, Stern, remained seated. He continued scribbling notes on a pad but didn't lift his head or acknowledge my presence.

"Thank you for waiting," DeFelice said.

Like I had a choice? I bit back that response. "How can I help?"

CHAPTER 26

As I drove home, Thor scurried back and forth across the rear seat, sticking his muzzle first out the left window then the right, tirelessly repeating the process. I felt as scattered as his actions. But at least he was tracing scents—while I was merely at sea. True, I'd done the right thing by calling the cops and getting Stacy arrested. But I didn't feel good about it. At least Felicity wouldn't be a suspect any longer. My stomach twisted. Right thing or not, Stacy seemed someone who was more to be pitied than punished.

When I pulled into my garage and opened the 4Runner's back door, Thor leapt out. Leaving him in the backyard, I went inside the house and roused the other dogs. After giving them pets and kisses, I took them through the kitchen slider to the yard. Sky snorted and wiggled her butt. Harlow's ruff deployed, and a low growl came from Noodle. A stranger was in their home territory. I crouched next to a nervous-looking Thor.

"It's okay, guys. We've got a new member of our pack." I

stroked the border collie's coat, then held out my hand to the other dogs. Sky and the Saint Berdoodle approached the border collie, but Harlow remained cautious. Noodle gave Thor a thorough sniffing, then wagged and drooled. After cocking her head and sampling the air, Harlow sat and woofed while Sky ran around like a dervish. I wasn't sure if the Frenchie realized this was Thor's first time joining them in the yard.

I found one of the tennis balls and tossed it. Harlow, Thor, and Sky took off after it. Thor got there first. I threw a second ball and happy chaos erupted. After the dogs had a chance to play and burn off some energy, they seemed to put aside their nervousness and fear.

When the Frenchie began to slow her pursuit of the ball, I leashed all four. Having figured out who killed Celeste, I decided it was time to get to the bottom of Izzy's lurking man. "Come on. We're all taking Sky home tonight." At the sound of her name, the Frenchie snorted.

Hoping to catch the guy loitering outside Izzy's, I circled the block, approaching her house from the opposite direction. Just like before, the tall man stood on the sidewalk across the street. When we were less than five feet away, I spoke. "Don't run. The dogs will chase you."

The man jumped, then turned. His jaw dropped, but no words came out.

"You're Kyle."

He nodded, then his gaze lasered in on Sky.

I told the dogs to sit. "And you're Izzy's ex?"

Once again, he nodded.

"She says you're here to steal Sky."

His Adam's apple bobbed, then he spoke, eyes still on the

Frenchie. "I just want to see Sky. I haven't gotten to visit with her since I left."

"When was that?"

"Two weeks ago. I've pleaded with Izzy, but she refuses to let me see the dog."

He had a slight accent, which I couldn't place. Eastern European maybe?

He crouched. "Hey, baby." The bulldog pulled on the leash.

"Hang on, girl." I dropped the leash and she ran to him.

Sky rolled onto her back. He rubbed her belly. "That's my pretty girl. I've missed you so much." The love-starved dog wiggled and snorted. He scooped her up and hugged her. "I brought you a treat." He pulled a biscuit from his pocket and looked up at me.

I nodded my permission. Noodle lurched forward, trying to horn in. Telling him to sit again, I gave the other three dogs treats of their own, then wiped drool from my palm. "Tell me the truth: Is the dog yours or Izzy's?"

"Technically, she's Izzy's. Because she paid for Sky. But that's only because I wanted to adopt a rescue dog. Izzy didn't want anything except a purebred. I said I'd pay the fee for a rescue but wasn't buying a dog. There are too many abandoned animals that need good homes."

This time, I nodded.

"My argument went nowhere and Izzy paid a breeder." He rubbed Sky's coat. "But I didn't know how wonderful you were going to be. No, I didn't." He looked up at me again. "I've offered to pay Izzy back. Hell, I offered to give her double what she paid for Sky. But she refused. She's still refusing. What makes it all worse is I never once saw her play with Sky. Or pet her. She doesn't care about the dog. She's just doing this to get back at me for leaving."

"Look, I'm not going to mediate between you and Izzy. I seriously doubt she'd listen to me anyway. But I can see the dog loves you." I pulled out my cell and checked the time. "We've got forty minutes before I have to get Sky home. But I don't want to hang out here in case Izzy returns earlier than usual. If you want to meet me a couple blocks from here, you can visit with Sky for thirty minutes. Sound good?"

His face lit up. "Yes."

"Did you drive or walk?"

"Drove." He pointed back the way I'd come. "I'm parked around the corner."

I gave him the address and my name, then headed off with the dogs. Wanting to get there before Kyle arrived, I picked up the pace. Too fast for the Frenchie. I lifted Sky and jogged to the alley. But instead of going to my house, I knocked on J. D.'s door.

He pulled it open, Buster at his side. "This is a nice surprise."

I introduced him and his dog to Thor. The border collie's tail wagged as did the boxer's. Once sure the pups were getting along, I straightened and checked the alley. No sign of Kyle yet. "I hope you still think this is a nice surprise in another couple minutes. You've got company coming over."

"Huh?" He stepped back and waved us inside.

I urged the dogs in and unhooked leashes as I explained the situation. "Sorry to rope you in. I wasn't comfortable giving a strange man my home address. Even though he truly seems to love Sky."

"Well, talking to Stalker Man was my idea."

"True."

He grinned. "Giving him my address was a smart move. I

know you can take care of yourself, but it never hurts to have backup." He led the way to the family room at the rear of the house. "What's the plan? You observe this guy, figure out if he's safe and stable, then let him hang out with Sky behind Izzy's back before you take her home every day?"

I huffed out a sigh. "I don't know. He looked so happy about getting to spend time with Sky. And she was ecstatic. Kyle told me Izzy's only keeping the dog out of spite."

J. D. called the dogs into the backyard, then closed the screen behind them. "You said she was unpleasant, but that's evil. It's not just mean to her ex, it's mean to the dog."

"I know. And from the way I've seen Izzy treat Sky, I've got no reason to doubt what Kyle said."

The doorbell rang. Buster, Harlow, and Noodle barked. J. D. raised his eyebrows. "Time to meet your new friend."

I trailed after him and stood back as he opened the front door.

Kyle's eyes widened. "Uh, sorry, I thought . . ." He spied me behind J. D. "Oh. Good. Thought I was at the wrong house."

J. D. waved him inside. "Let's get you and Sky together. By the way, I'm J. D."

"Hi."

He led Kyle past the dining room and atrium to the family room. "Why don't we give you and Sky some time away from us and the other dogs?"

"Sounds good." He turned to me and nodded. "Thank you."

"No problem."

J. D. opened the screen to the slider and called the dogs inside. When Sky approached, he told her to stay. The big dogs tumbled into the room. He turned to Kyle. "The yard is yours. Help yourself to any of the toys out there."

Kyle stepped outside and dropped to his knees to hug the

Frenchie. Letting go, he stood and found a ball, then tossed it across the small lawn. She scrambled after it, her short legs a blur. After fifteen minutes of watching man and dog, J. D. said, "Gotta say, he seems like a good guy."

"Yep." How was I supposed to handle this? Izzy had never shown any affection or interest in the dog, but from my previous attempts, I knew she wouldn't listen to me about what was best for Sky.

J. D. told the milling dogs to sit. Grabbing my hand, he headed for the hall. Startled, I stared at his fingers twined with mine, then began following a half second later. Stopping when we reached the stairs, he retrieved Sky's leash from where I'd draped it on the banister.

Turning to me, he said, "You know, we could solve everyone's problem right now."

"How?"

He released my hand and pulled a multi-tool from the pocket of his jeans. After selecting the knife blade, he gestured at the pink leather.

"What are you trying to say?"

"We damage the leash. Start a small cut here, then pull on it until it snaps. You go to Izzy's tonight and tell her you were walking Sky when the leash broke. Sky ran off. Tell her you've been search-ing for the dog all afternoon and evening but haven't found her."

"J. D. . . ."

"Molly . . ."

I placed my hands on my hips. "Great, we've proved we know each other's name. Yay us, but your idea's . . ."

J. D. dropped the leash and peeled one hand off my hip. "It's perfect."

"I was going to say 'mean.' I don't want to worry Izzy."

"You really think she'll lose any sleep over it?"

"I . . . You're right. She'll be angry at my incompetence, but she's not going to care about Sky's safety."

"You already know Izzy isn't giving Sky the attention she needs."

"True."

"And you have good reason to suspect she's kicked the dog. At least once."

I chewed my lower lip. "Also true."

He waved toward the hall and the back of the house. "I get why you gave this guy a chance to play with Sky. He loves that dog. And Sky loves him. Why not let them be together? They'll both be happier."

"You're right. But she's not my dog to give away. I don't want to get accused of dog-napping."

"From everything you've told me, it doesn't sound like Izzy's attached to the dog. If she only laid claim to Sky to keep her ex from having her, how upset will she actually be?"

"Let me give it some thought." I squeezed his hand, then pulled free and walked back down the wide hall to the family room. Harlow and Noodle trotted over to me while Thor investigated something beneath the couch. I crouched to pet the two larger dogs and peered through the slider. Sky and Kyle were running around in the yard.

I heard J. D.'s soft tread behind me and turned. "You're right—those two belong together. But lying to Izzy?" I shook my head. "Seems like a bad idea."

"Hang on." J. D. tucked the multi-tool back inside his pocket and held up a finger. "Don't decide anything yet." He left the room, Buster at his heels.

Familiar visitors at J. D.'s, Harlow and Noodle sprawled on the floor while Thor stayed in investigative mode, sniffing along the room's baseboards. The border collie looked engaged, not nervous. I brought my attention back to the yard.

When J. D. returned, he carried a glass of wine in each hand. "I liberated a kick-ass chardonnay from the wine library. Let's have a drink while you consider my proposal."

"Oh, sure. Alcohol will really help my critical thinking skills."

"You do way too much critical thinking. I want you to shut off that brain of yours for a few minutes and go with your gut."

I took the offered glass of wine. "Okay." I moved to the sofa. As soon as I sat, Harlow hopped up beside me. Noodle settled on the tiles by my feet as Thor continued nosing his way around the room. "Thank goodness you opened a white wine and didn't have to let it breathe."

"I know you're not a fan of that."

"Patience may be a virtue, but it isn't one of mine." I took a sip. "Wow."

"Right? I have to admit, my dad's got impeccable taste where wine's concerned." J. D. sat on the other side of Harlow.

We each took another sip while Buster pawed at the screen. "Not now, boy," he said. The boxer whined and sent an eager look at J. D. "We'll play later."

My shoulders relaxed and my back sank deeper into the leather cushion. The wine was doing its job. I took another drink as I watched Kyle and Sky play tug-of-war with a braided rope. Exploration apparently completed, Thor jumped into the arm-chair and circled.

J. D. chuckled. "Guess he's ready to make himself at home." He gazed at me over his glass. "Why is he with you? Got another dog-sitting client?"

"I can't believe I didn't tell you right away. Thor is Stacy Marinkovic's dog. Tonight she confessed to killing Celeste."

"Whoa. Did she say why?"

"All murders are sad, but this . . ." I shook my head. "Stacy killed Celeste because the woman belittled her daughter to the point where the girl stopped eating. She eventually died."

The cushion shifted as J. D. straightened. "That's terrible."

"Yep. According to Stacy, Celeste felt zero guilt about what she'd done."

"So Stacy losing her daughter . . . is that why you're taking in her dog?"

"In part. She thought it was what Ramona would've wanted. For Thor to have a good home." At the sound of his name, the border collie raised his head.

"That's a smart fellow."

"I suspect he's going to keep me on my toes."

"He doesn't seem stressed about being with someone new. How about you?"

"Border collies are high-energy dogs. Which means I'll be doing agility with both him and Harlow."

"That's a lot of work."

"Yep, but it'll be fun, too."

"You know, maybe you should change your business cards from 'Molly Madison, Dog Wrangler,' to 'Molly Madison, Dog Collector.'"

I snort-laughed, chardonnay burning my nasal passages.

J. D. nodded toward the yard. Kyle had picked up Sky and was nuzzling her again. "What do you think?" J. D. said, turning to me with a grin. "Is it time to 'cut' Sky loose?"

Warmth filled my chest as I smiled back. "You're becoming a bad influence on me."

ACKNOWLEDGMENTS

Thank you to all the readers of this series, and to the librarians, booksellers, and reviewers who have recommended my books.

As always, thank you to my agent, Melissa Jeglinski. When I approached her with the idea for this series, concerned there were already a lot of mysteries featuring dogs out there, she told me, "You can never have too many dogs." (This book may challenge that theory!) Another big thank-you to Kristine Swartz, editor extraordinaire, for always making the story stronger. Thanks also to the amazing people at Berkley—Mary Baker, Yazmine Hassan, Christine Legon—plus many others I've yet to meet. The Berkley team made this book a reality.

I'm grateful for the love and support of my family and friends, whose encouragement and kind words have helped me stay the course. And, once again, a big thank-you goes out to my good friend Nancy Withrow, for answering all my questions about agility training and barn hunt. Any mistakes on these topics are my own!

Thank you also to Wrona Gall, for reading and providing feedback for this novel—from messy first draft to final version—and to the Sunday Morning Writers: Ann Brady, Kathleen Coatta, Anne Riffenburgh, and Howard Rosenberg. You have all made my writing journey a wonderful experience.